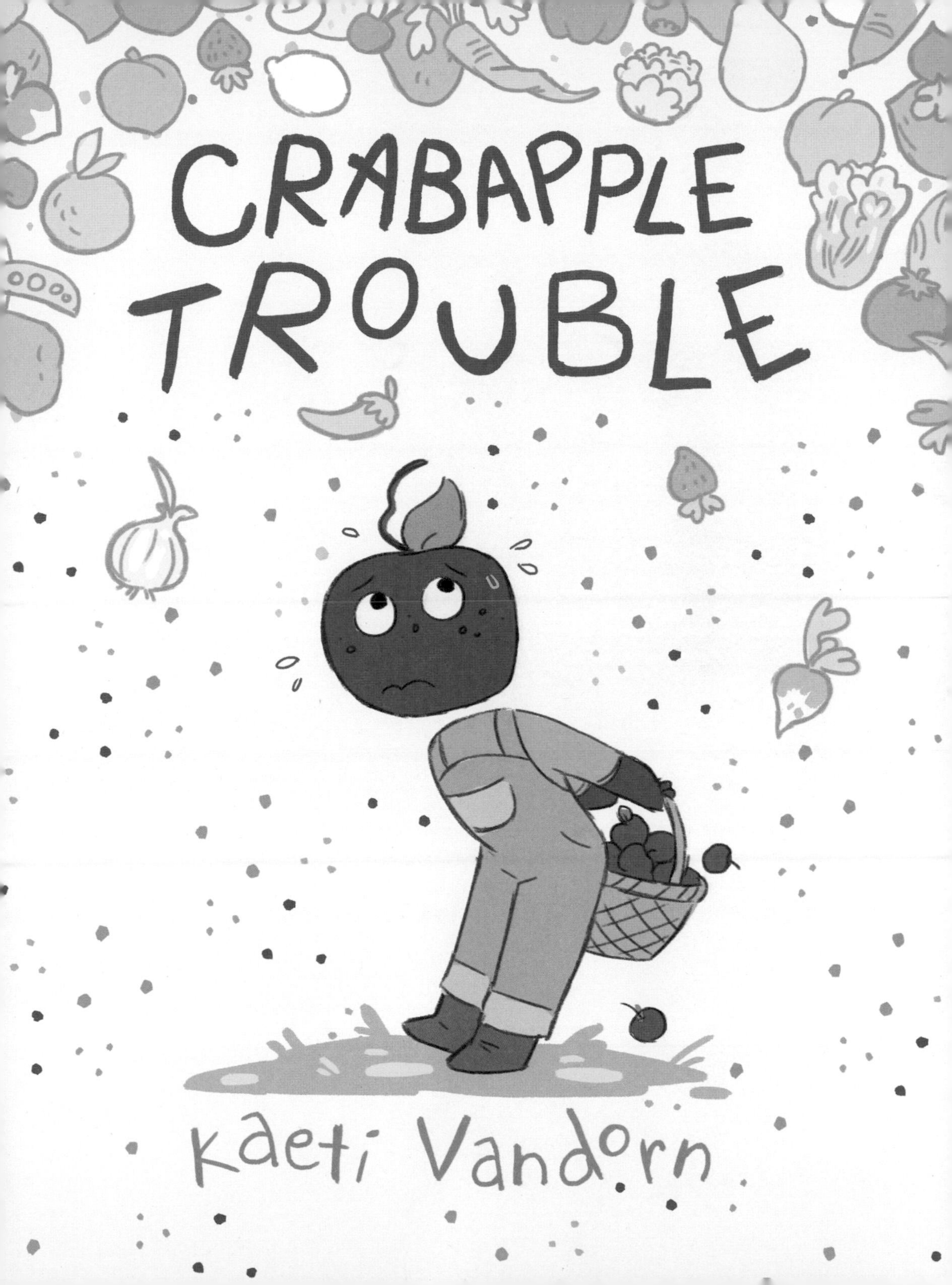
CRABAPPLE TROUBLE
Kaeti Vandorn

Cover art, text, and interior illustrations copyright © 2020 by Kaeti Vandorn

All rights reserved. Published in the United States by RH Graphic, an imprint of Random House Children's Books, a division of Penguin Random House LLC, New York.

RH Graphic with the book design is a trademark of Penguin Random House LLC.

Visit us on the Web! RHKidsGraphic.com • @RHKidsGraphic

Educators and librarians, for a variety of teaching tools, visit us at RHTeachersLibrarians.com

Library of Congress Cataloging-in-Publication Data
Names: Vandorn, Kaeti, author, artist.
Title: Crabapple trouble / Kaeti Vandorn.
Description: First edition. | New York : RH Graphic, [2020] | Audience: Ages 5–7 | Audience: Grades 2–3 |
Summary: "Callaway just wants to help her friends but the pressure of an
upcoming contest is giving her anxiety"—Provided by publisher.
Identifiers: LCCN 2019026171 | ISBN 978-1-9848-9680-3 (hardcover)
ISBN 978-0-593-12526-7 (library binding) | ISBN 978-1-9848-9681-0 (ebook)
Subjects: LCSH: Graphic novels. | CYAC: Graphic novels. | Contests—Fiction. |
Friendship—Fiction. | Anxiety—Fiction.
Classification: LCC PZ7.7.V24 Cr 2020 | DDC 741.5/973—dc23

Designed by Patrick Crotty

MANUFACTURED IN CHINA
10 9 8 7 6 5 4 3 2 1
First Edition

A comic on every bookshelf.

CRABAPPLE TROUBLE

Kaeti Vandorn

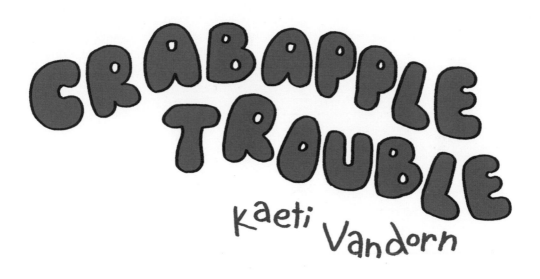

CRABAPPLE TROUBLE WAS DRAWN WITH CUSTOMIZED BRUSHES IN ADOBE PHOTOSHOP USING A WACOM CINTIQ. THE BOOK WAS LETTERED DIGITALLY WITH A FONT CALLED MILK MUSTACHE.

FOR MOM AND DAD

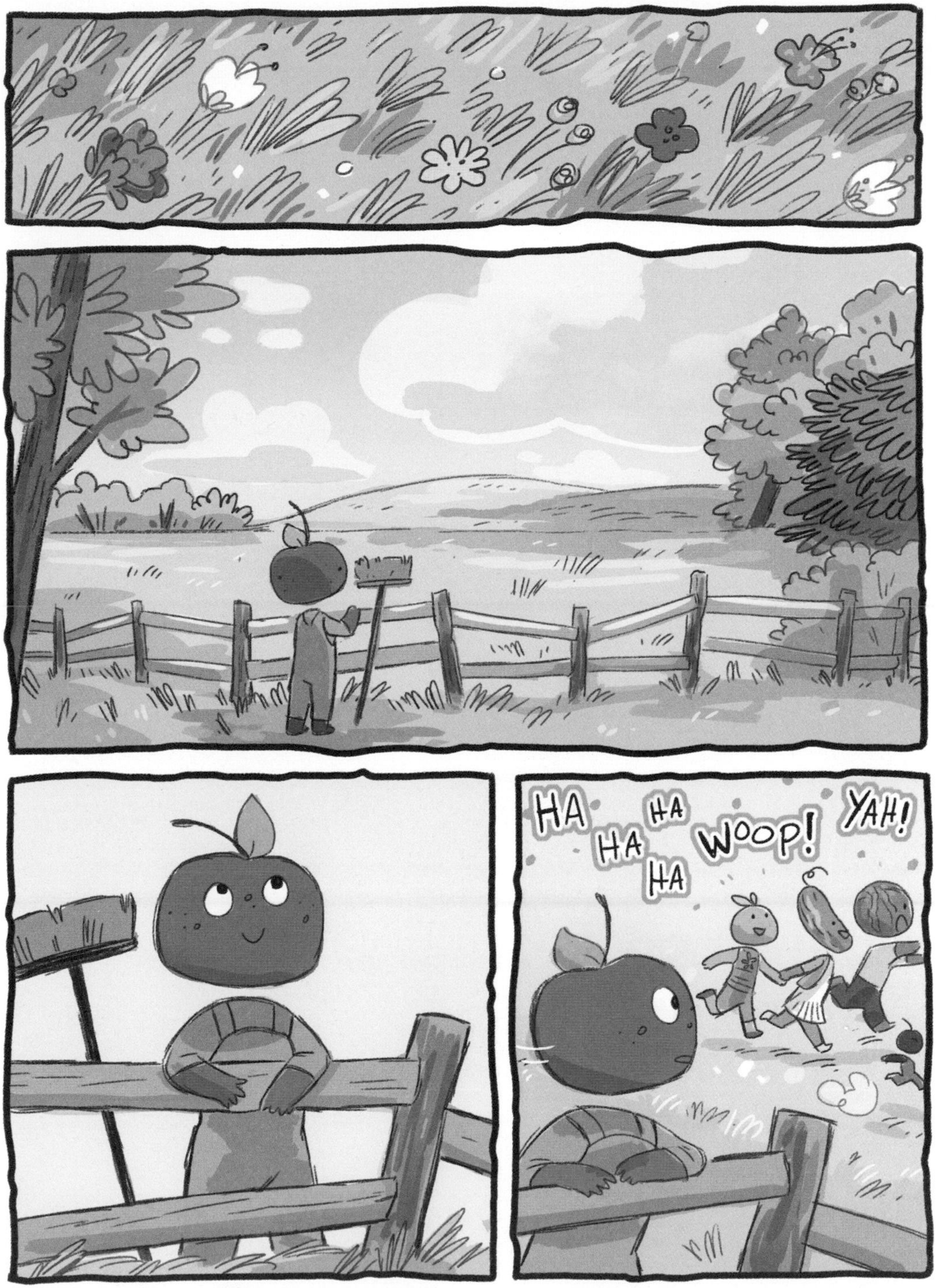
HA
HA
HA
HA
WOOP!
YAH!

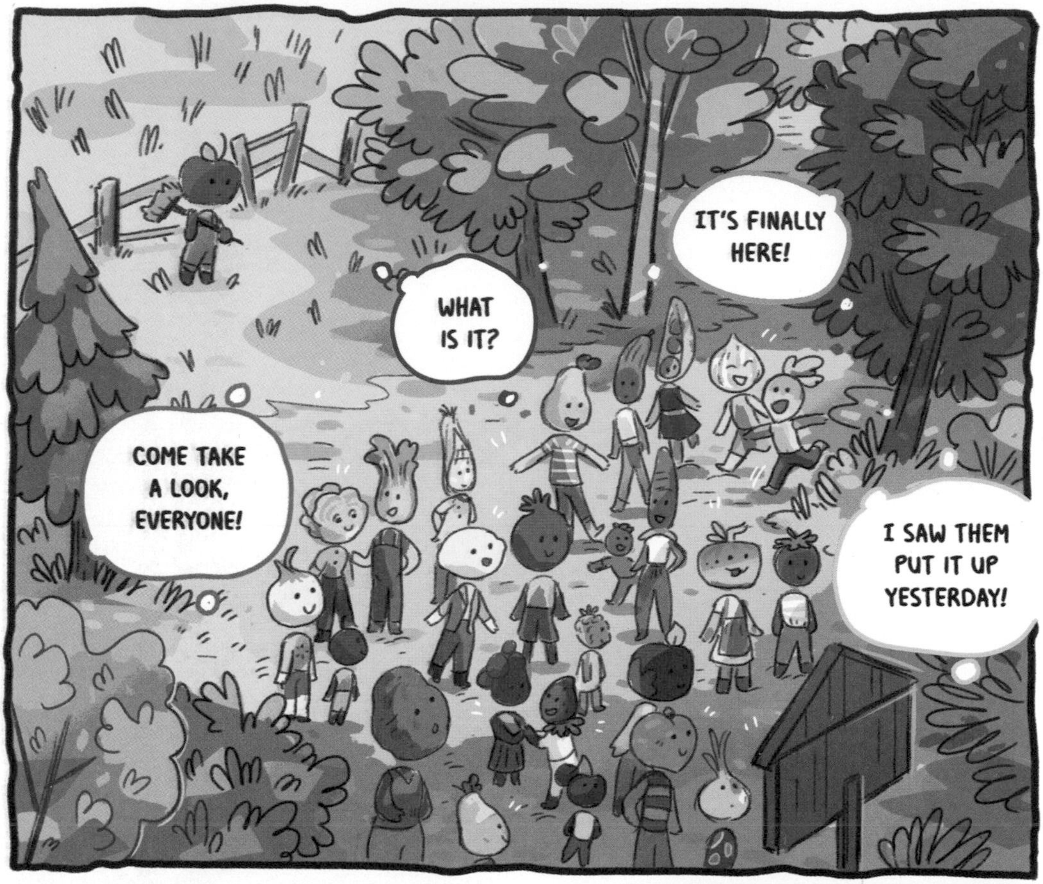
IT'S FINALLY HERE!
WHAT IS IT?
COME TAKE A LOOK, EVERYONE!
I SAW THEM PUT IT UP YESTERDAY!

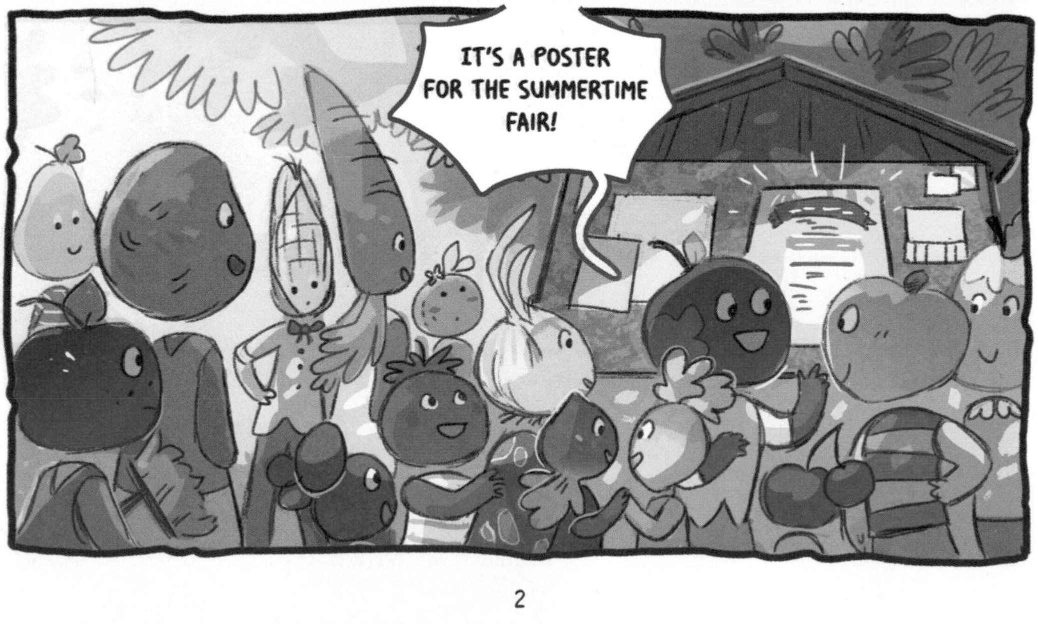
IT'S A POSTER FOR THE SUMMERTIME FAIR!

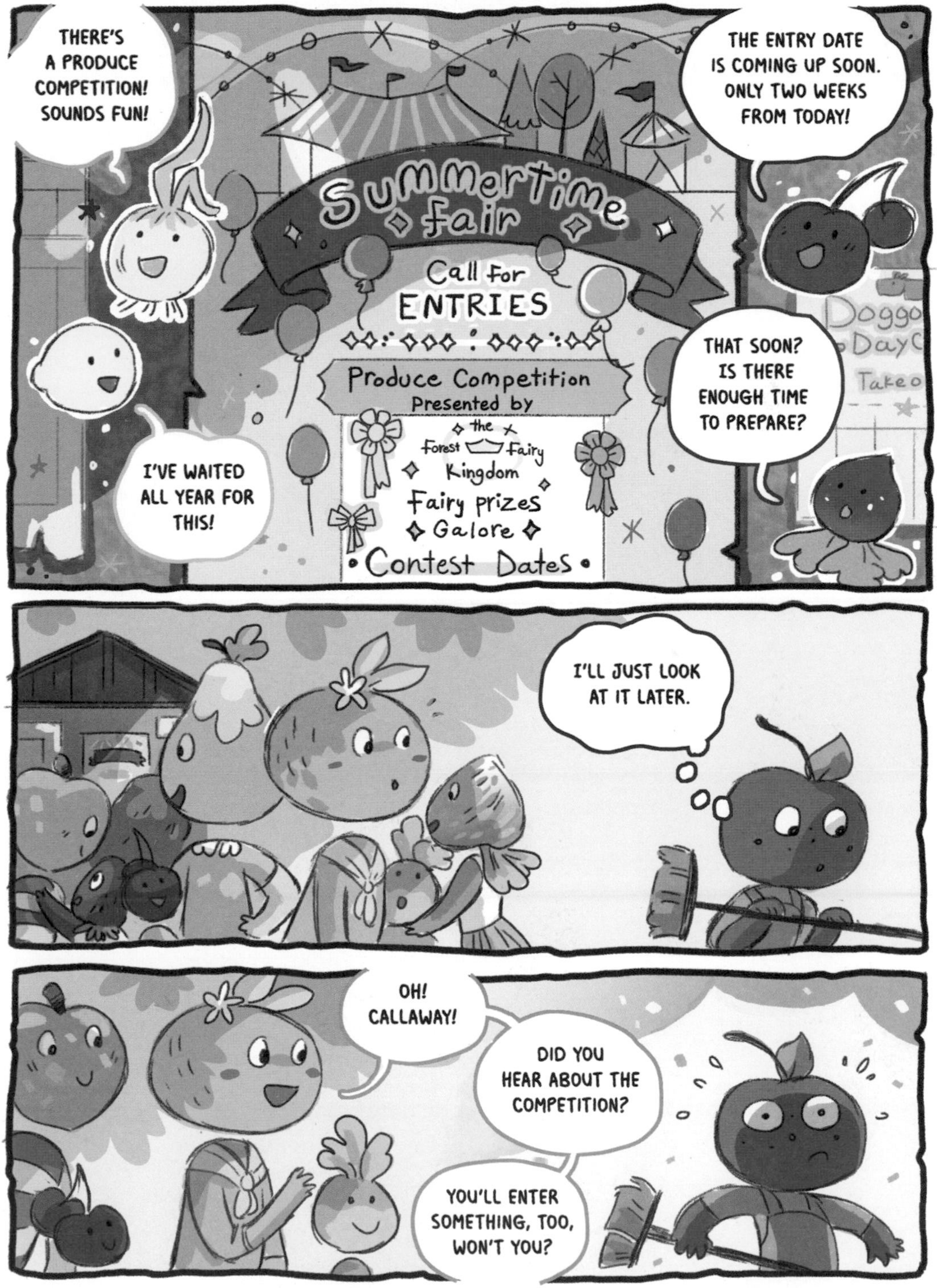
THERE'S A PRODUCE COMPETITION! SOUNDS FUN!
Summertime fair
Call for ENTRIES
Produce Competition Presented by the Forest Fairy Kingdom
Fairy prizes Galore
Contest Dates
THE ENTRY DATE IS COMING UP SOON. ONLY TWO WEEKS FROM TODAY!
I'VE WAITED ALL YEAR FOR THIS!
THAT SOON? IS THERE ENOUGH TIME TO PREPARE?
I'LL JUST LOOK AT IT LATER.
OH! CALLAWAY!
DID YOU HEAR ABOUT THE COMPETITION?
YOU'LL ENTER SOMETHING, TOO, WON'T YOU?

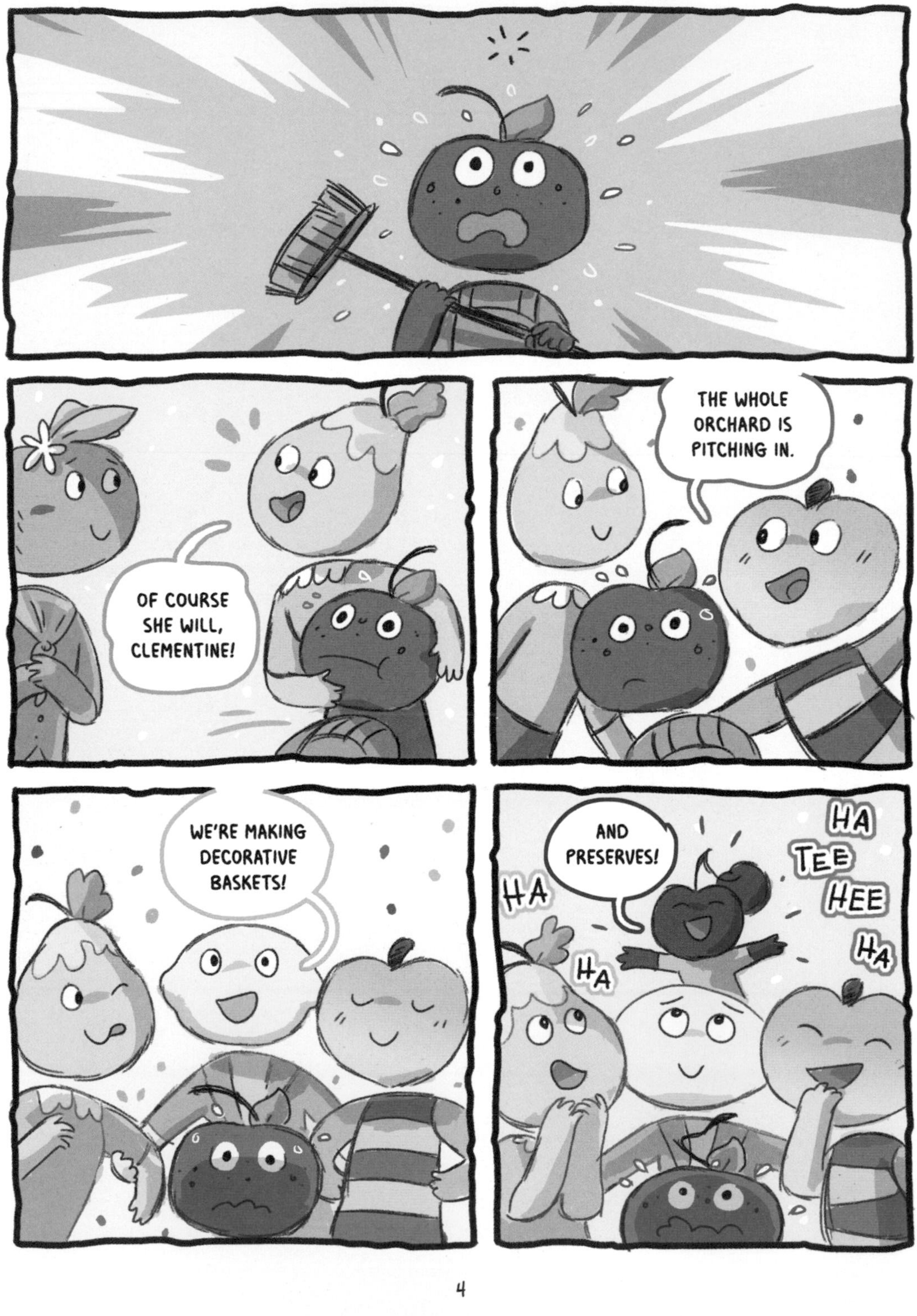
OF COURSE SHE WILL, CLEMENTINE!
THE WHOLE ORCHARD IS PITCHING IN.
WE'RE MAKING DECORATIVE BASKETS!
AND PRESERVES!
HA
HA
HA
TEE
HEE
HA

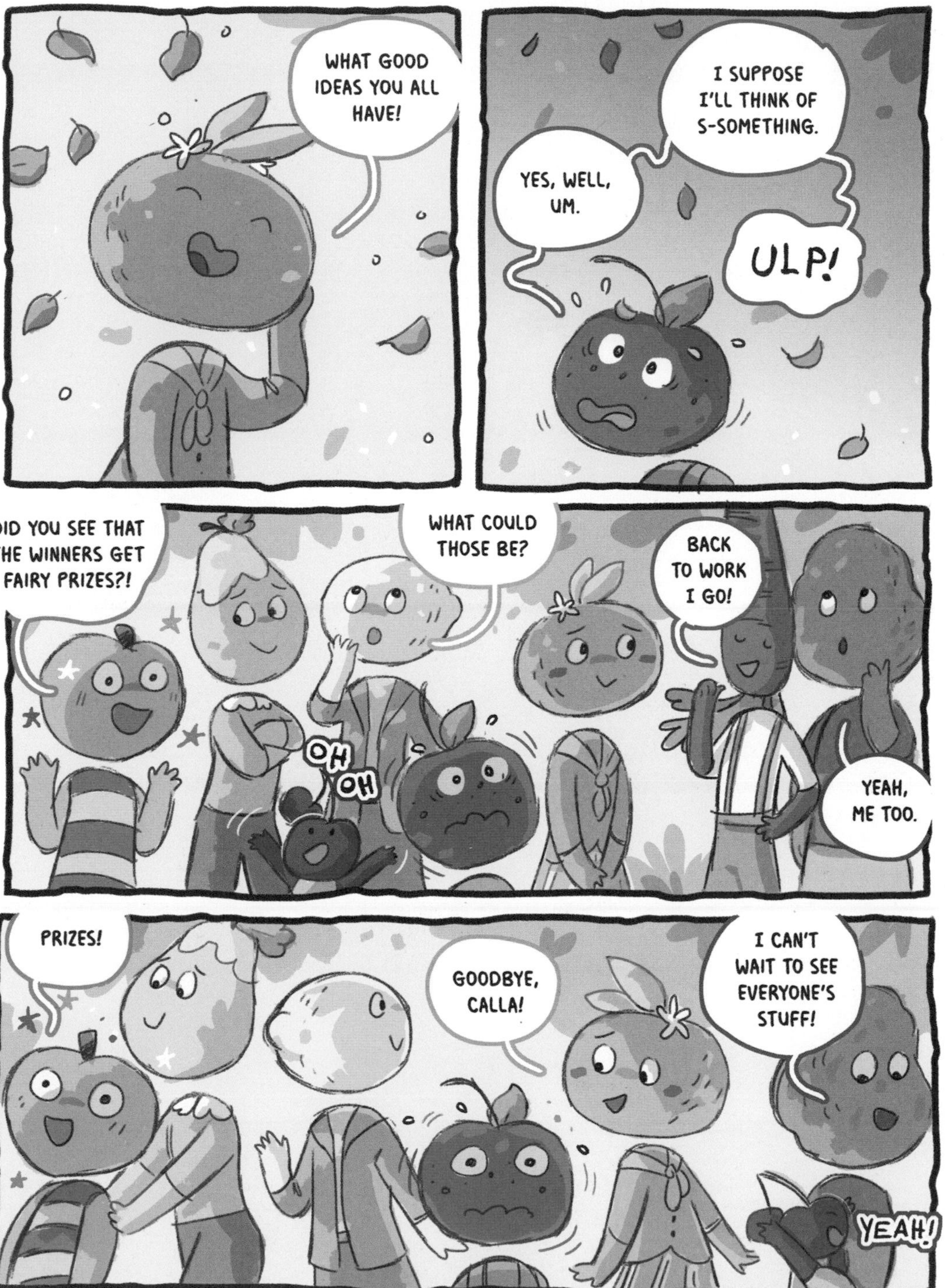
WHAT GOOD IDEAS YOU ALL HAVE!
YES, WELL, UM.
I SUPPOSE I'LL THINK OF S-SOMETHING.
ULP!
DID YOU SEE THAT THE WINNERS GET FAIRY PRIZES?!
WHAT COULD THOSE BE?
OH OH
BACK TO WORK I GO!
YEAH, ME TOO.
PRIZES!
GOODBYE, CALLA!
I CAN'T WAIT TO SEE EVERYONE'S STUFF!
YEAH!

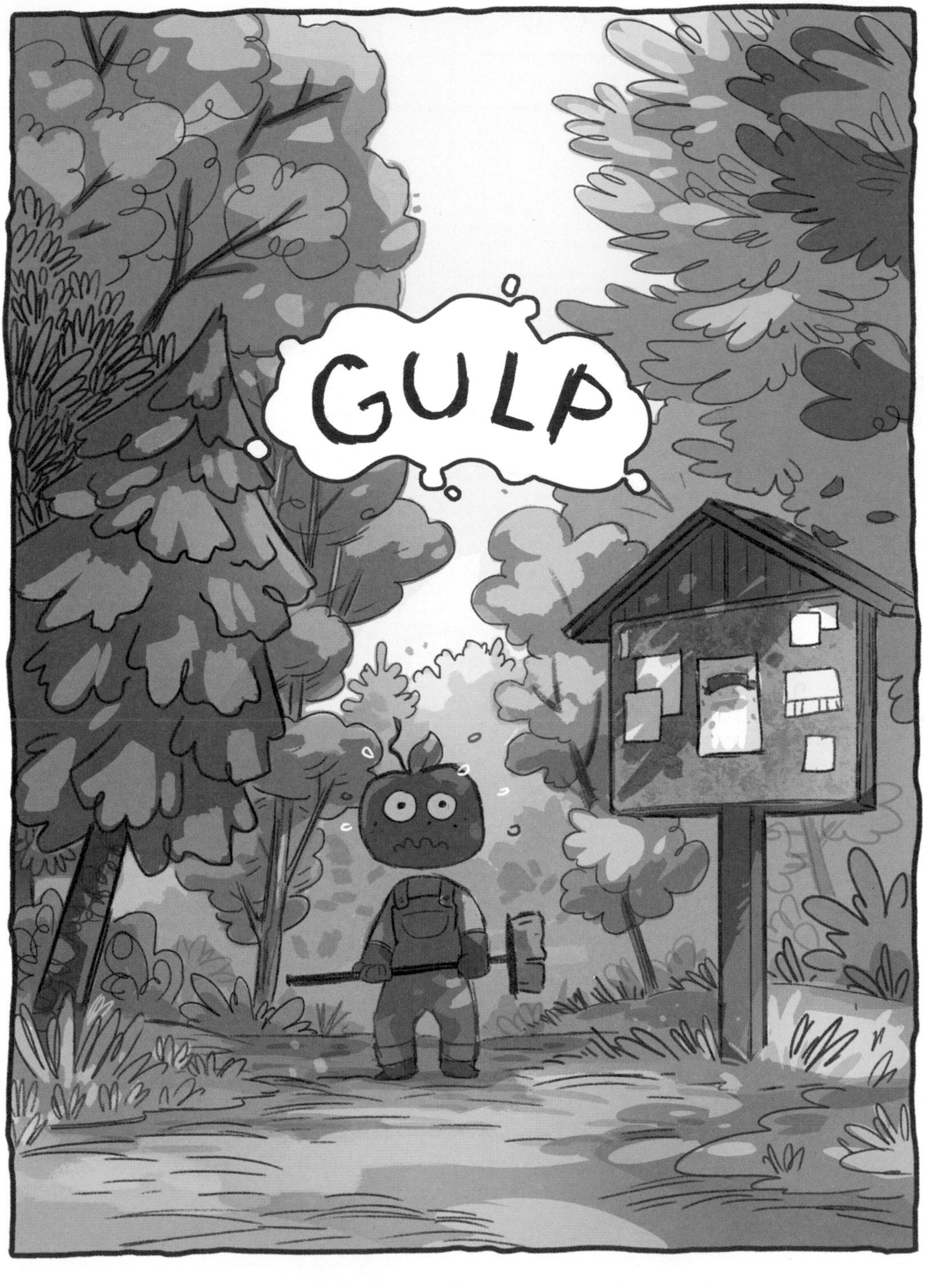
GULP

CHAPTER 1

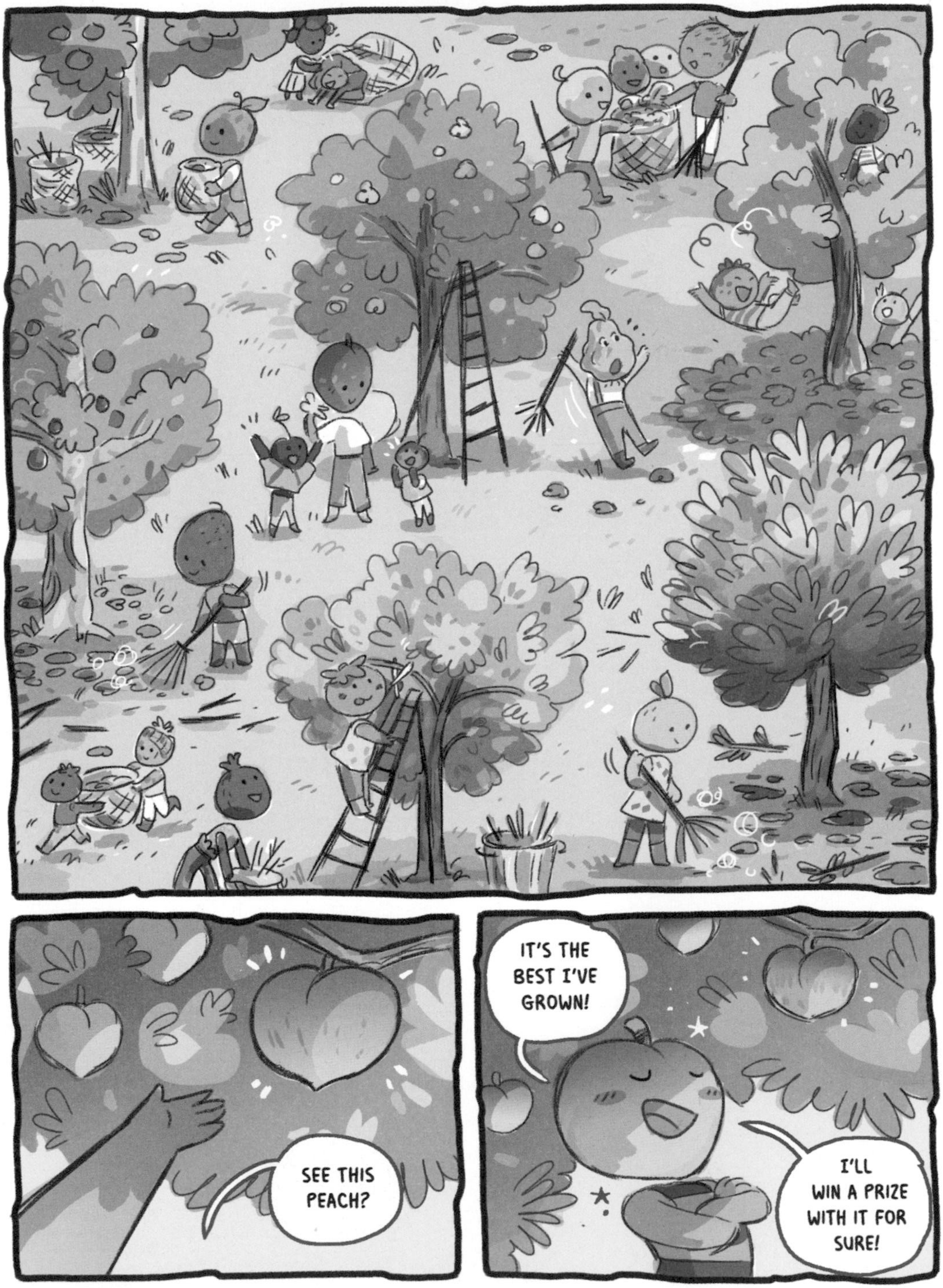

SEE THIS PEACH?
IT'S THE BEST I'VE GROWN!
I'LL WIN A PRIZE WITH IT FOR SURE!

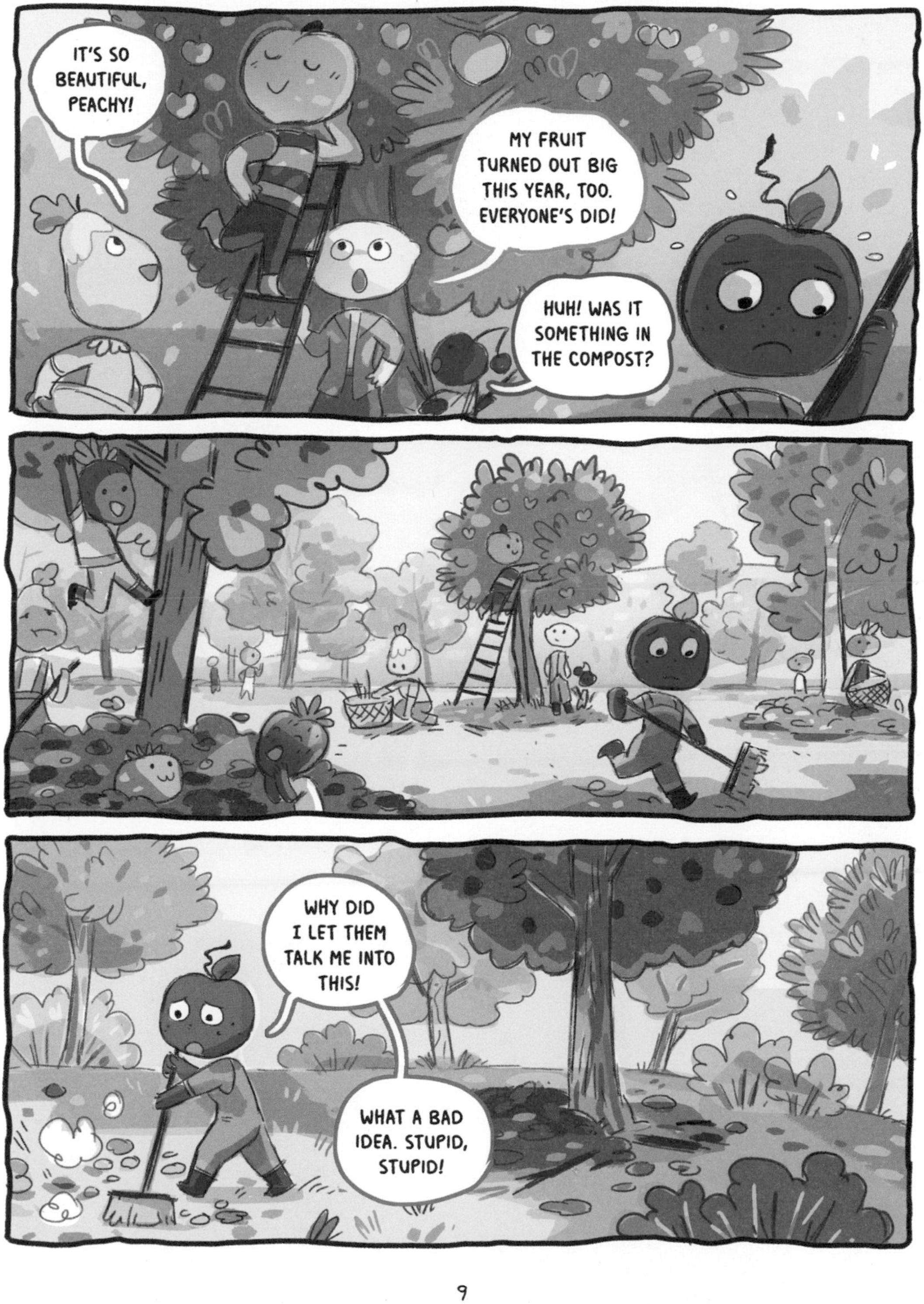
IT'S SO BEAUTIFUL, PEACHY!
MY FRUIT TURNED OUT BIG THIS YEAR, TOO. EVERYONE'S DID!
HUH! WAS IT SOMETHING IN THE COMPOST?
WHY DID I LET THEM TALK ME INTO THIS!
WHAT A BAD IDEA. STUPID, STUPID!

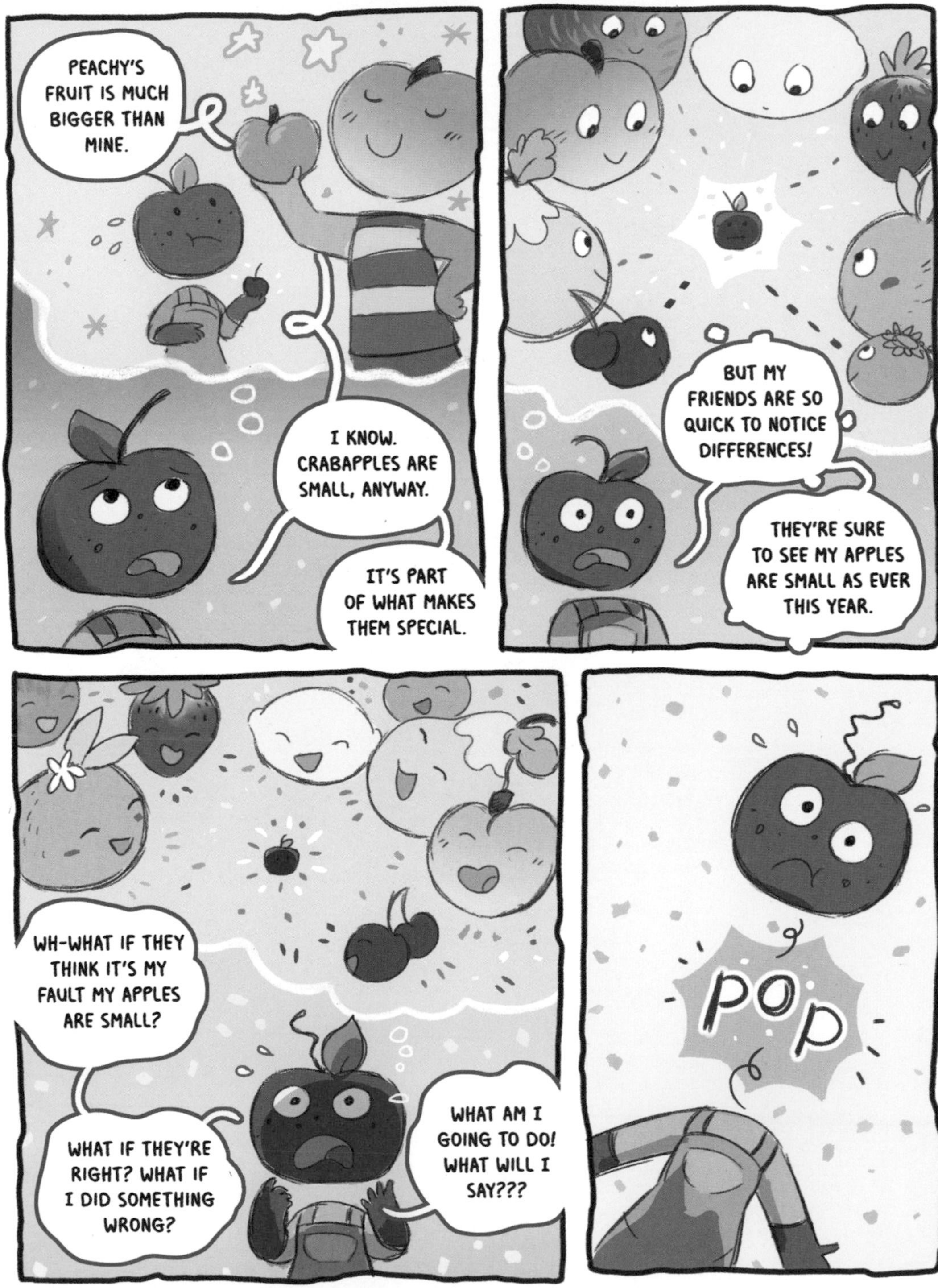
PEACHY'S FRUIT IS MUCH BIGGER THAN MINE.
I KNOW. CRABAPPLES ARE SMALL, ANYWAY.
IT'S PART OF WHAT MAKES THEM SPECIAL.
BUT MY FRIENDS ARE SO QUICK TO NOTICE DIFFERENCES!
THEY'RE SURE TO SEE MY APPLES ARE SMALL AS EVER THIS YEAR.
WH-WHAT IF THEY THINK IT'S MY FAULT MY APPLES ARE SMALL?
WHAT IF THEY'RE RIGHT? WHAT IF I DID SOMETHING WRONG?
WHAT AM I GOING TO DO! WHAT WILL I SAY???
POP

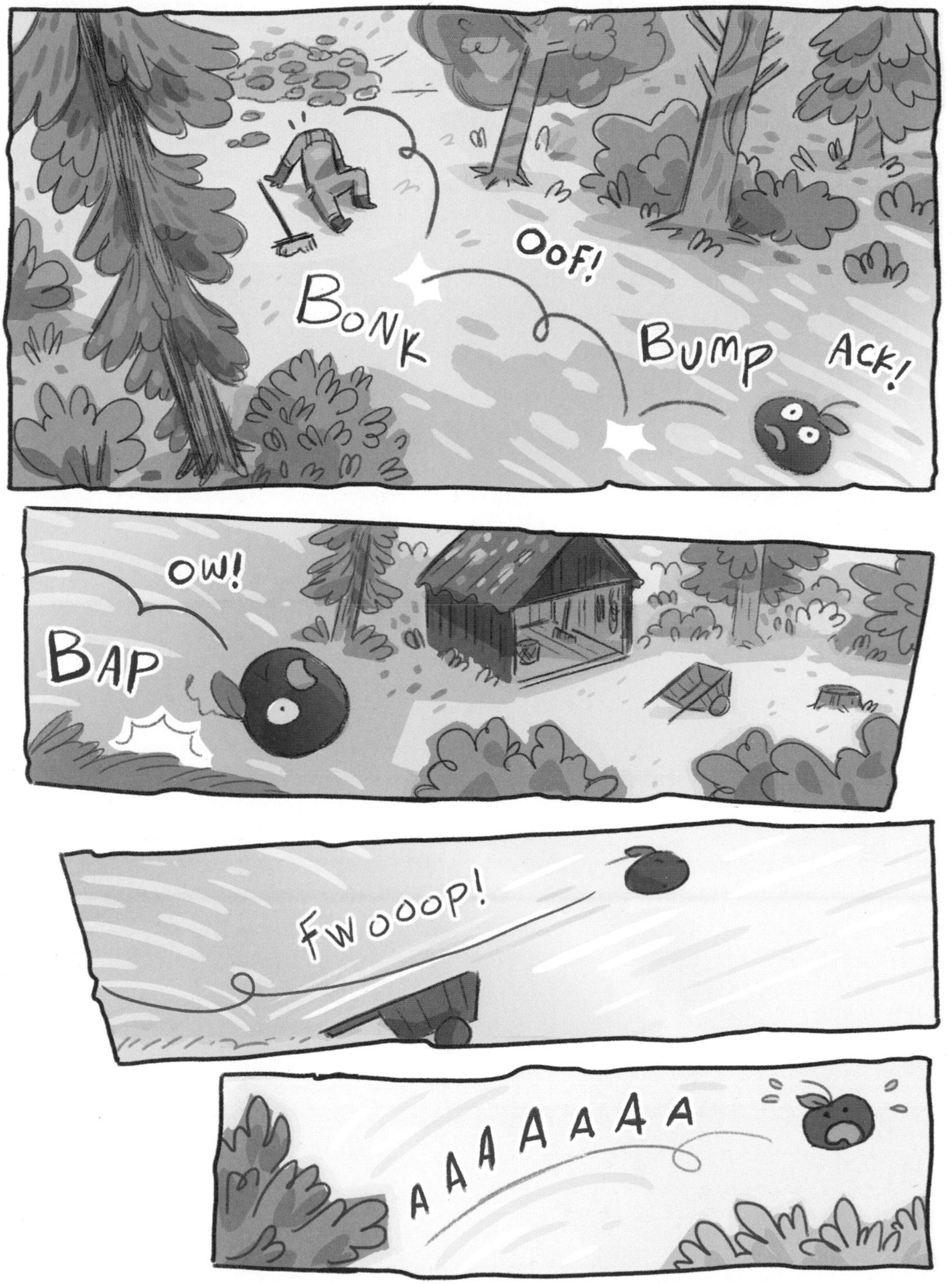
BONK
OOF!
BUMP
ACK!
BAP
OW!
FWOOOP!
AAAAAAAA

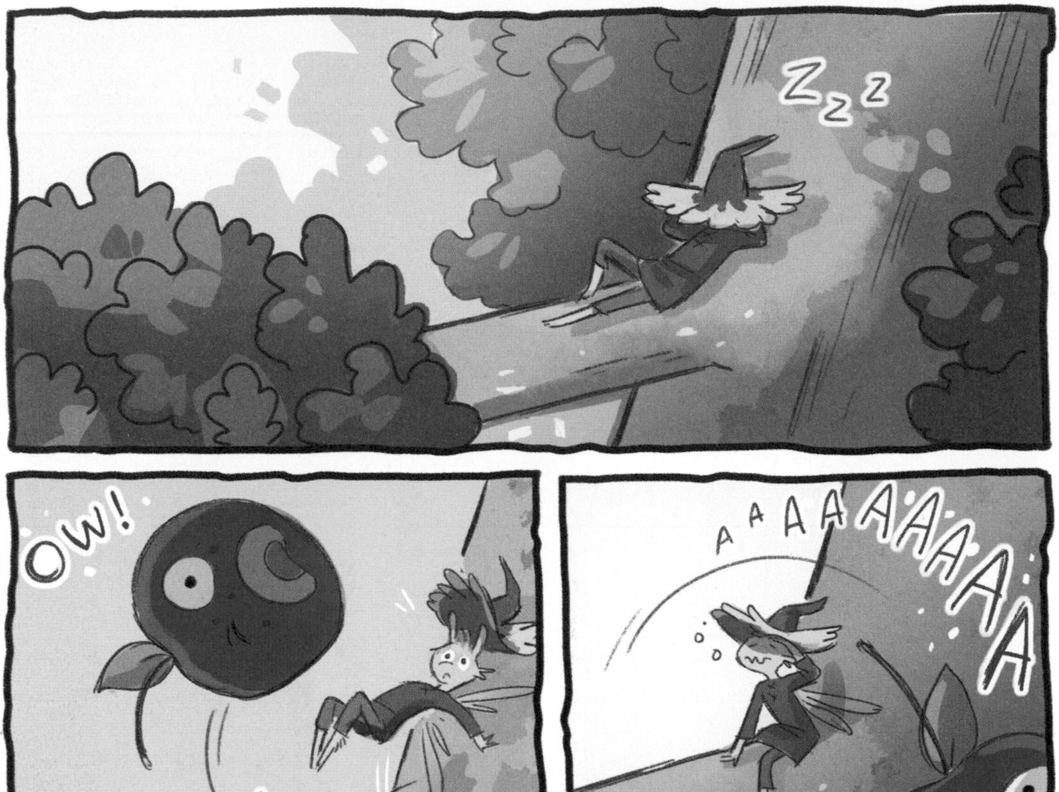
Z z z
OW!
AAAAAAAAAAAA
FOOOMP

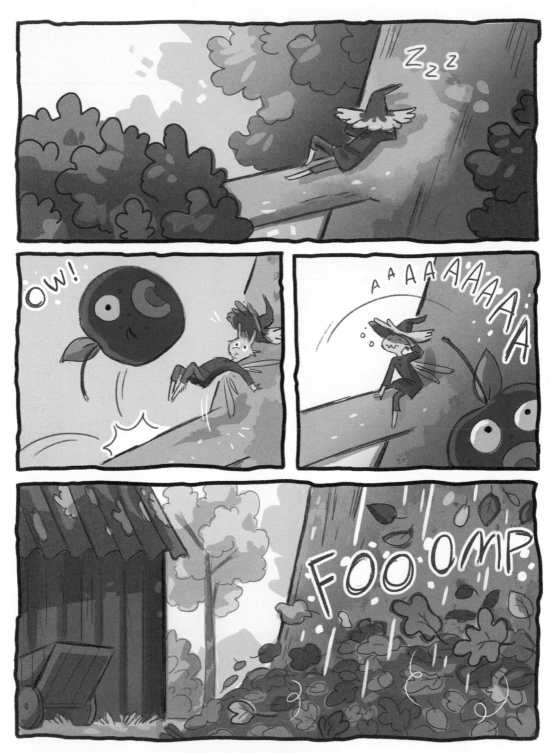

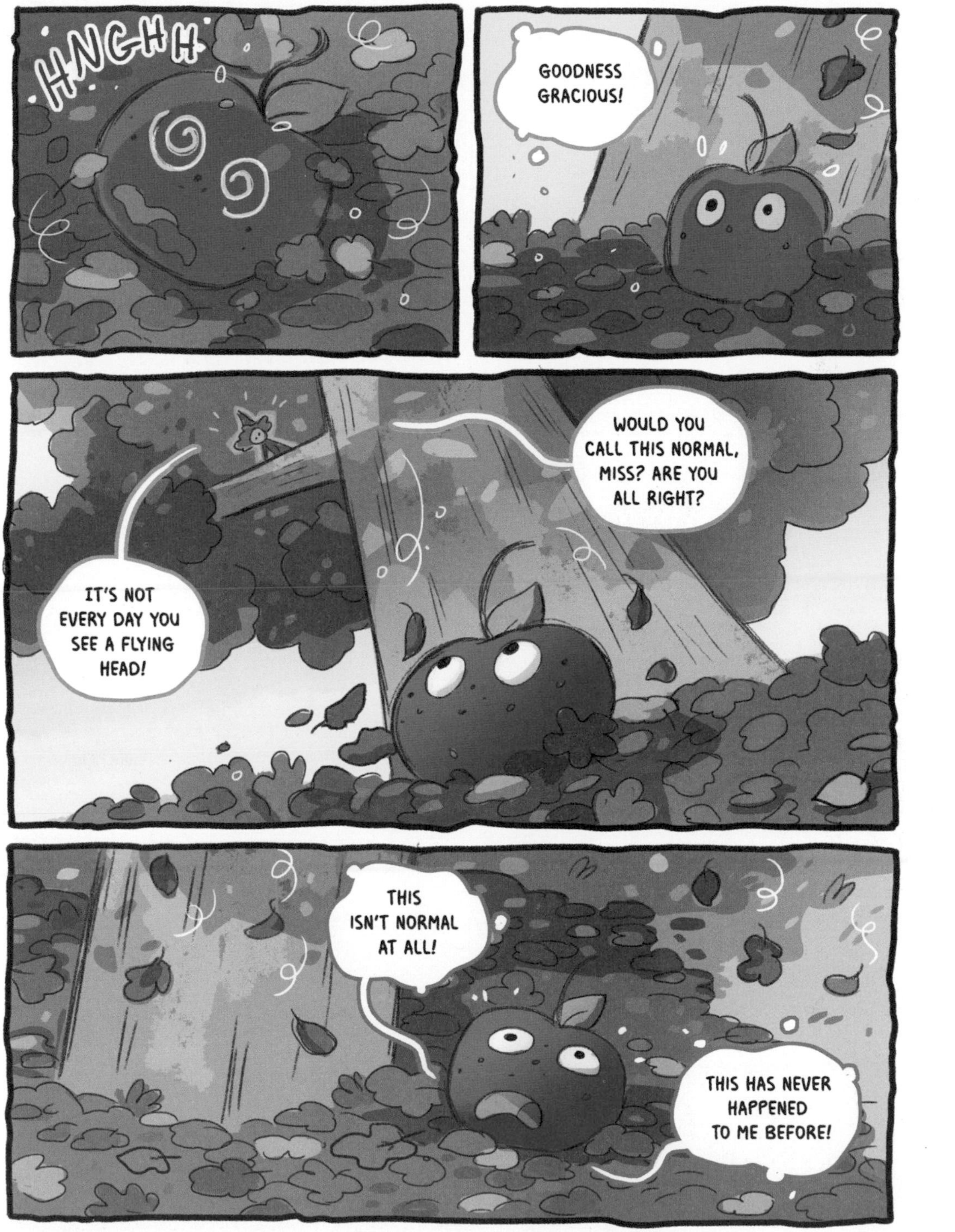
HNGHH
GOODNESS GRACIOUS!
WOULD YOU CALL THIS NORMAL, MISS? ARE YOU ALL RIGHT?
IT'S NOT EVERY DAY YOU SEE A FLYING HEAD!
THIS ISN'T NORMAL AT ALL!
THIS HAS NEVER HAPPENED TO ME BEFORE!

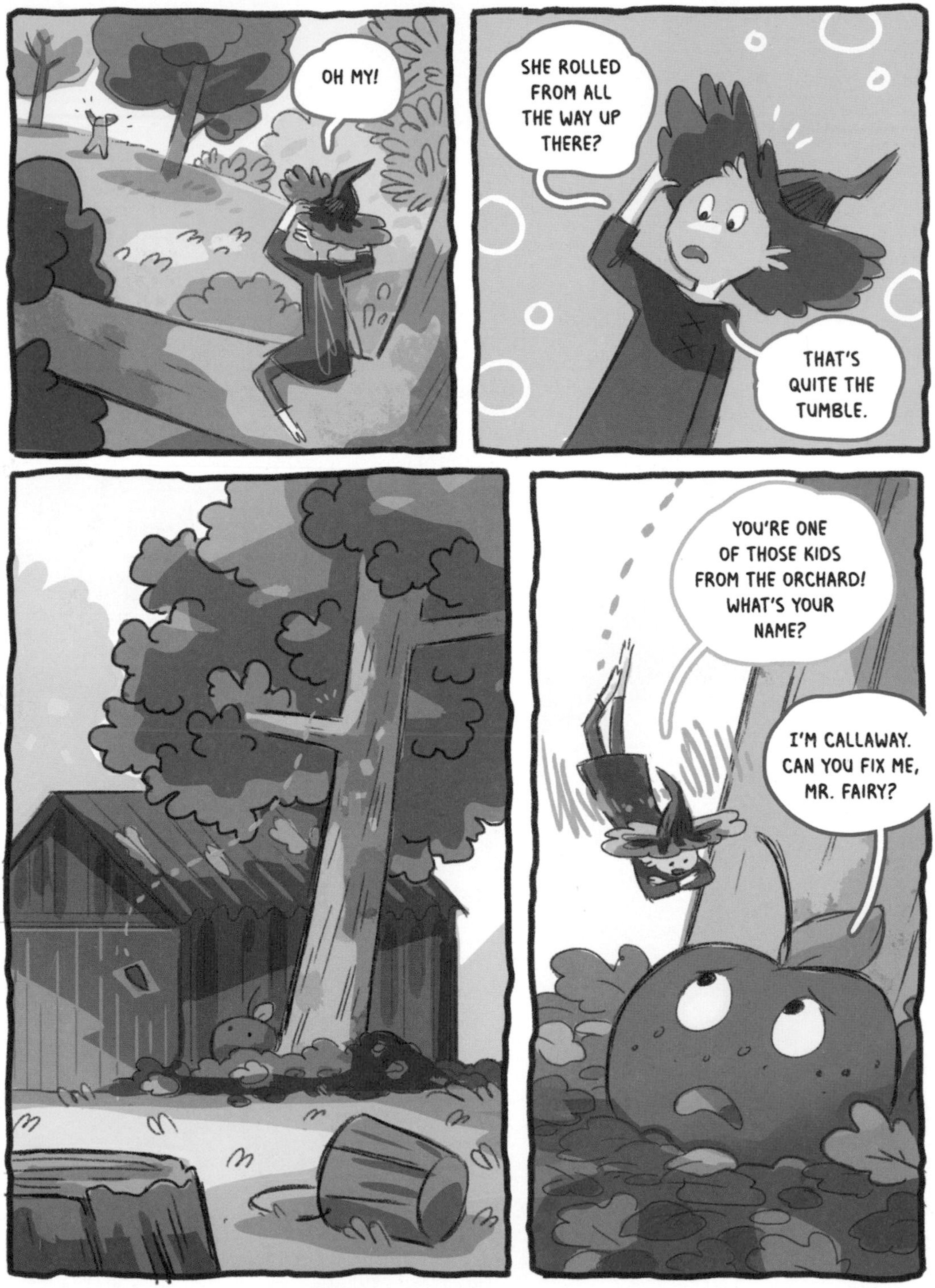
OH MY!
SHE ROLLED FROM ALL THE WAY UP THERE?
THAT'S QUITE THE TUMBLE.
YOU'RE ONE OF THOSE KIDS FROM THE ORCHARD! WHAT'S YOUR NAME?
I'M CALLAWAY. CAN YOU FIX ME, MR. FAIRY?

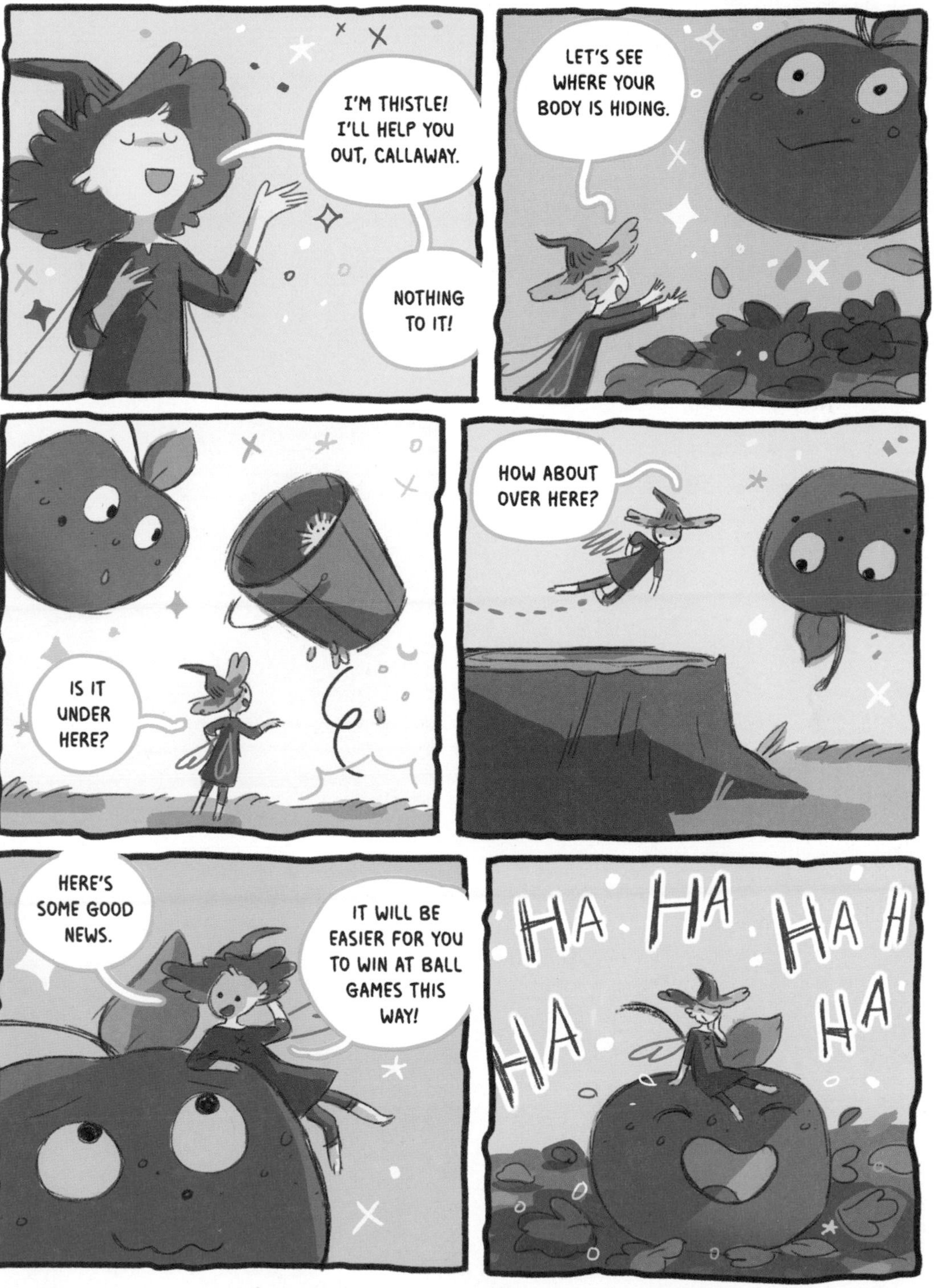
I'M THISTLE! I'LL HELP YOU OUT, CALLAWAY.
NOTHING TO IT!
LET'S SEE WHERE YOUR BODY IS HIDING.
IS IT UNDER HERE?
HOW ABOUT OVER HERE?
HERE'S SOME GOOD NEWS.
IT WILL BE EASIER FOR YOU TO WIN AT BALL GAMES THIS WAY!
HA HA HA H
HA HA

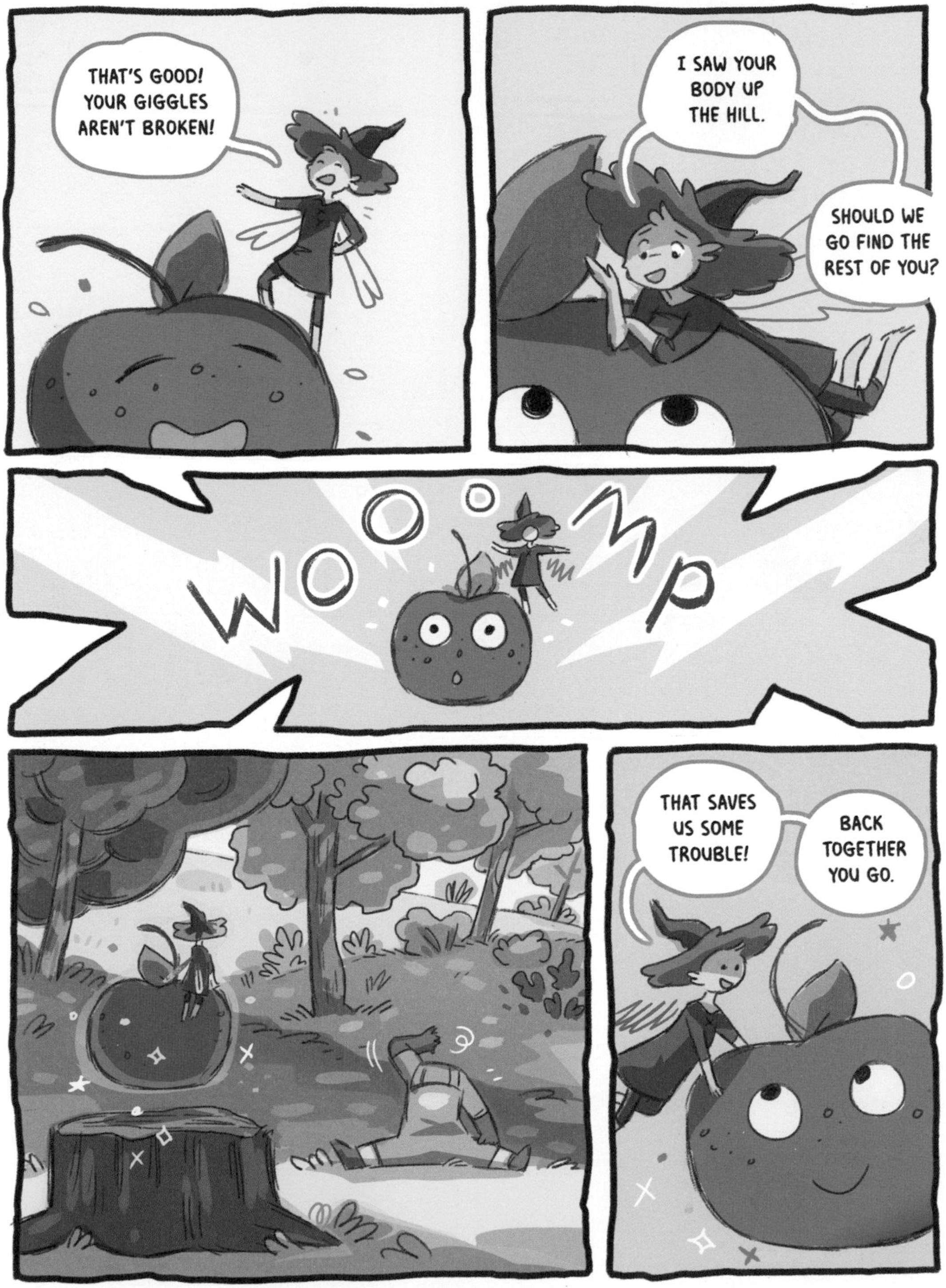
THAT'S GOOD! YOUR GIGGLES AREN'T BROKEN!
I SAW YOUR BODY UP THE HILL.
SHOULD WE GO FIND THE REST OF YOU?
WOOOOMP
THAT SAVES US SOME TROUBLE!
BACK TOGETHER YOU GO.

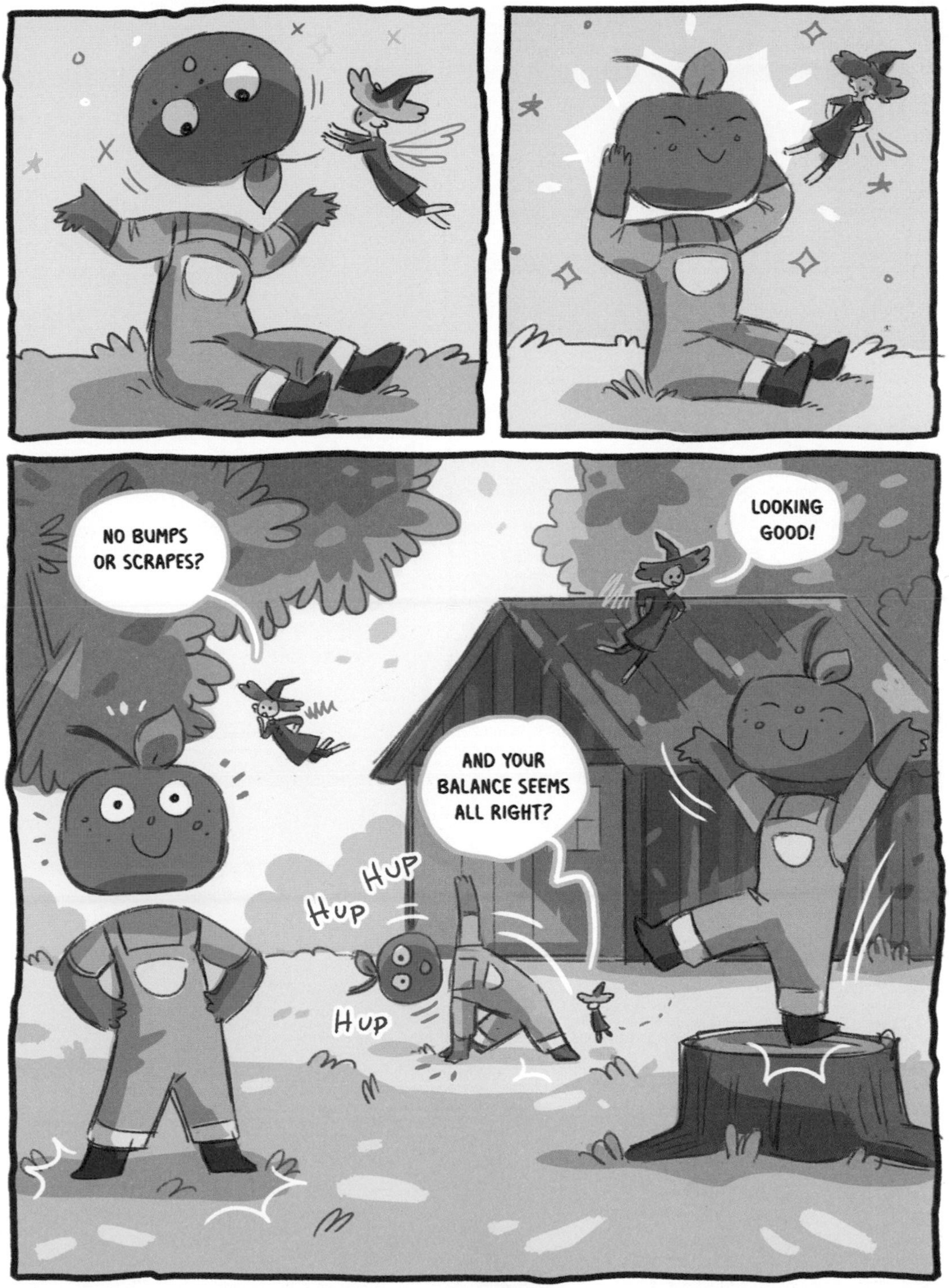
NO BUMPS OR SCRAPES?
LOOKING GOOD!
AND YOUR BALANCE SEEMS ALL RIGHT?
HUP
HUP
HUP

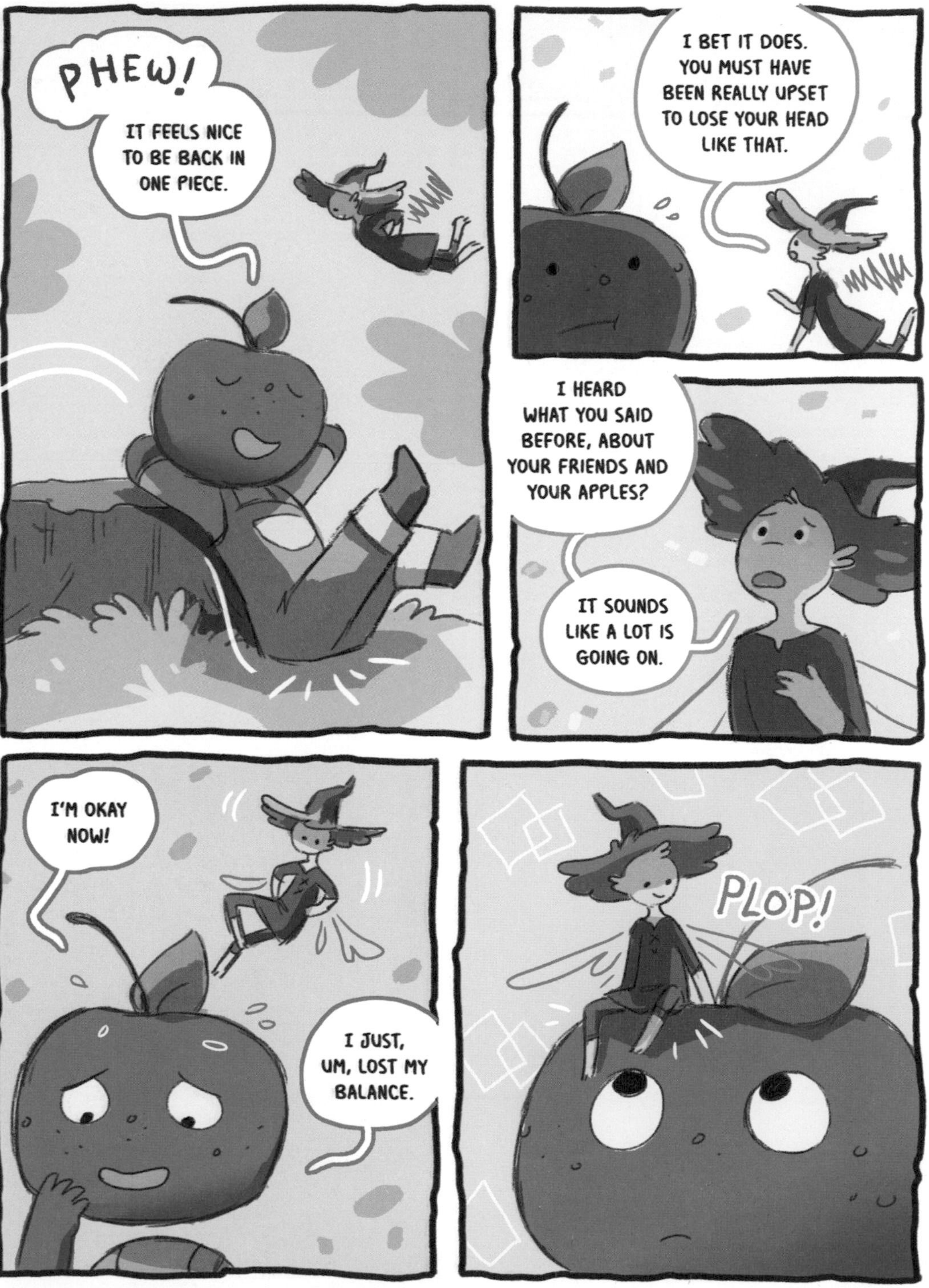
PHEW!
IT FEELS NICE TO BE BACK IN ONE PIECE.
I BET IT DOES. YOU MUST HAVE BEEN REALLY UPSET TO LOSE YOUR HEAD LIKE THAT.
I HEARD WHAT YOU SAID BEFORE, ABOUT YOUR FRIENDS AND YOUR APPLES?
IT SOUNDS LIKE A LOT IS GOING ON.
I'M OKAY NOW!
I JUST, UM, LOST MY BALANCE.
PLOP!

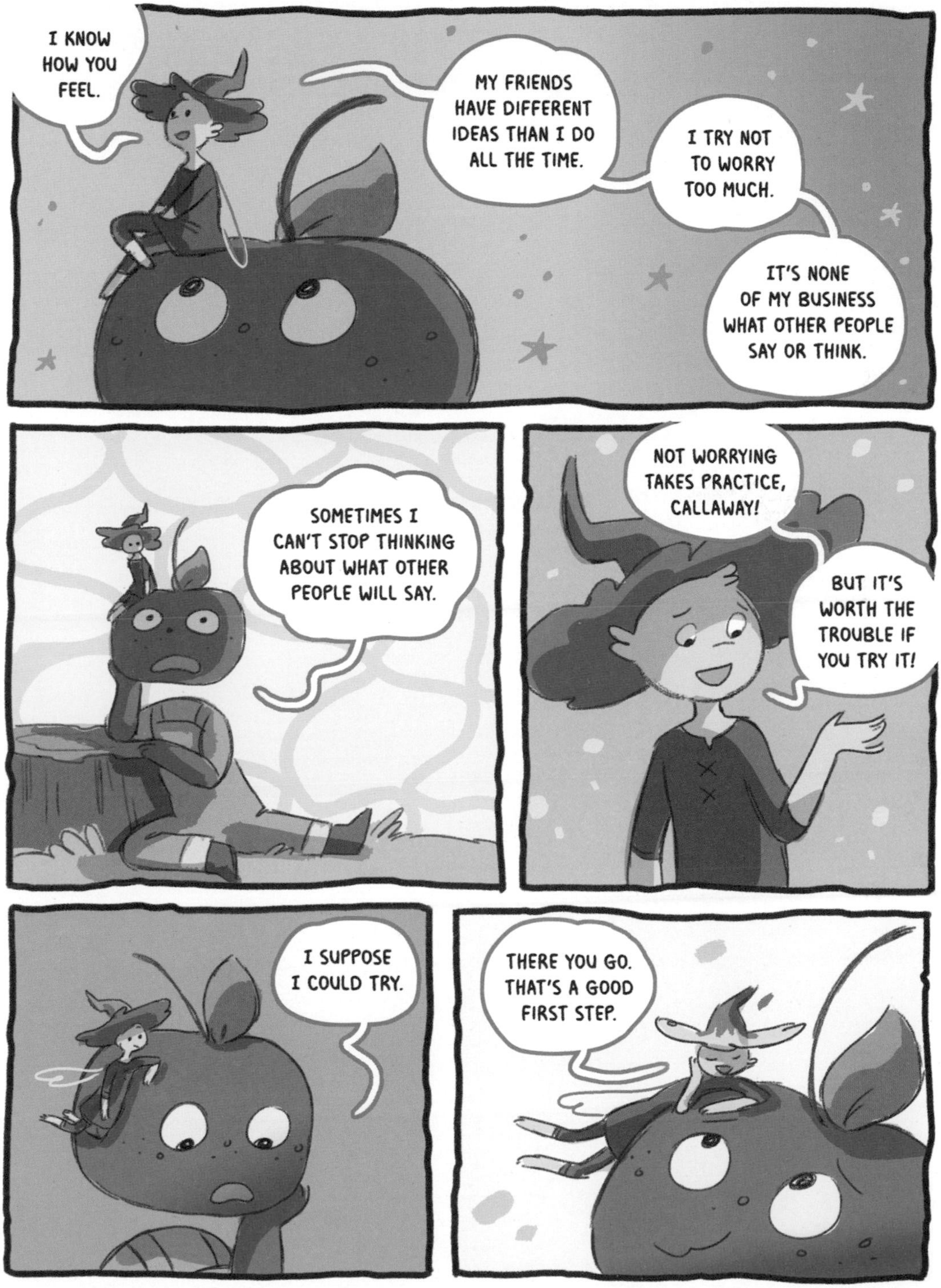
I KNOW HOW YOU FEEL.
MY FRIENDS HAVE DIFFERENT IDEAS THAN I DO ALL THE TIME.
I TRY NOT TO WORRY TOO MUCH.
IT'S NONE OF MY BUSINESS WHAT OTHER PEOPLE SAY OR THINK.
SOMETIMES I CAN'T STOP THINKING ABOUT WHAT OTHER PEOPLE WILL SAY.
NOT WORRYING TAKES PRACTICE, CALLAWAY!
BUT IT'S WORTH THE TROUBLE IF YOU TRY IT!
I SUPPOSE I COULD TRY.
THERE YOU GO. THAT'S A GOOD FIRST STEP.

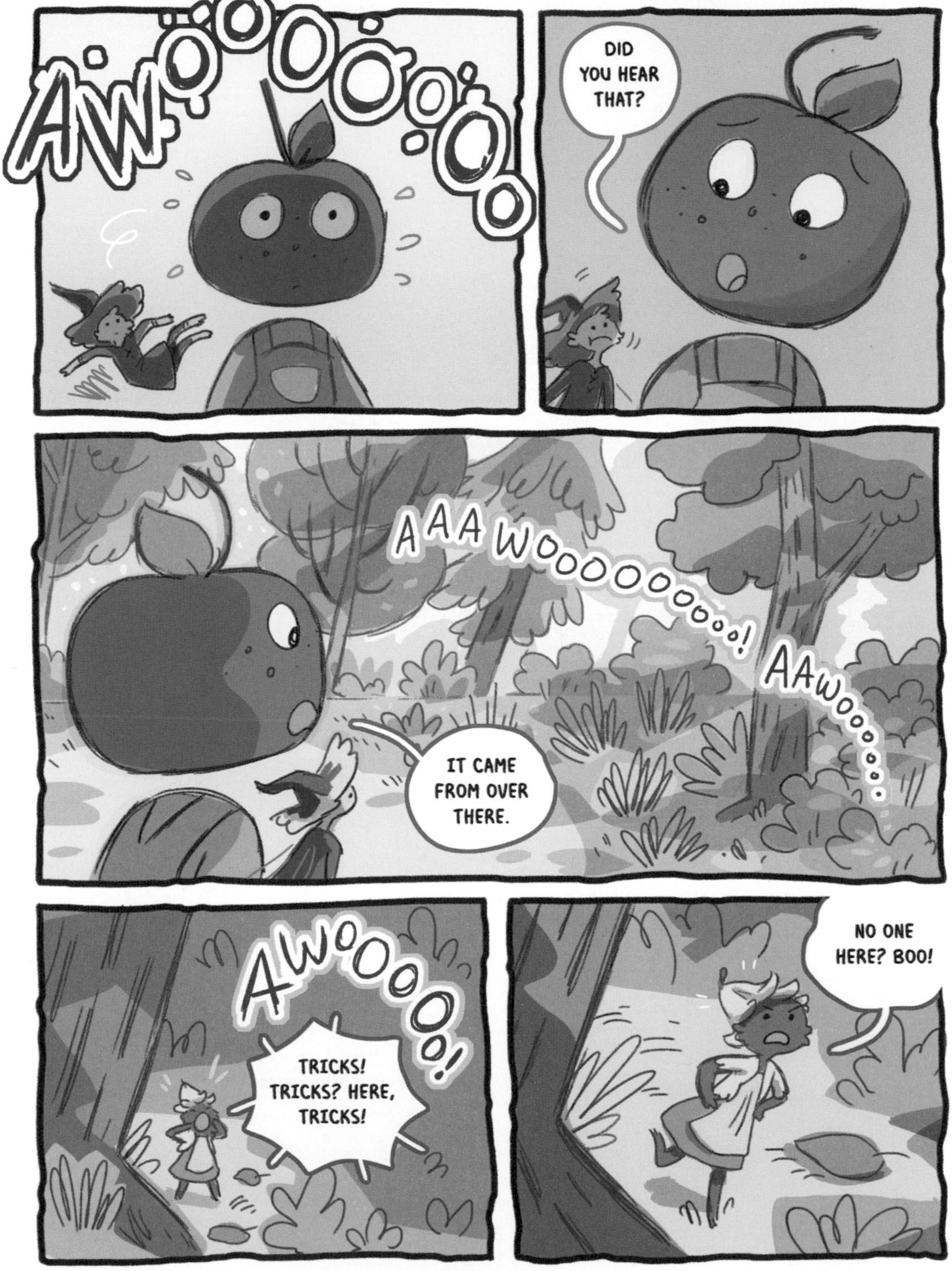
AWÖOOOOOOO
DID YOU HEAR THAT?
AAA WOOOOOOOooo!
AAWoooooo
IT CAME FROM OVER THERE.
AWOOOOo!
TRICKS! TRICKS? HERE, TRICKS!
NO ONE HERE? BOO!

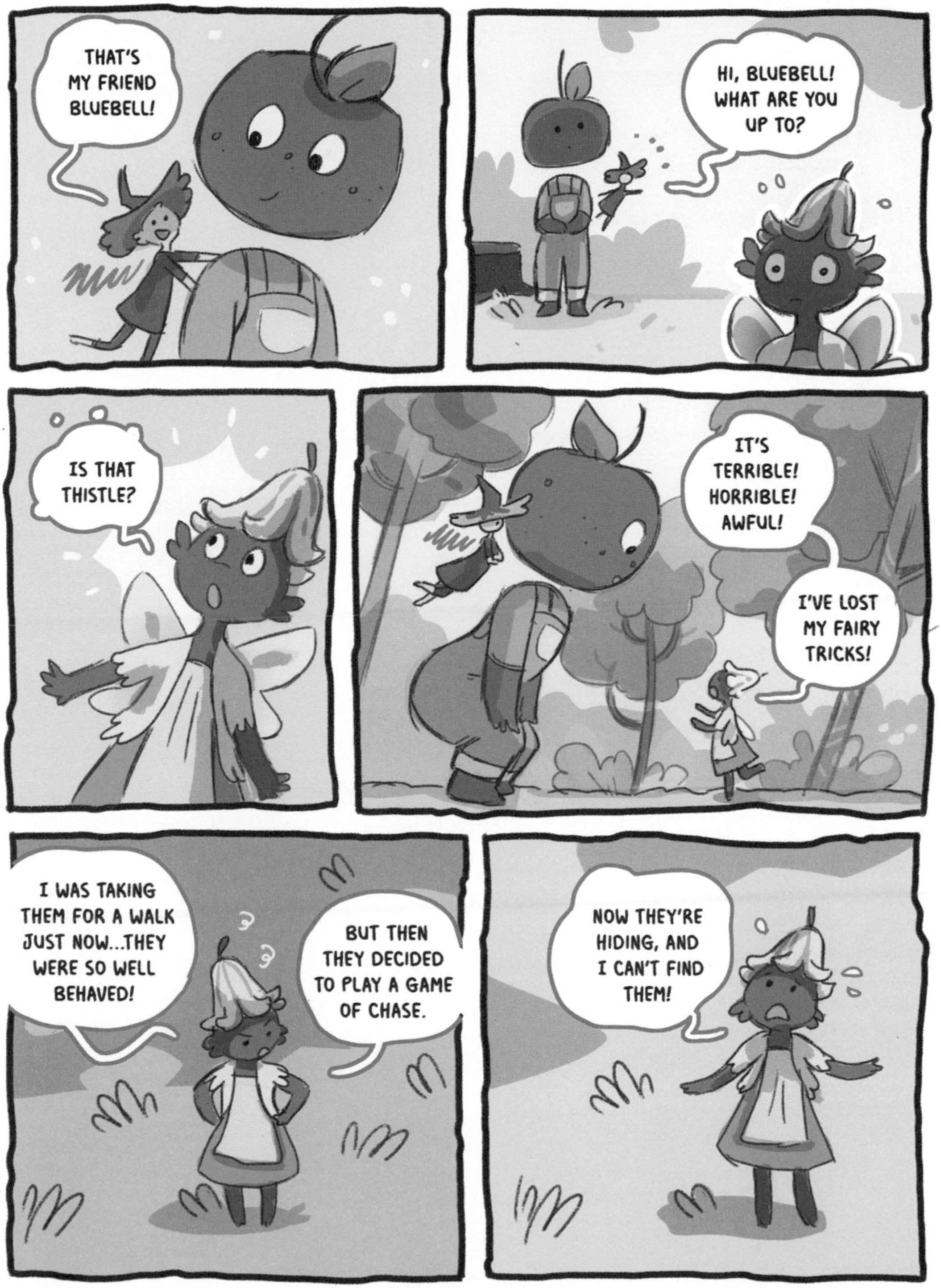
THAT'S MY FRIEND BLUEBELL!
HI, BLUEBELL! WHAT ARE YOU UP TO?
IS THAT THISTLE?
IT'S TERRIBLE! HORRIBLE! AWFUL!
I'VE LOST MY FAIRY TRICKS!
I WAS TAKING THEM FOR A WALK JUST NOW...THEY WERE SO WELL BEHAVED!
BUT THEN THEY DECIDED TO PLAY A GAME OF CHASE.
NOW THEY'RE HIDING, AND I CAN'T FIND THEM!

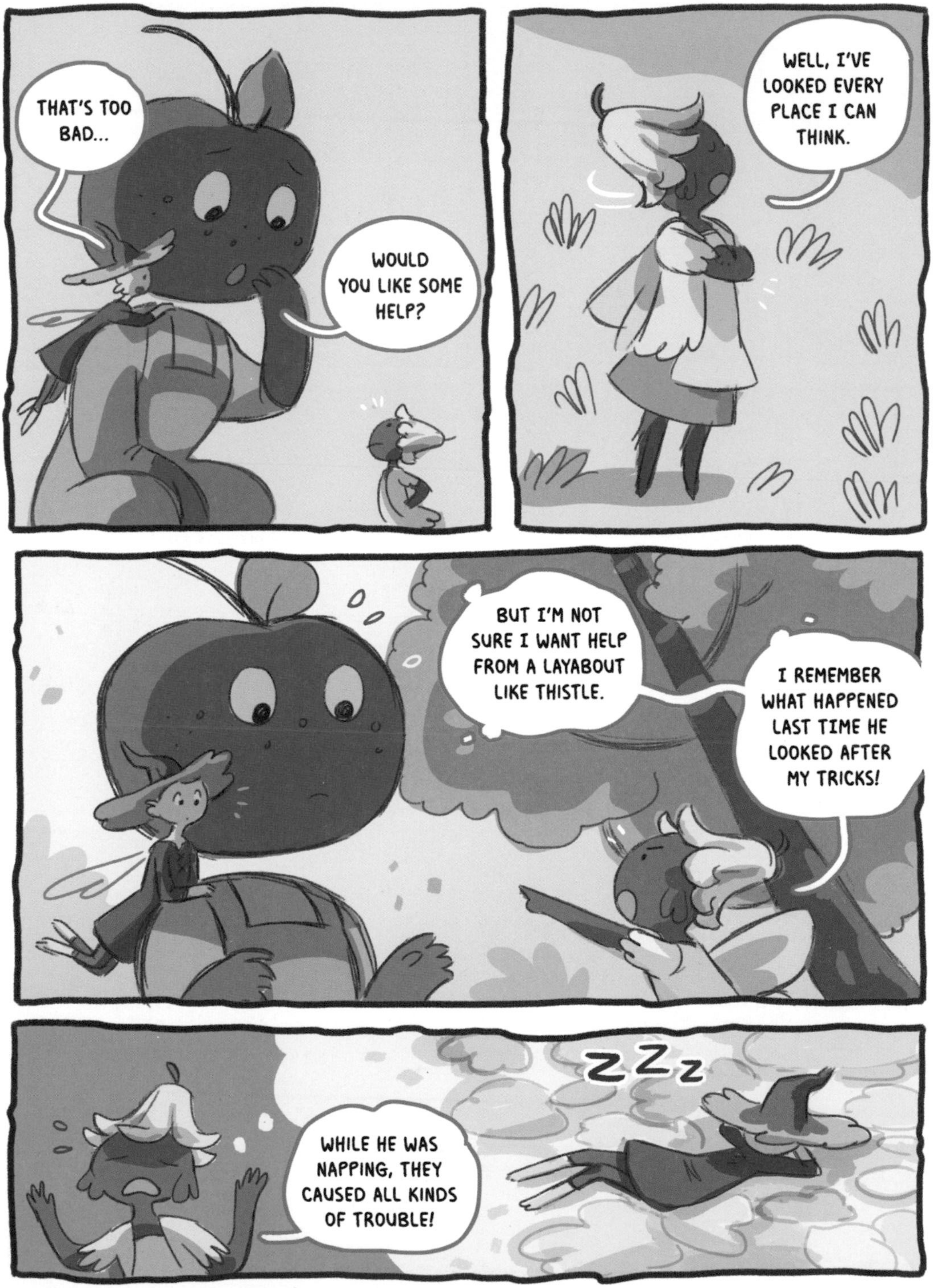
THAT'S TOO BAD...
WOULD YOU LIKE SOME HELP?
WELL, I'VE LOOKED EVERY PLACE I CAN THINK.
BUT I'M NOT SURE I WANT HELP FROM A LAYABOUT LIKE THISTLE.
I REMEMBER WHAT HAPPENED LAST TIME HE LOOKED AFTER MY TRICKS!
ZZZ
WHILE HE WAS NAPPING, THEY CAUSED ALL KINDS OF TROUBLE!

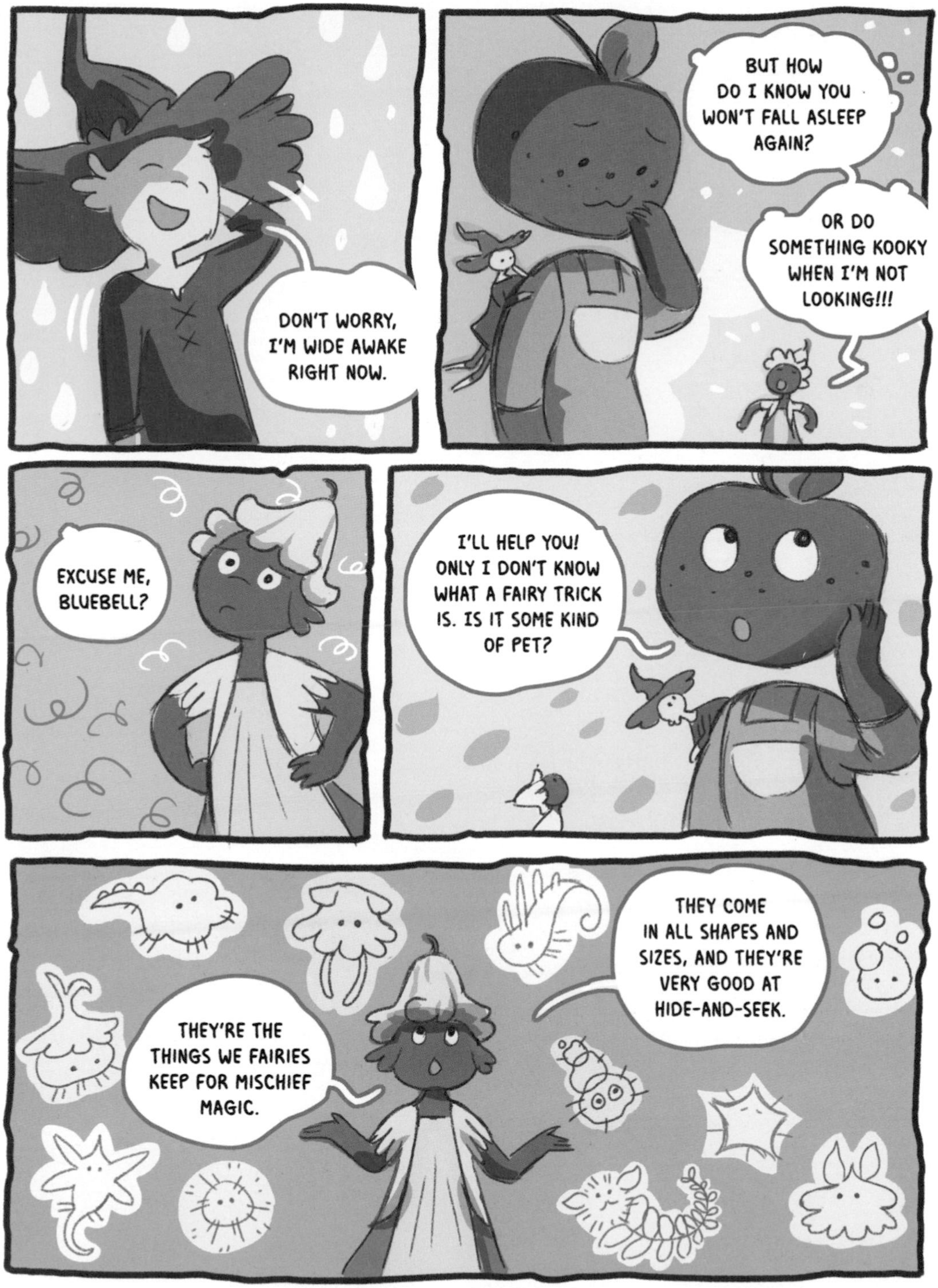
DON'T WORRY, I'M WIDE AWAKE RIGHT NOW.
BUT HOW DO I KNOW YOU WON'T FALL ASLEEP AGAIN?
OR DO SOMETHING KOOKY WHEN I'M NOT LOOKING!!!
EXCUSE ME, BLUEBELL?
I'LL HELP YOU! ONLY I DON'T KNOW WHAT A FAIRY TRICK IS. IS IT SOME KIND OF PET?
THEY'RE THE THINGS WE FAIRIES KEEP FOR MISCHIEF MAGIC.
THEY COME IN ALL SHAPES AND SIZES, AND THEY'RE VERY GOOD AT HIDE-AND-SEEK.

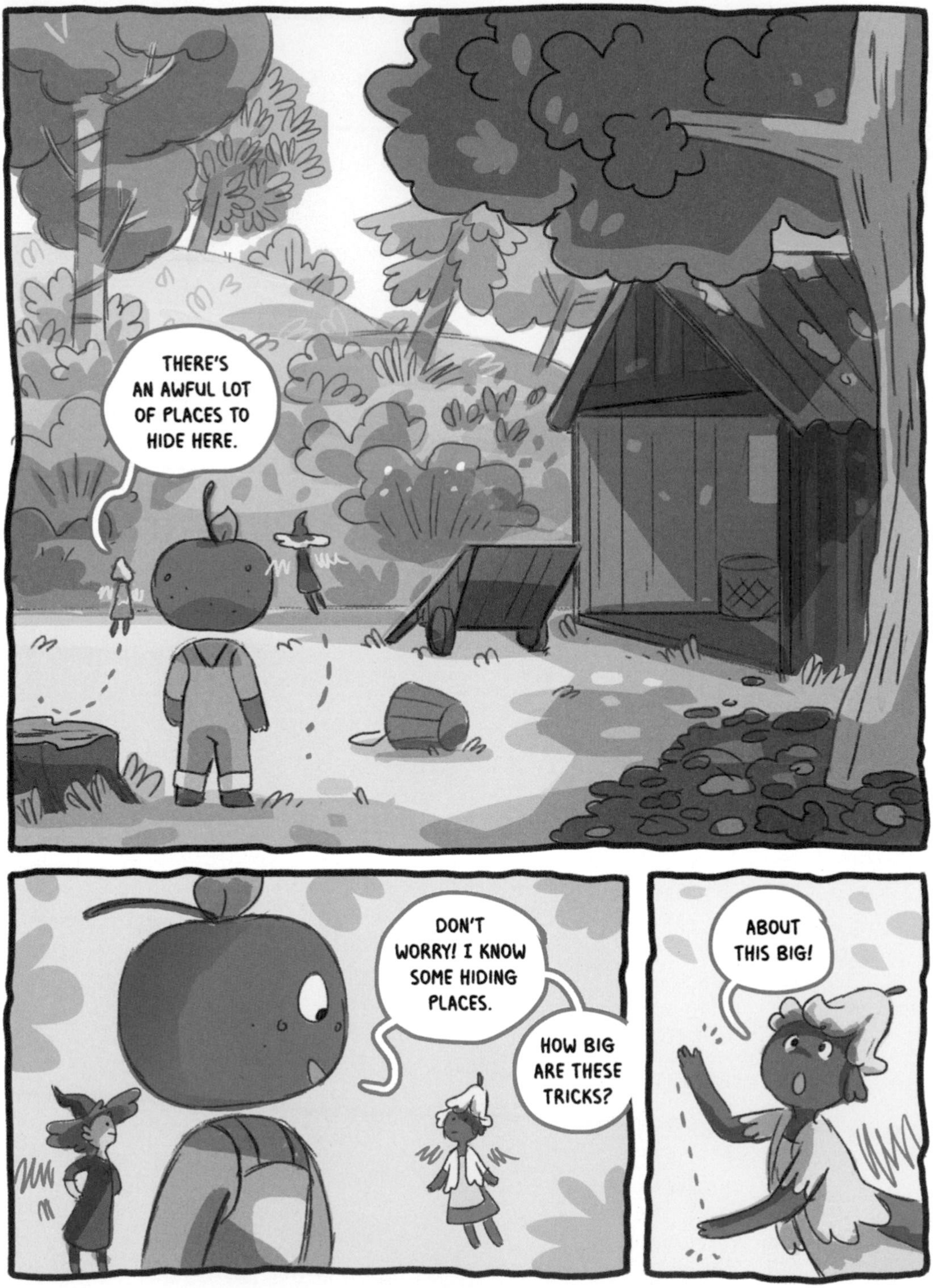
THERE'S AN AWFUL LOT OF PLACES TO HIDE HERE.
DON'T WORRY! I KNOW SOME HIDING PLACES.
HOW BIG ARE THESE TRICKS?
ABOUT THIS BIG!

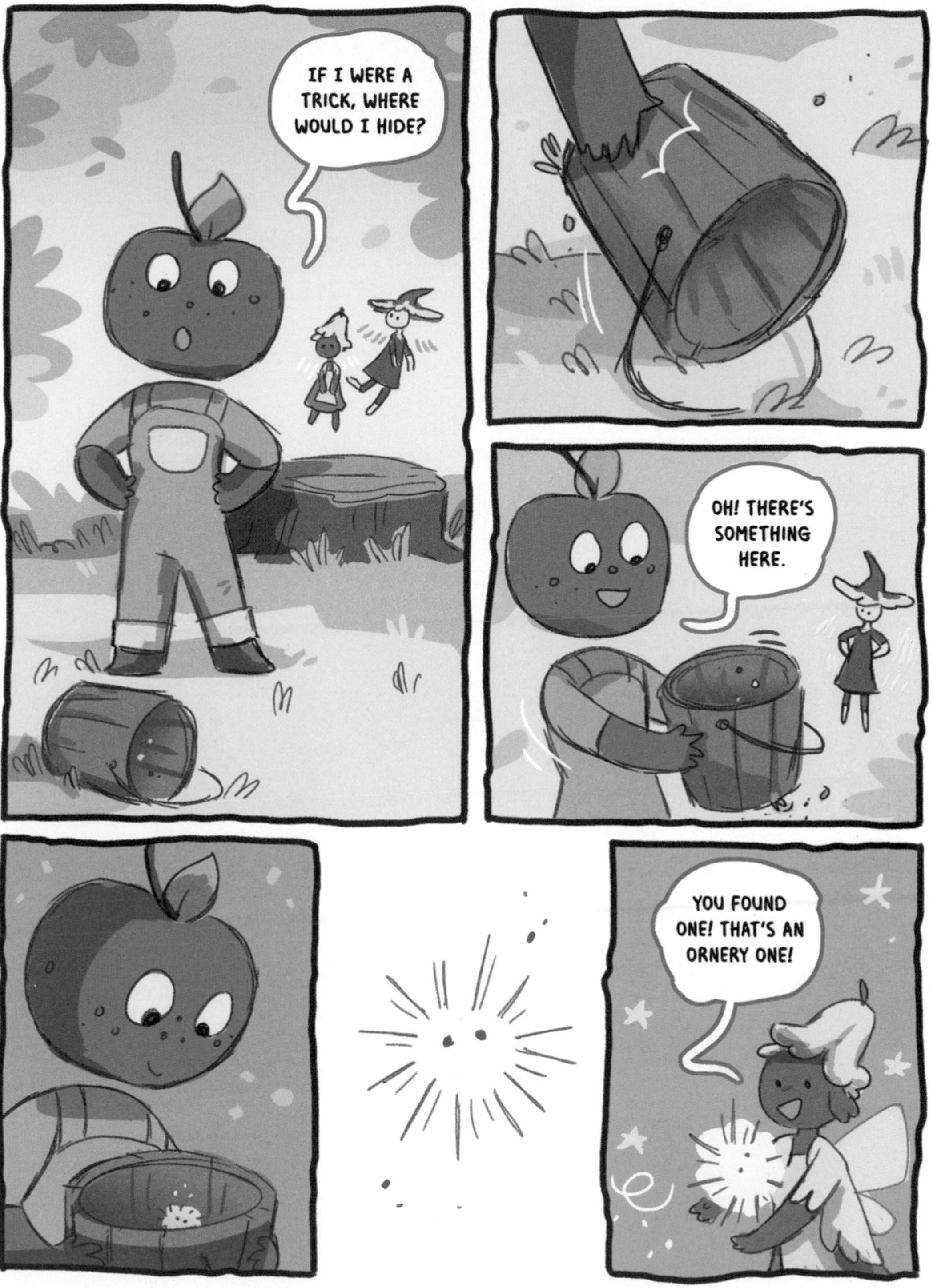
IF I WERE A TRICK, WHERE WOULD I HIDE?
OH! THERE'S SOMETHING HERE.
YOU FOUND ONE! THAT'S AN ORNERY ONE!

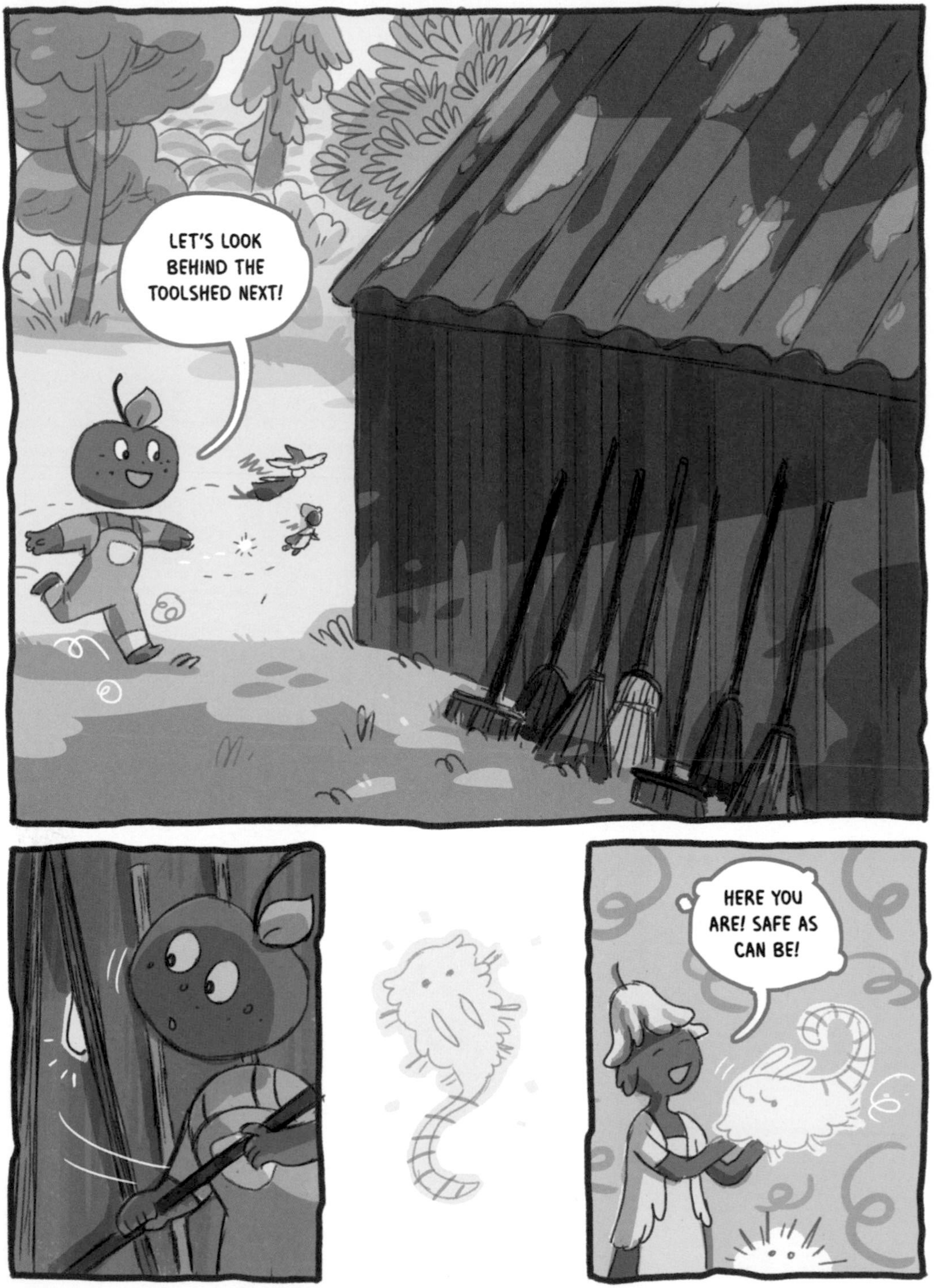
LET'S LOOK BEHIND THE TOOLSHED NEXT!
HERE YOU ARE! SAFE AS CAN BE!

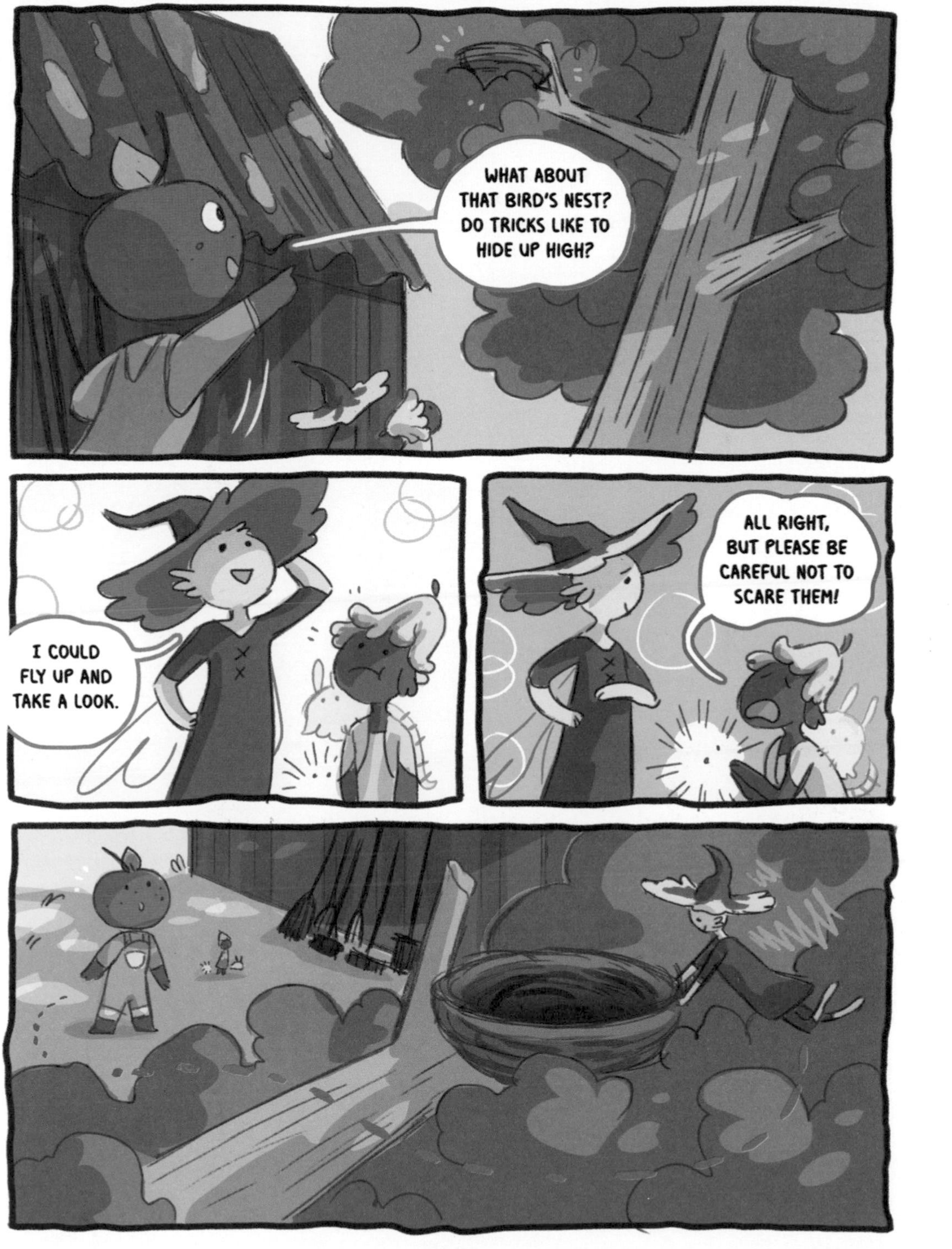
WHAT ABOUT THAT BIRD'S NEST? DO TRICKS LIKE TO HIDE UP HIGH?
I COULD FLY UP AND TAKE A LOOK.
ALL RIGHT, BUT PLEASE BE CAREFUL NOT TO SCARE THEM!

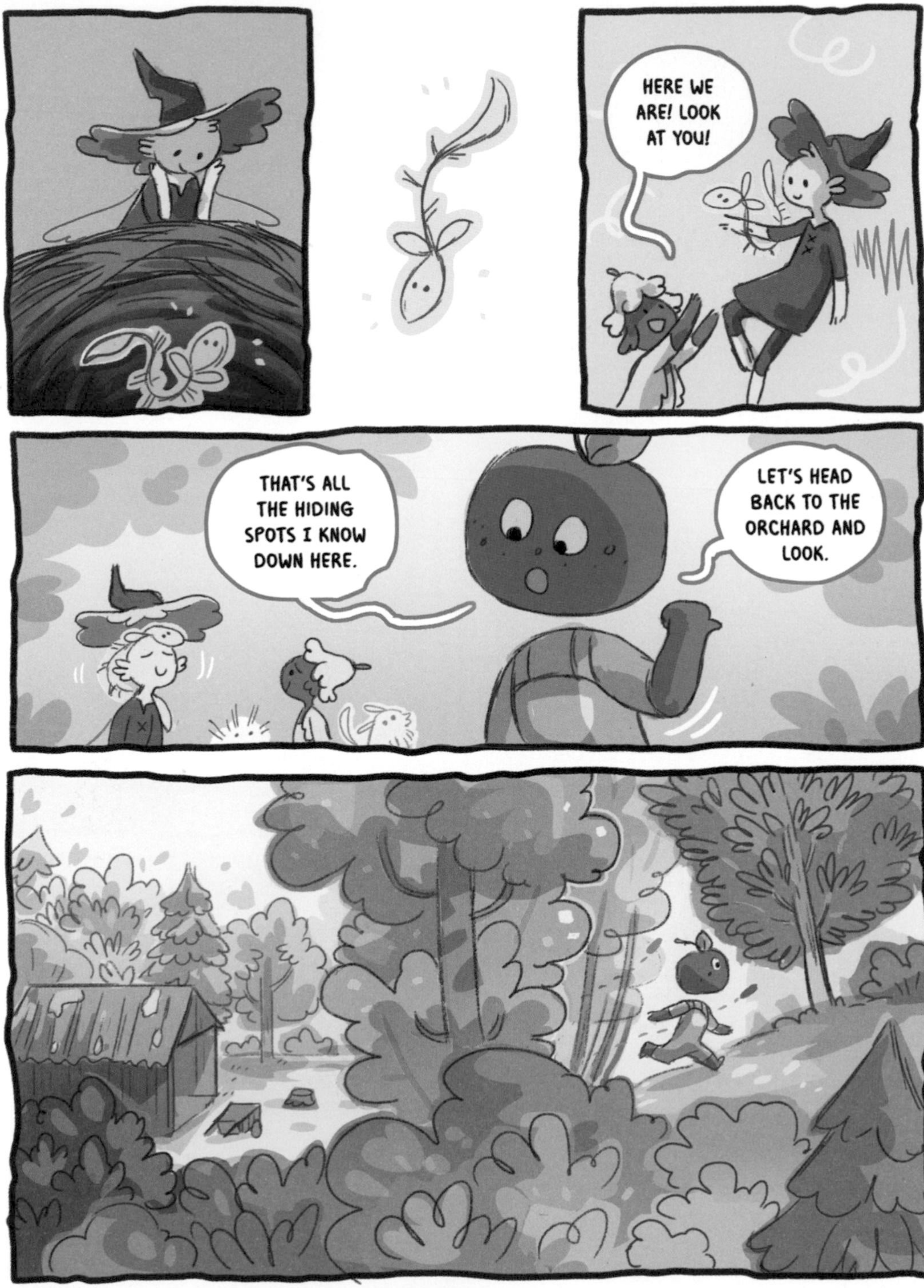
HERE WE ARE! LOOK AT YOU!
THAT'S ALL THE HIDING SPOTS I KNOW DOWN HERE.
LET'S HEAD BACK TO THE ORCHARD AND LOOK.

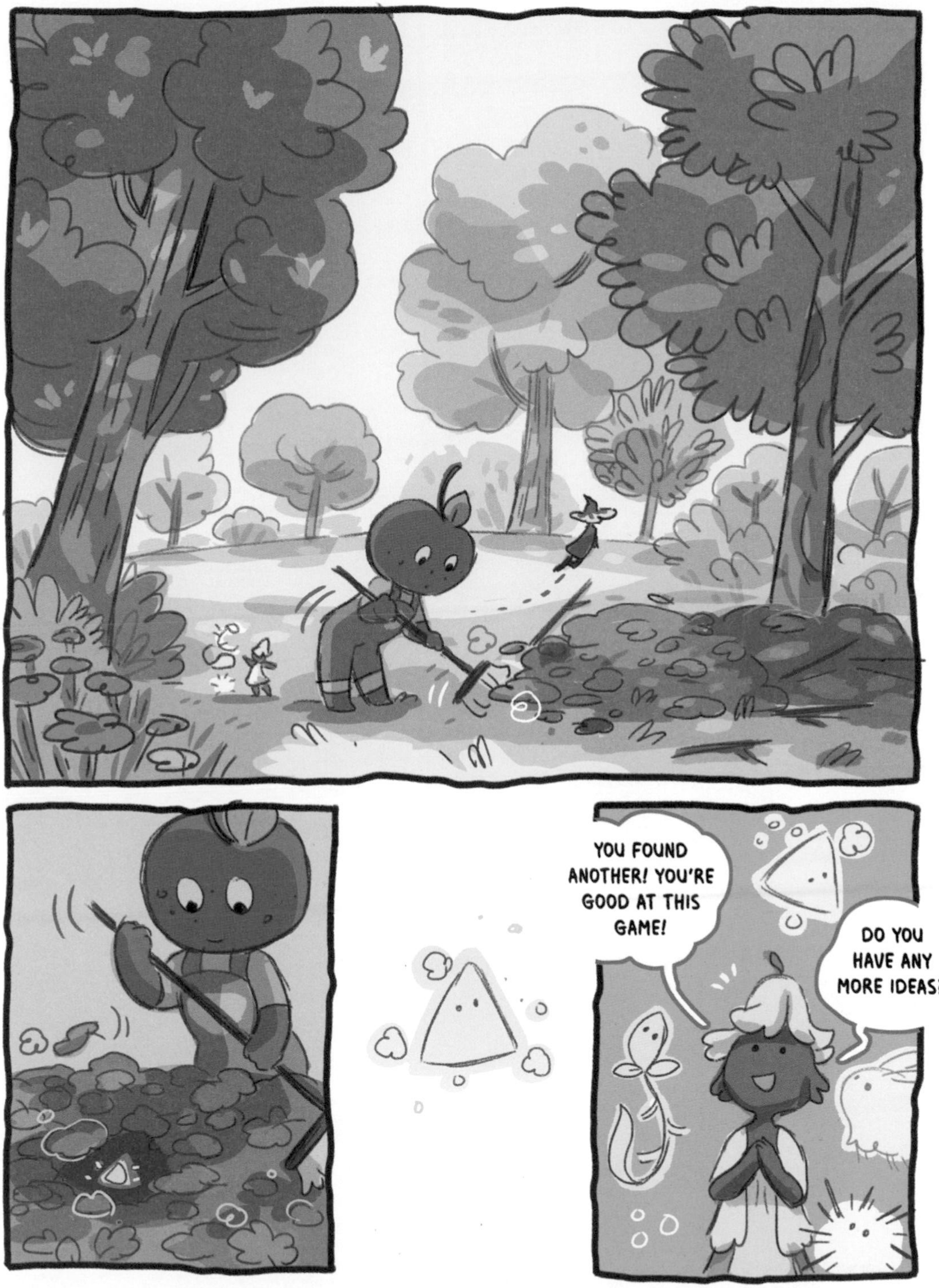
YOU FOUND ANOTHER! YOU'RE GOOD AT THIS GAME!
DO YOU HAVE ANY MORE IDEAS?

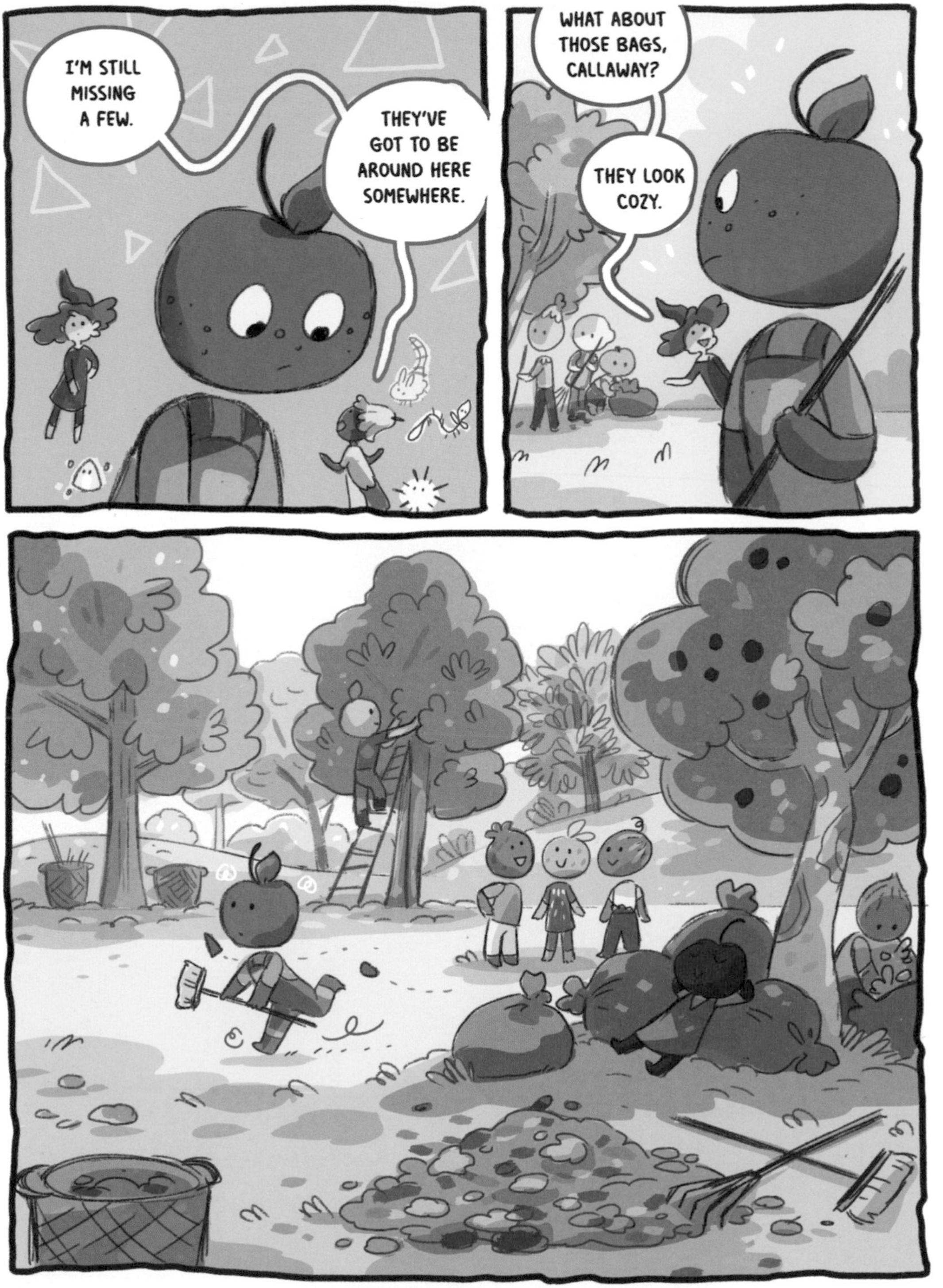
I'M STILL MISSING A FEW.
THEY'VE GOT TO BE AROUND HERE SOMEWHERE.
WHAT ABOUT THOSE BAGS, CALLAWAY?
THEY LOOK COZY.

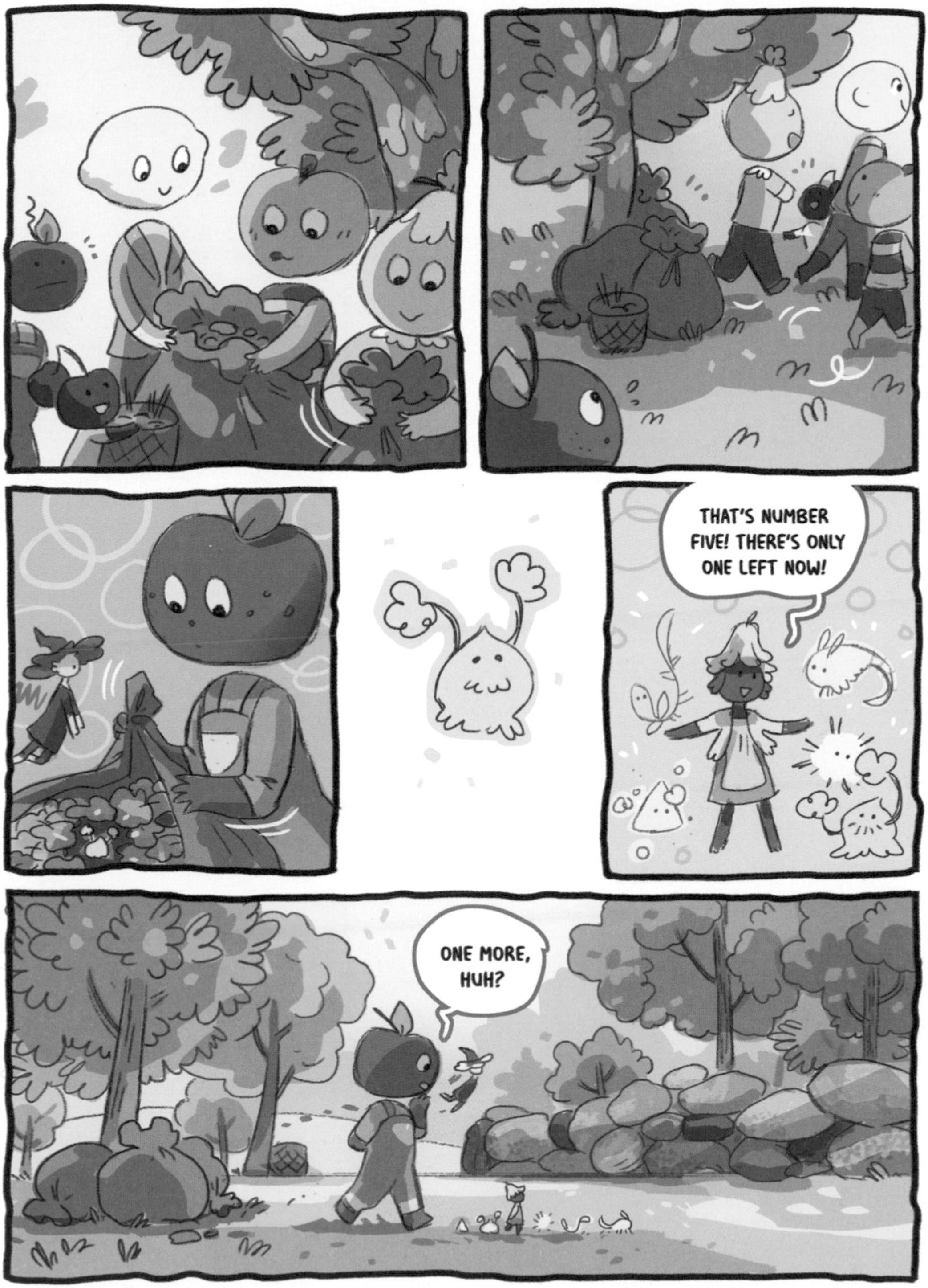
THAT'S NUMBER FIVE! THERE'S ONLY ONE LEFT NOW!
ONE MORE, HUH?

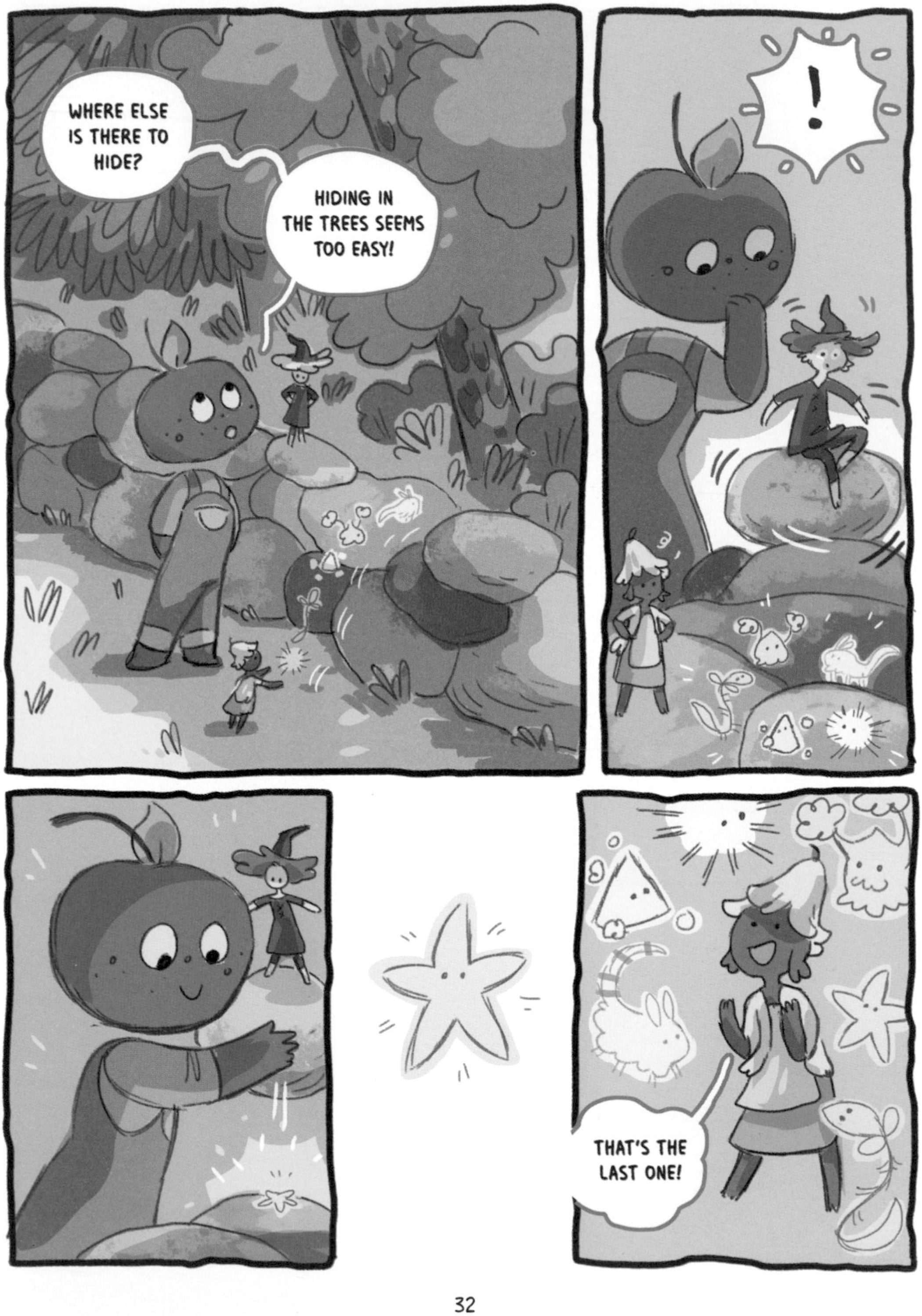
WHERE ELSE IS THERE TO HIDE?
HIDING IN THE TREES SEEMS TOO EASY!
!
THAT'S THE LAST ONE!

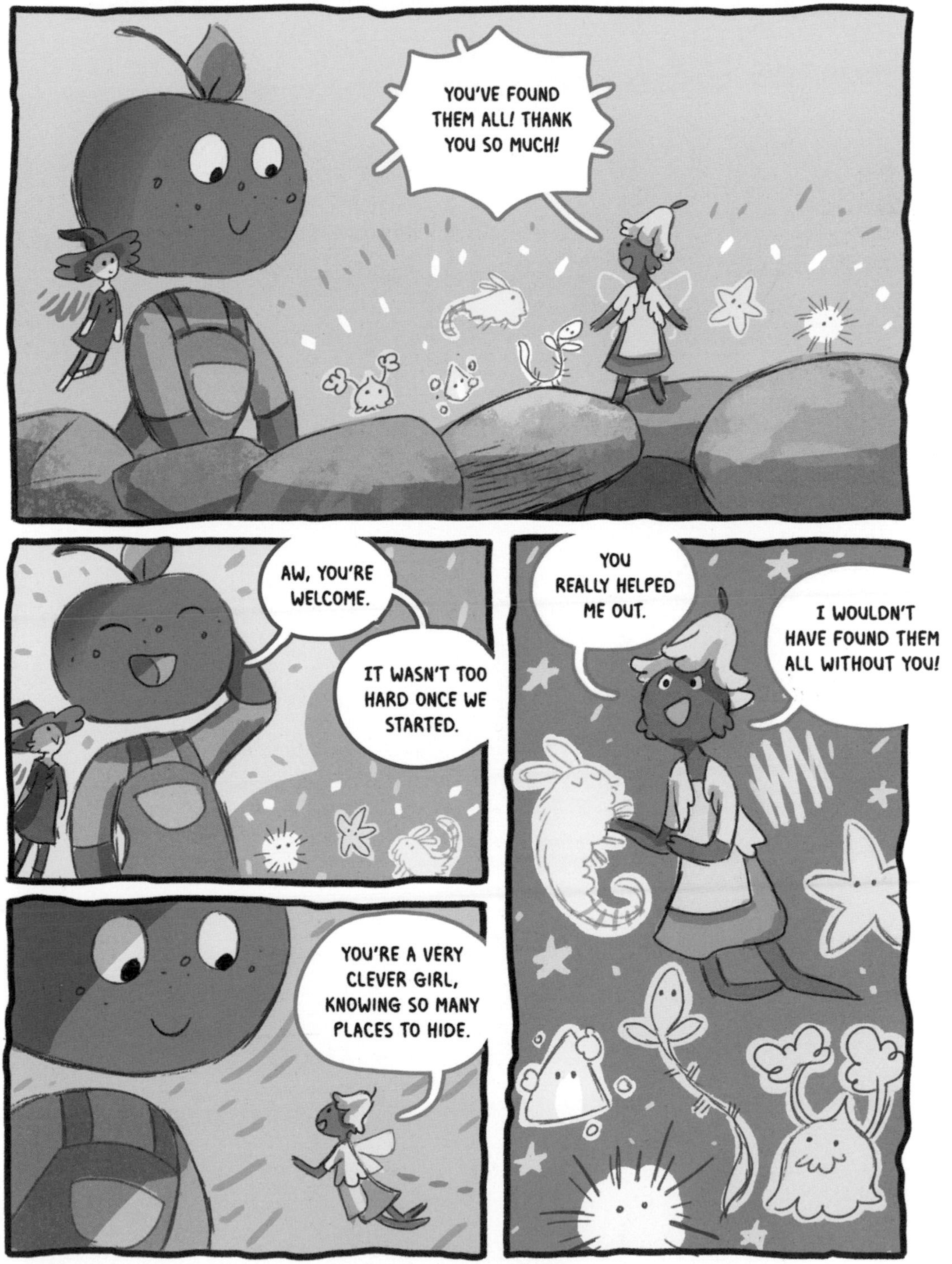
YOU'VE FOUND THEM ALL! THANK YOU SO MUCH!
AW, YOU'RE WELCOME.
IT WASN'T TOO HARD ONCE WE STARTED.
YOU'RE A VERY CLEVER GIRL, KNOWING SO MANY PLACES TO HIDE.
YOU REALLY HELPED ME OUT.
I WOULDN'T HAVE FOUND THEM ALL WITHOUT YOU!

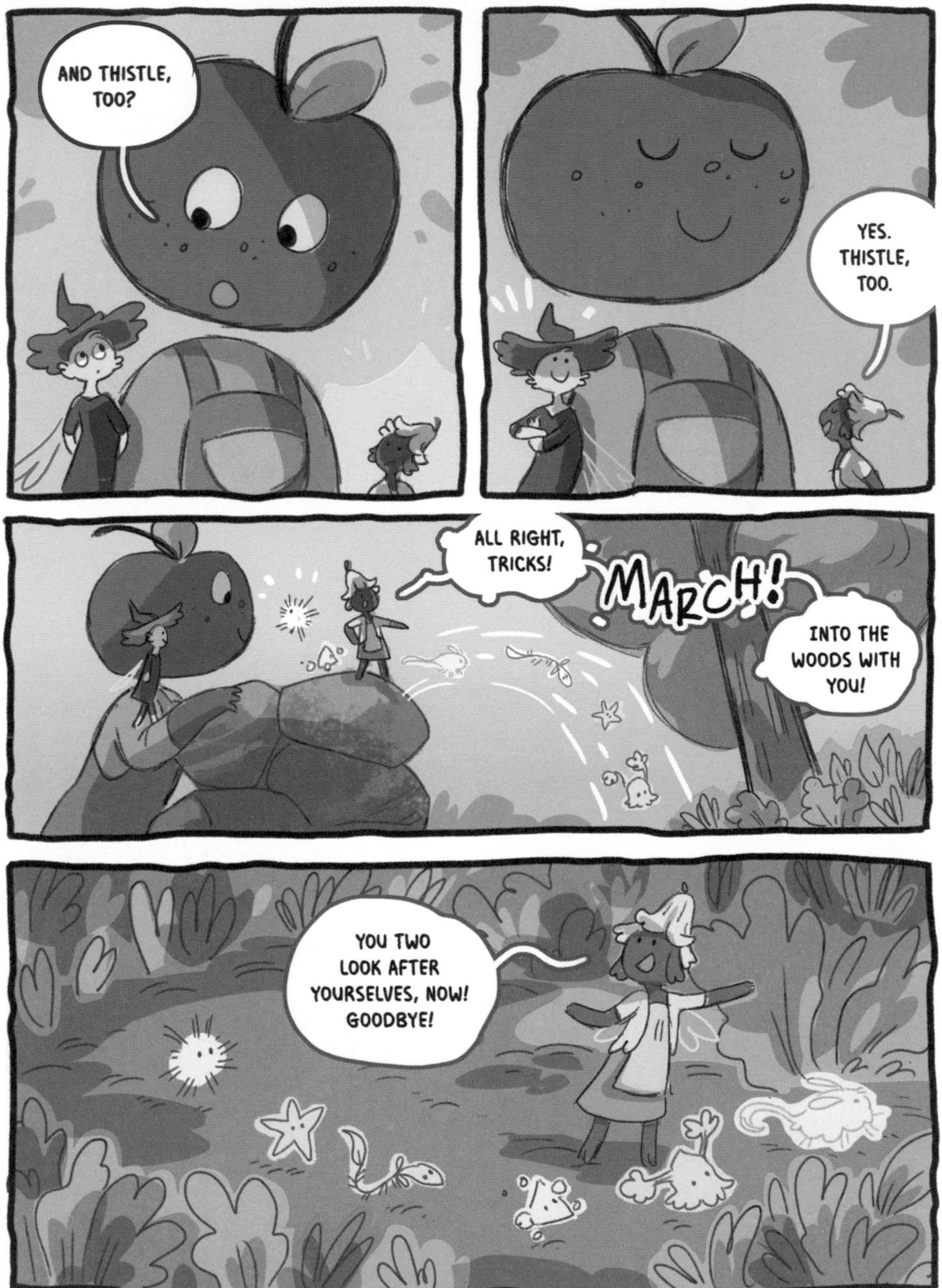
AND THISTLE, TOO?
YES. THISTLE, TOO.
ALL RIGHT, TRICKS!
MARCH!
INTO THE WOODS WITH YOU!
YOU TWO LOOK AFTER YOURSELVES, NOW! GOODBYE!

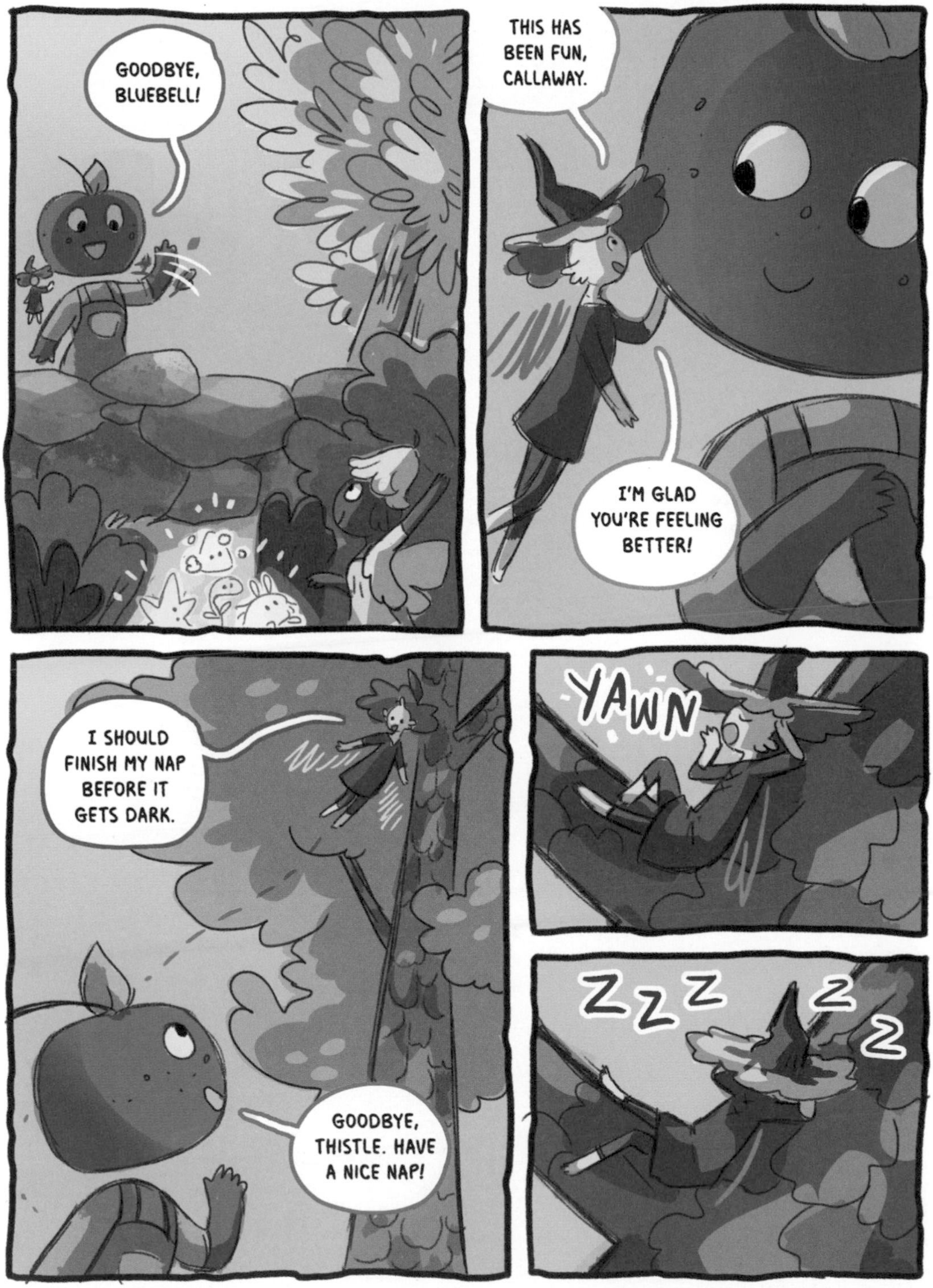
GOODBYE, BLUEBELL!
THIS HAS BEEN FUN, CALLAWAY.
I'M GLAD YOU'RE FEELING BETTER!
I SHOULD FINISH MY NAP BEFORE IT GETS DARK.
GOODBYE, THISTLE. HAVE A NICE NAP!
YAWN
Z Z Z Z Z

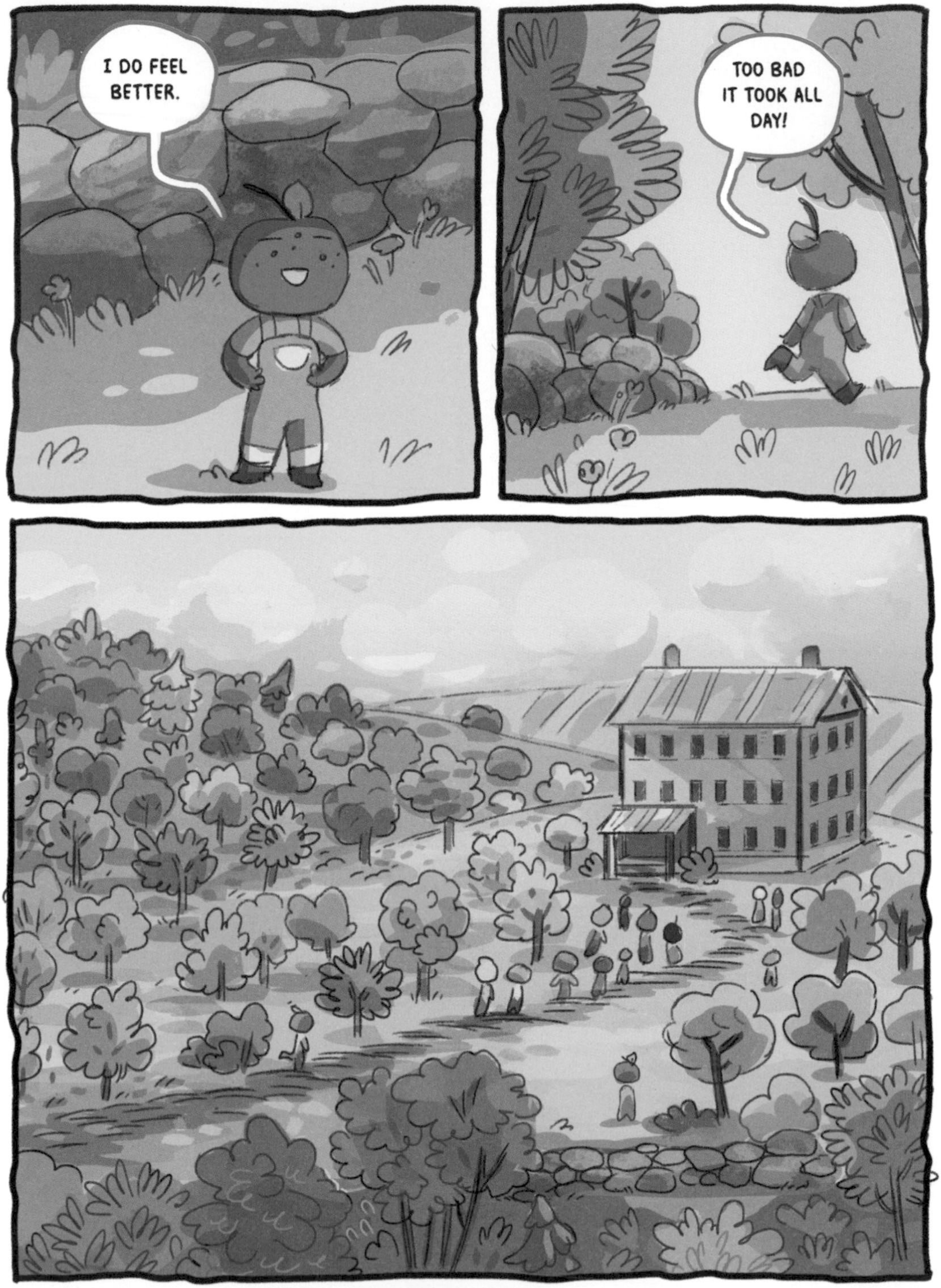
I DO FEEL BETTER.
TOO BAD IT TOOK ALL DAY!

CHAPTER 2

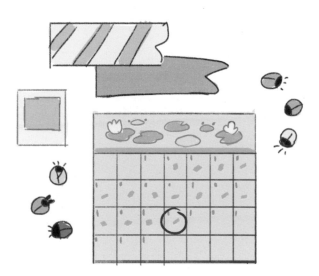

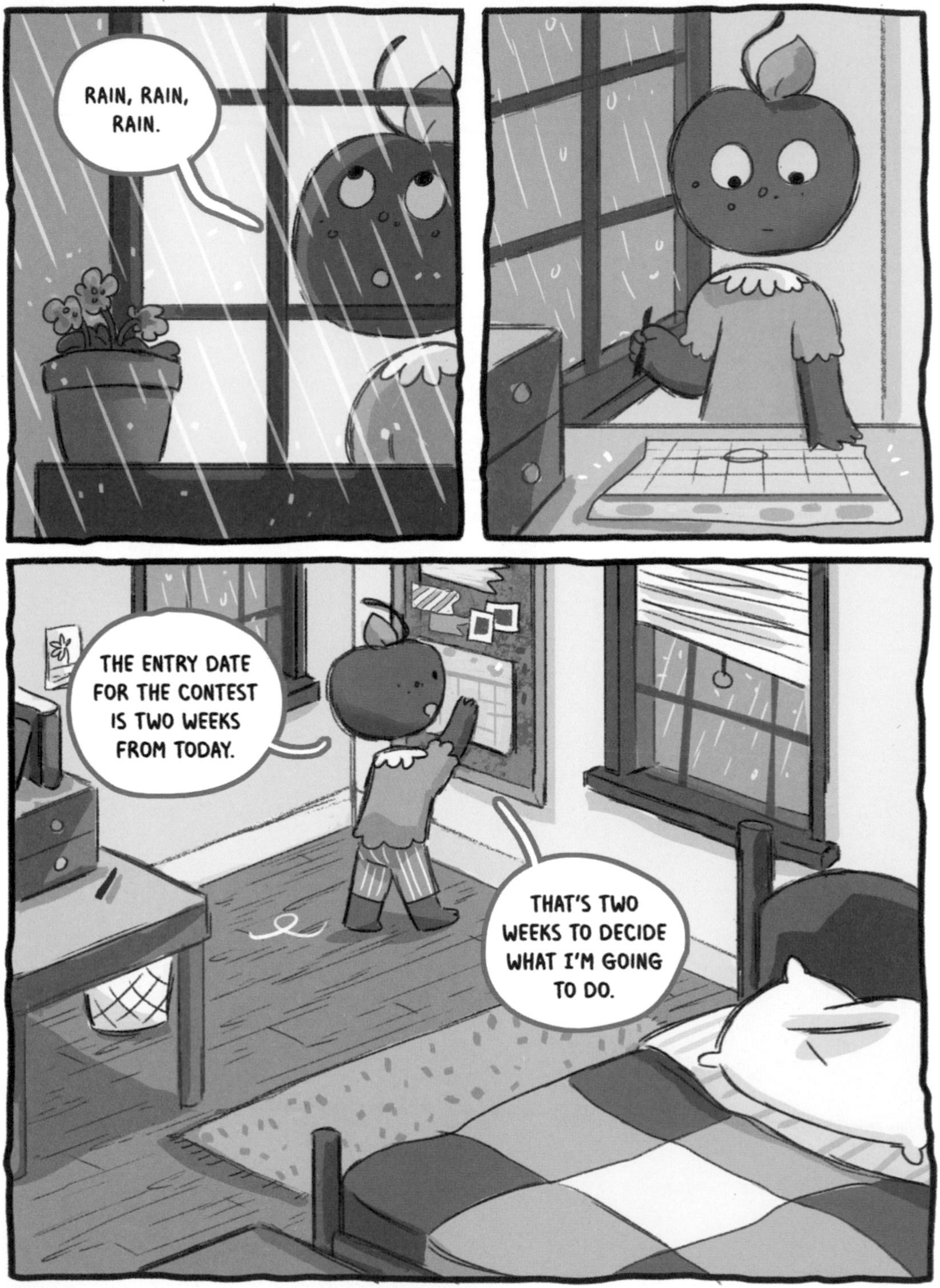
RAIN, RAIN, RAIN.
THE ENTRY DATE FOR THE CONTEST IS TWO WEEKS FROM TODAY.
THAT'S TWO WEEKS TO DECIDE WHAT I'M GOING TO DO.

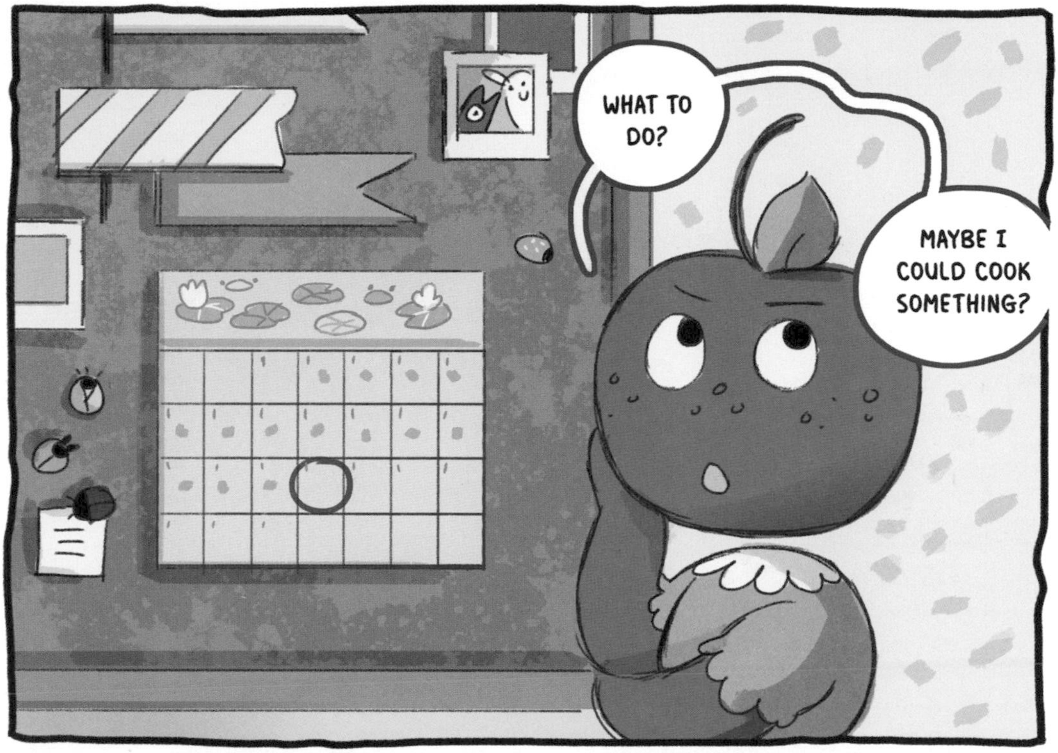
WHAT TO DO?
MAYBE I COULD COOK SOMETHING?

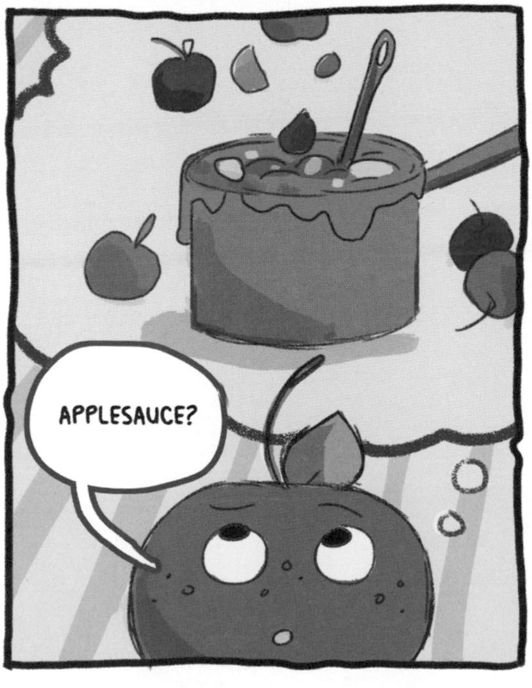
APPLESAUCE?

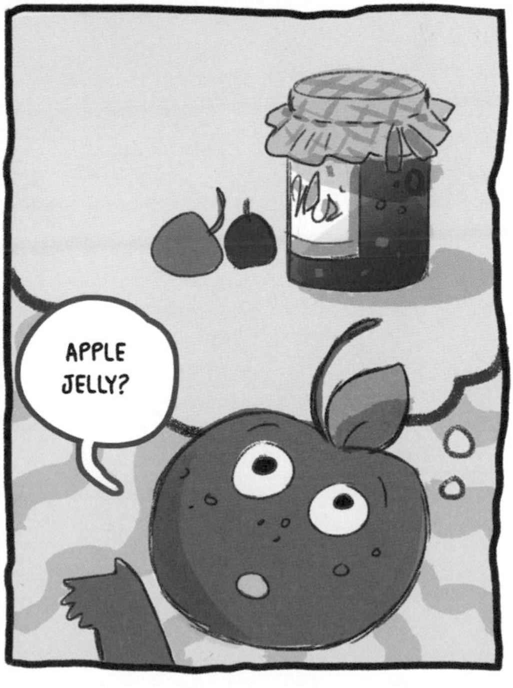
APPLE JELLY?

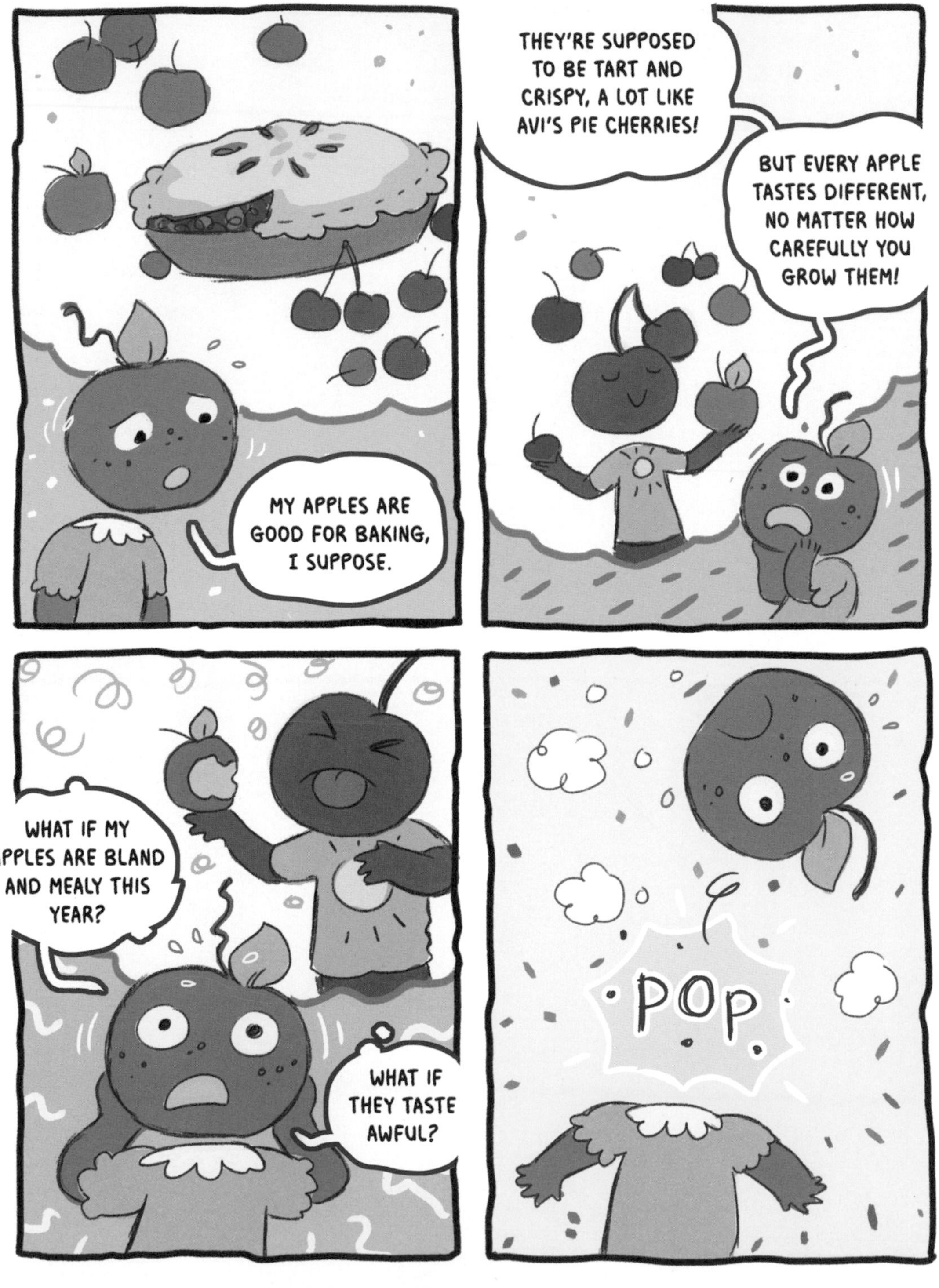

MY APPLES ARE GOOD FOR BAKING, I SUPPOSE.
THEY'RE SUPPOSED TO BE TART AND CRISPY, A LOT LIKE AVI'S PIE CHERRIES!
BUT EVERY APPLE TASTES DIFFERENT, NO MATTER HOW CAREFULLY YOU GROW THEM!
WHAT IF MY APPLES ARE BLAND AND MEALY THIS YEAR?
WHAT IF THEY TASTE AWFUL?
POP

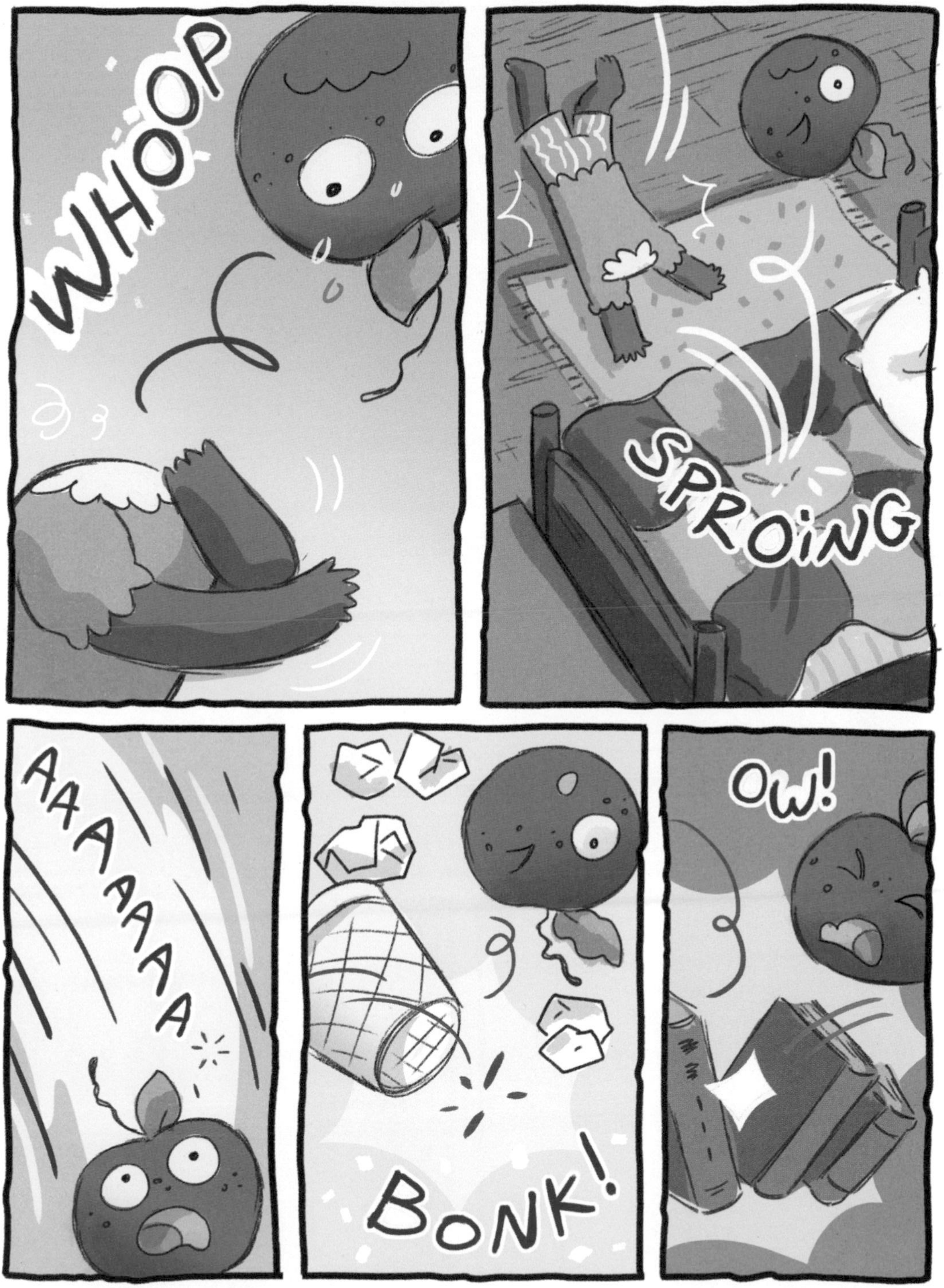
WHOOP
SPROING
AAAAAAAA
BONK!
OW!

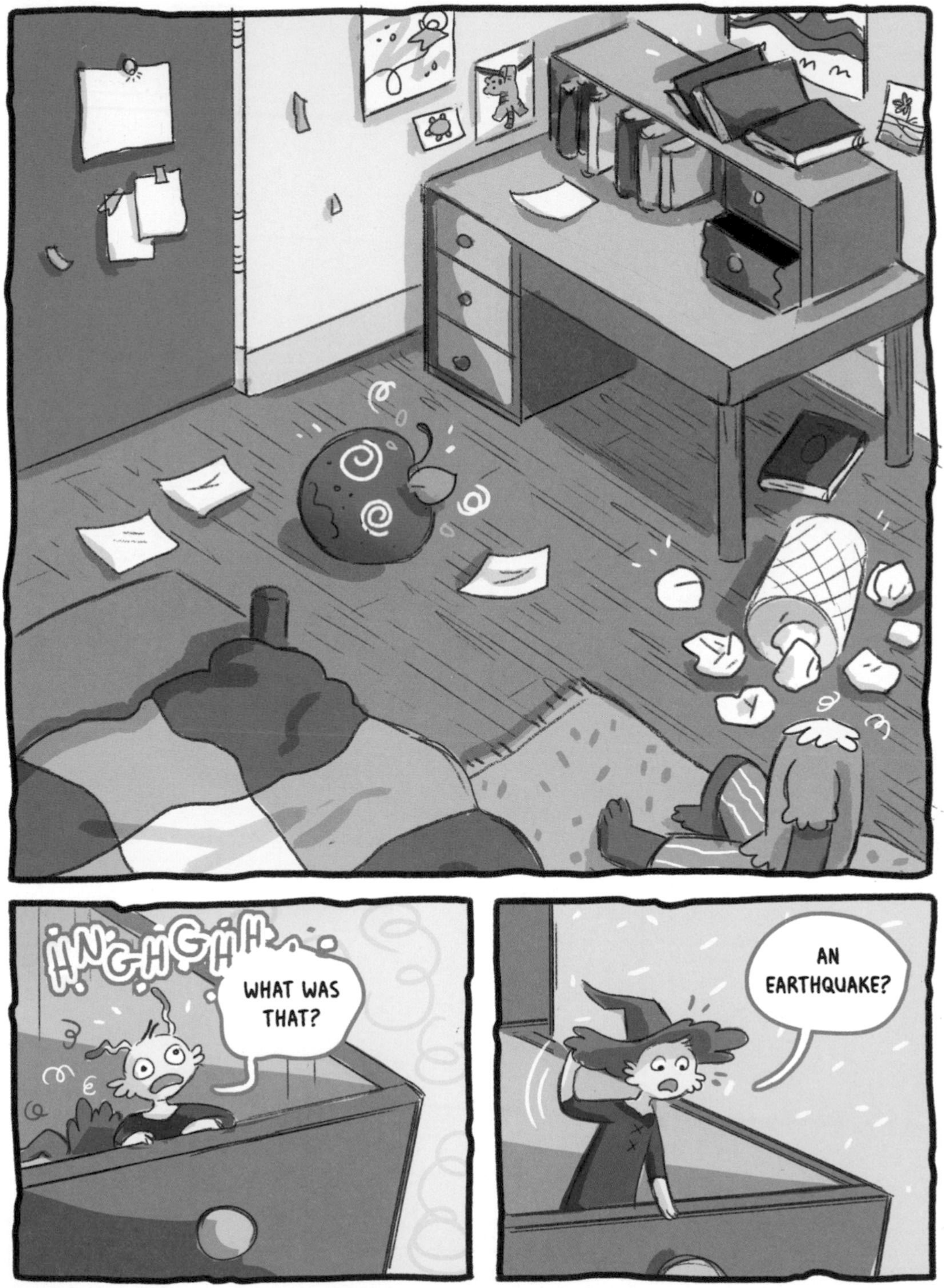
HNGHGHH
WHAT WAS THAT?
AN EARTHQUAKE?

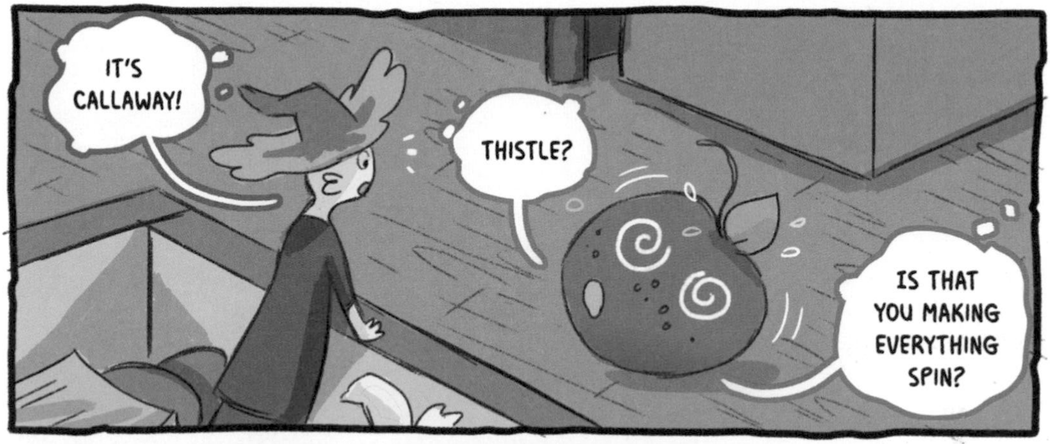
IT'S CALLAWAY!
THISTLE?
IS THAT YOU MAKING EVERYTHING SPIN?

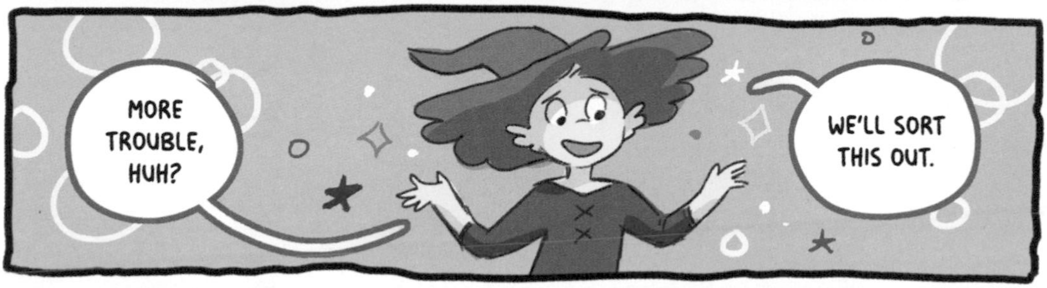
MORE TROUBLE, HUH?
WE'LL SORT THIS OUT.

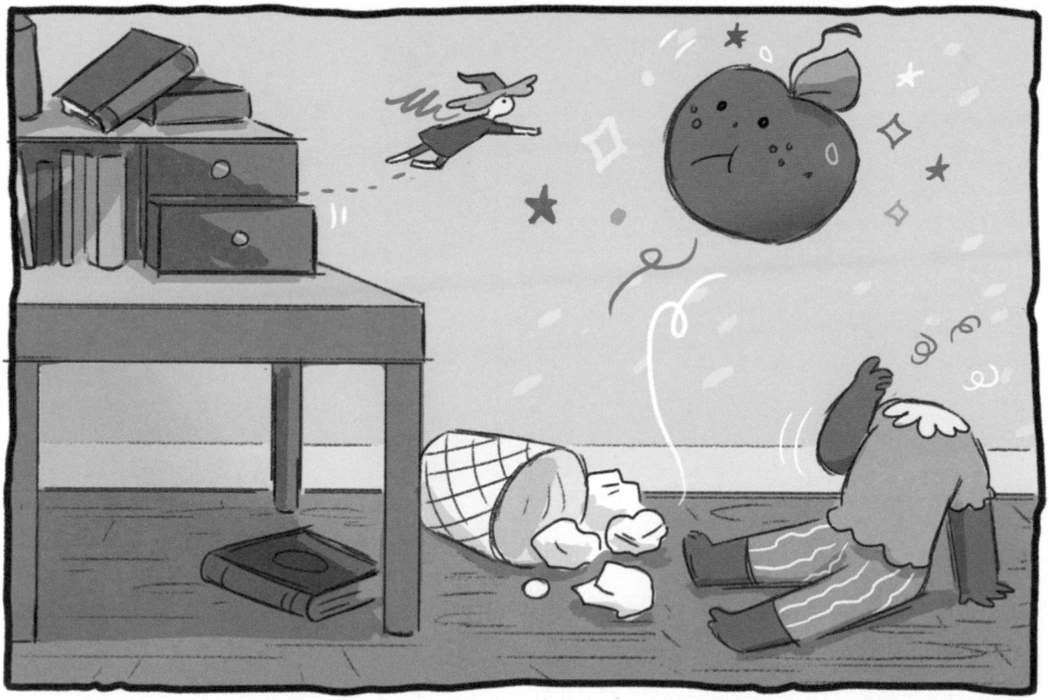

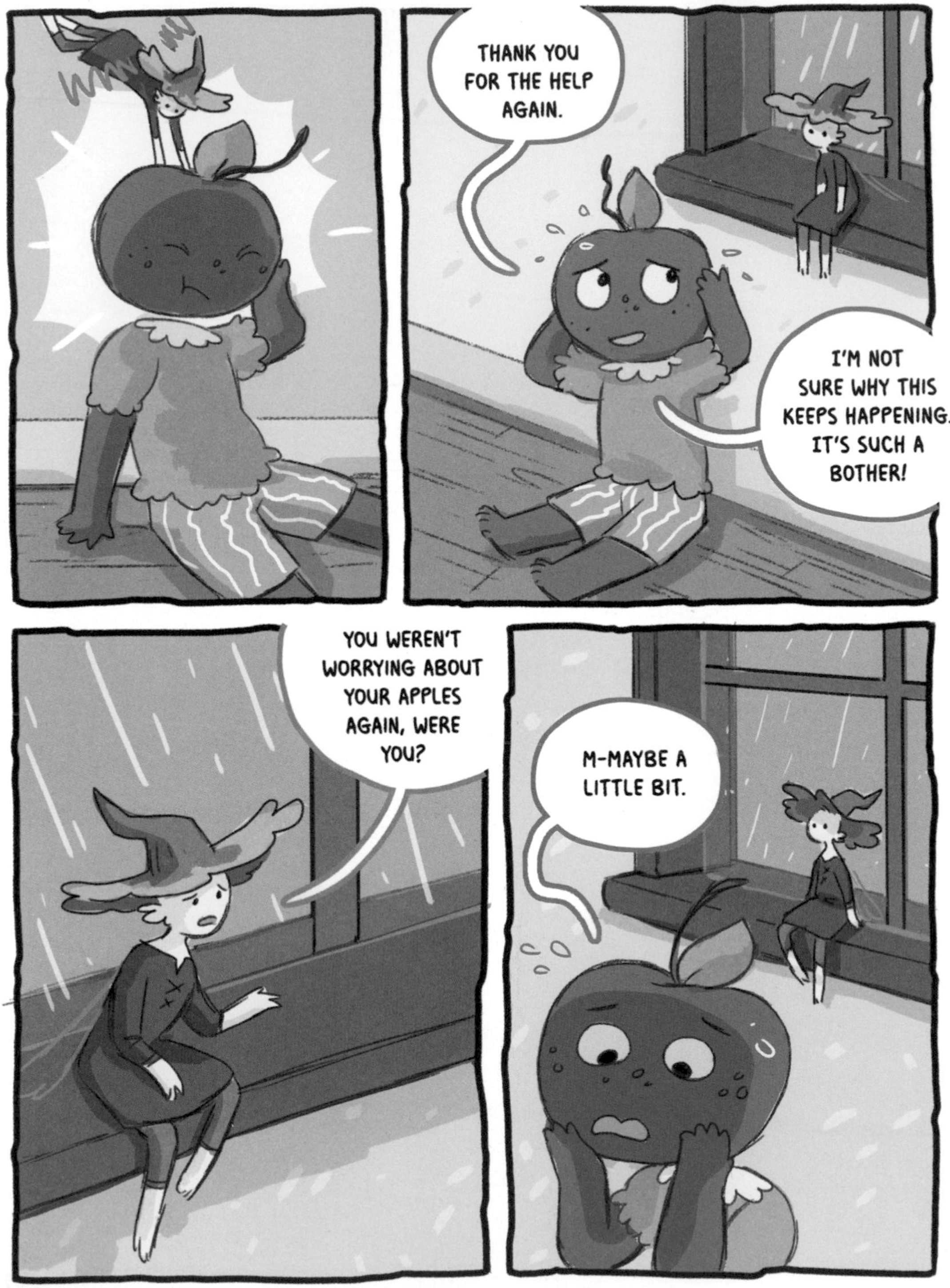
THANK YOU FOR THE HELP AGAIN.
I'M NOT SURE WHY THIS KEEPS HAPPENING. IT'S SUCH A BOTHER!
YOU WEREN'T WORRYING ABOUT YOUR APPLES AGAIN, WERE YOU?
M-MAYBE A LITTLE BIT.

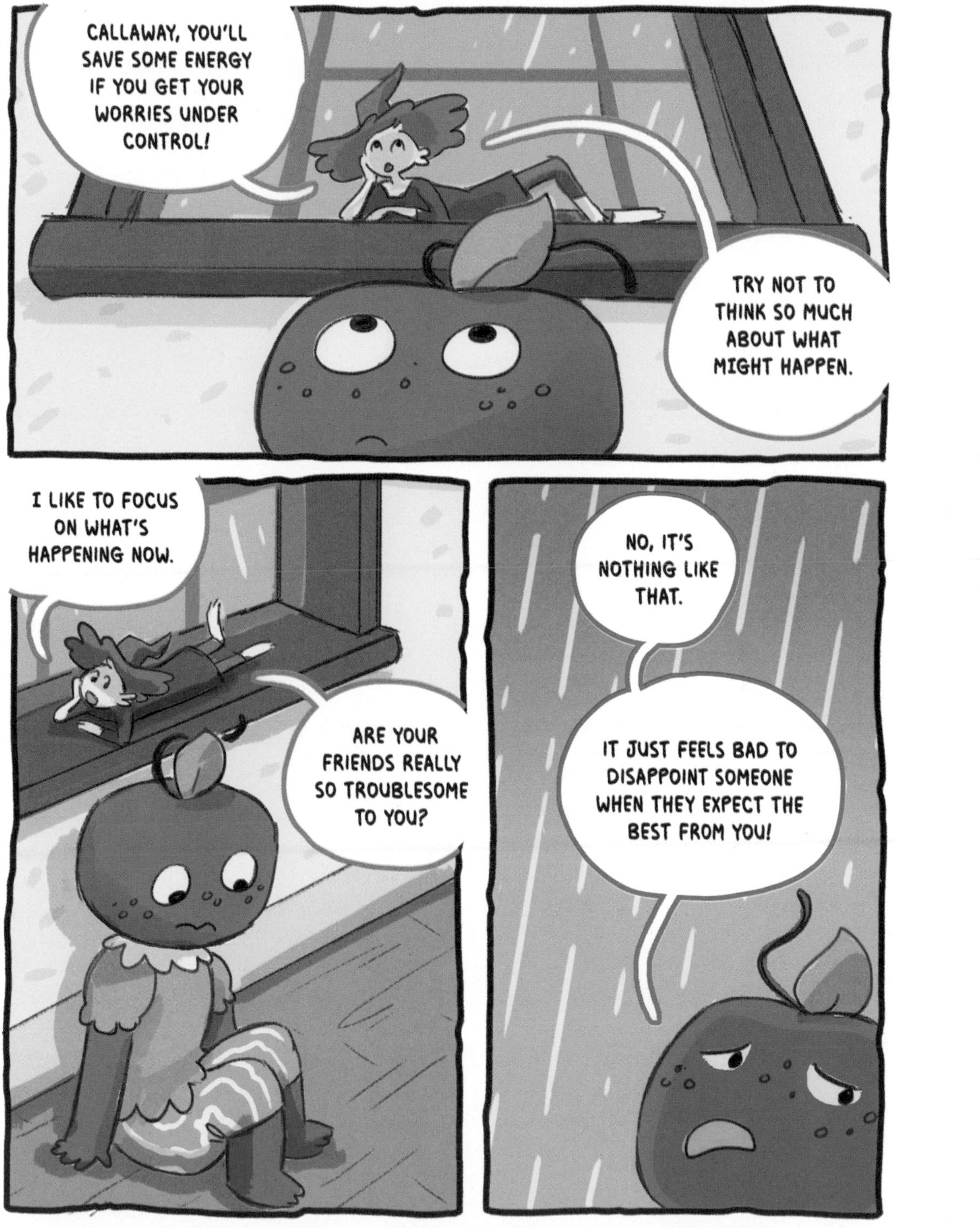
CALLAWAY, YOU'LL SAVE SOME ENERGY IF YOU GET YOUR WORRIES UNDER CONTROL!
TRY NOT TO THINK SO MUCH ABOUT WHAT MIGHT HAPPEN.
I LIKE TO FOCUS ON WHAT'S HAPPENING NOW.
ARE YOUR FRIENDS REALLY SO TROUBLESOME TO YOU?
NO, IT'S NOTHING LIKE THAT.
IT JUST FEELS BAD TO DISAPPOINT SOMEONE WHEN THEY EXPECT THE BEST FROM YOU!

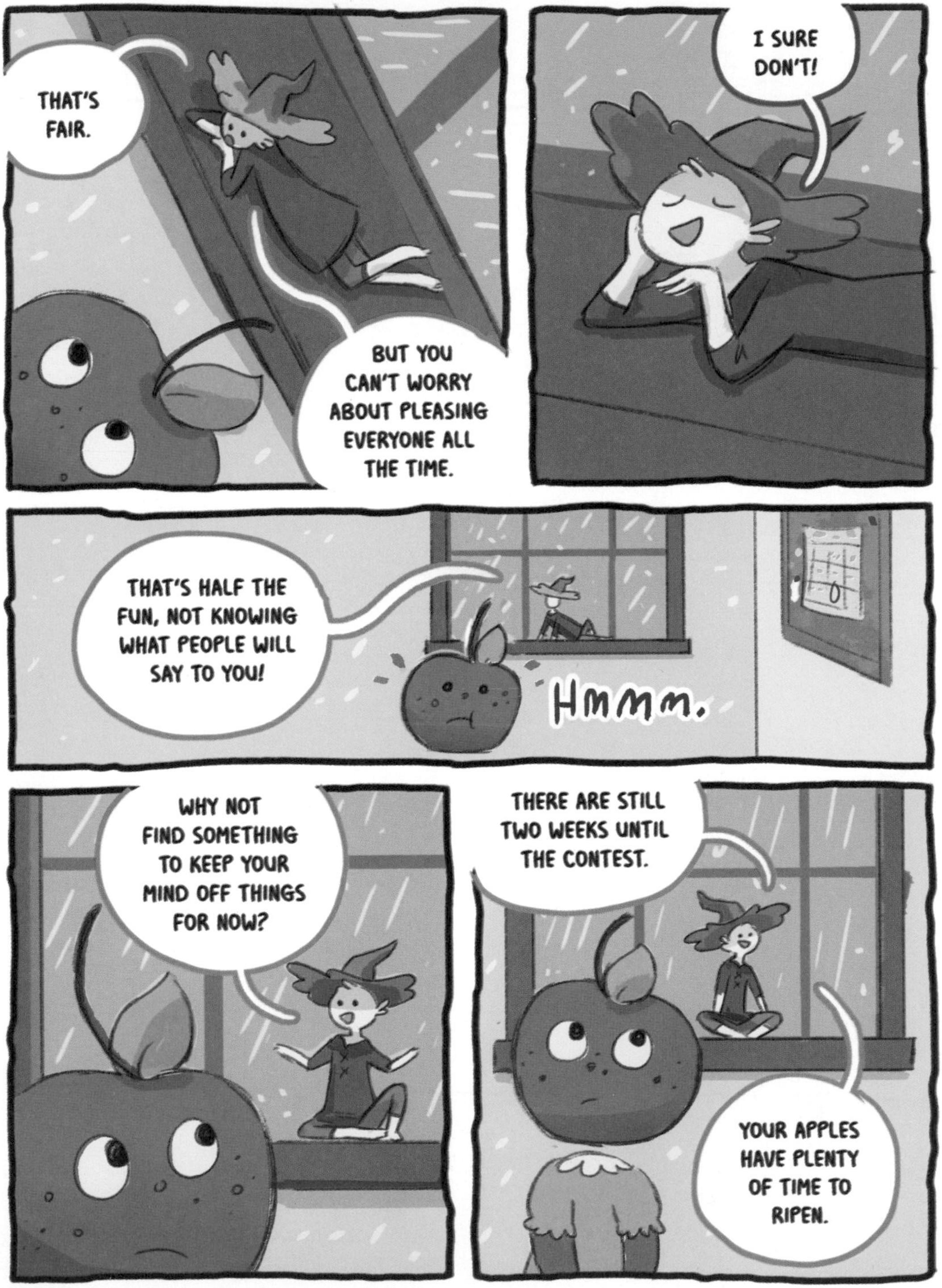
THAT'S FAIR.
BUT YOU CAN'T WORRY ABOUT PLEASING EVERYONE ALL THE TIME.
I SURE DON'T!
THAT'S HALF THE FUN, NOT KNOWING WHAT PEOPLE WILL SAY TO YOU!
Hmmm.
WHY NOT FIND SOMETHING TO KEEP YOUR MIND OFF THINGS FOR NOW?
THERE ARE STILL TWO WEEKS UNTIL THE CONTEST.
YOUR APPLES HAVE PLENTY OF TIME TO RIPEN.

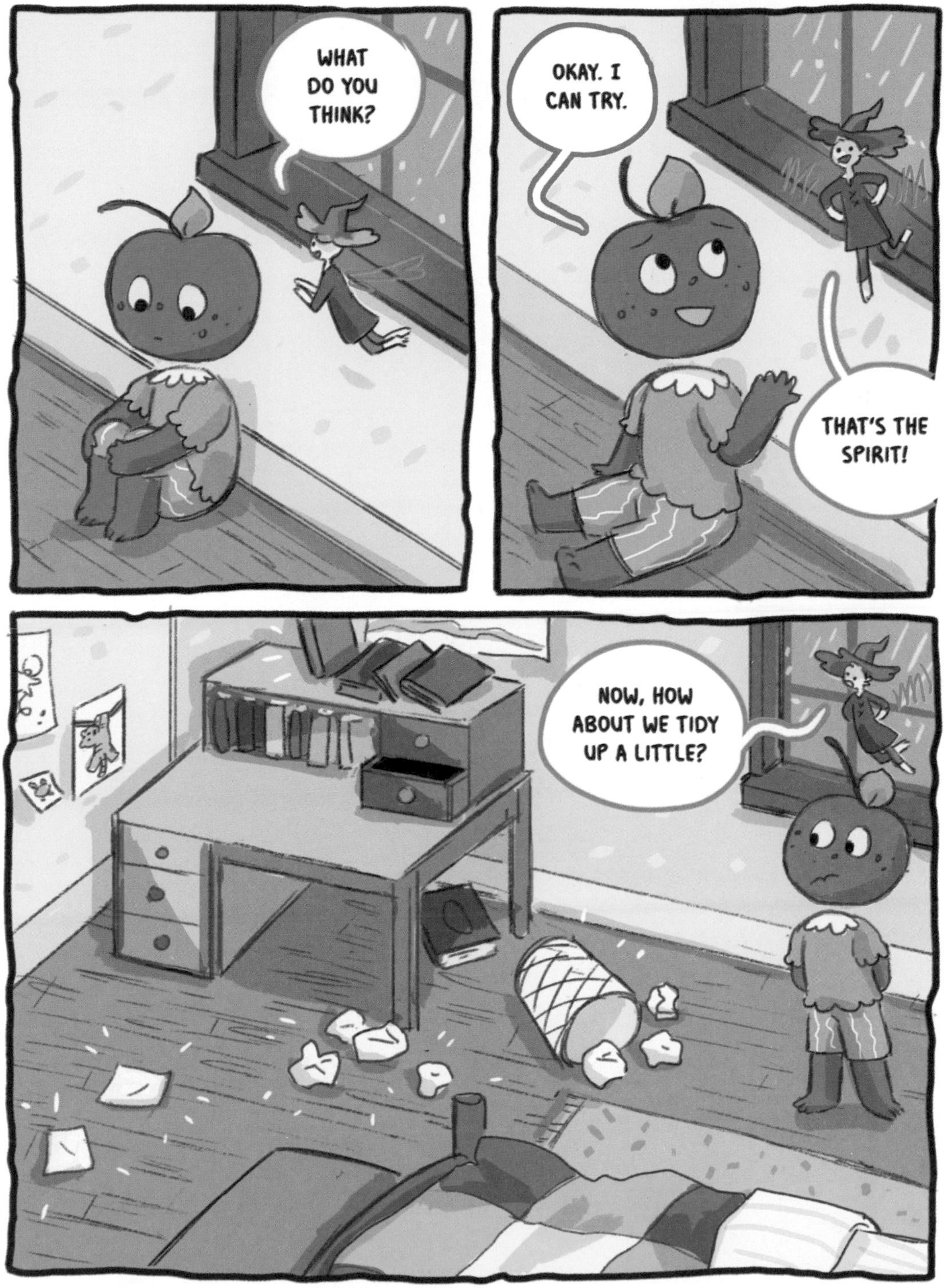
WHAT DO YOU THINK?
OKAY. I CAN TRY.
THAT'S THE SPIRIT!
NOW, HOW ABOUT WE TIDY UP A LITTLE?

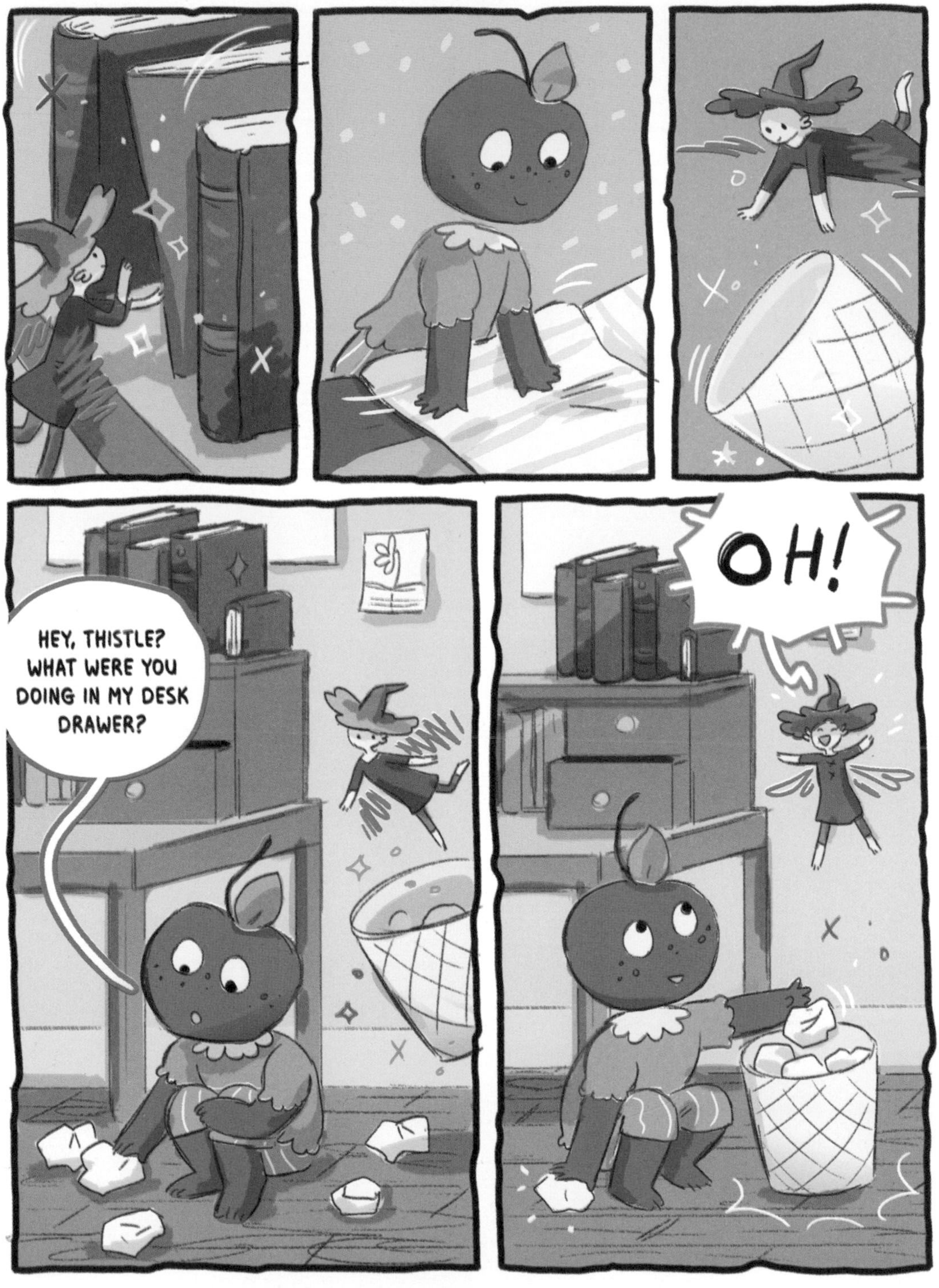
HEY, THISTLE? WHAT WERE YOU DOING IN MY DESK DRAWER?
OH!

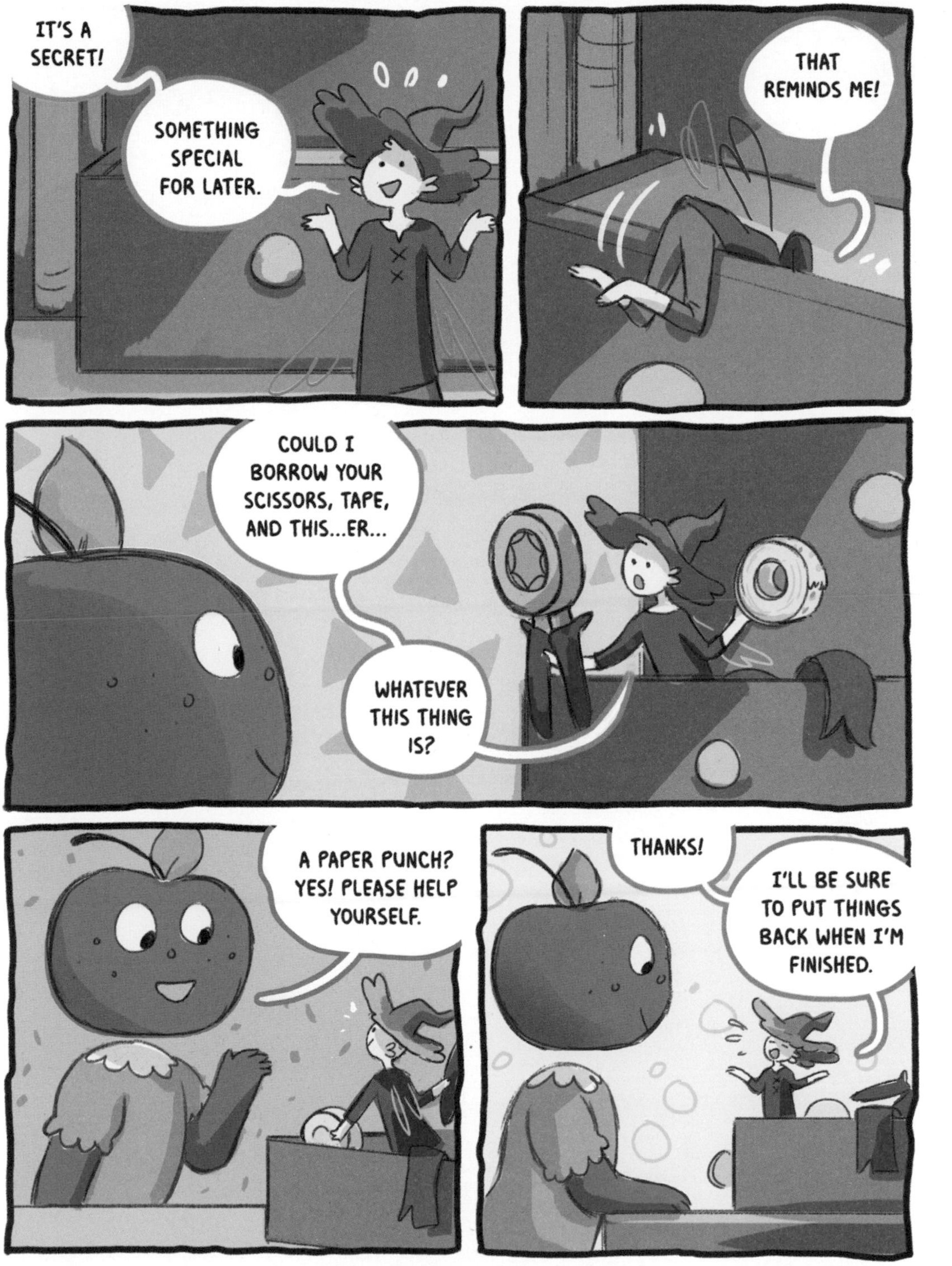
IT'S A SECRET!
SOMETHING SPECIAL FOR LATER.
THAT REMINDS ME!
COULD I BORROW YOUR SCISSORS, TAPE, AND THIS...ER...
WHATEVER THIS THING IS?
A PAPER PUNCH? YES! PLEASE HELP YOURSELF.
THANKS!
I'LL BE SURE TO PUT THINGS BACK WHEN I'M FINISHED.

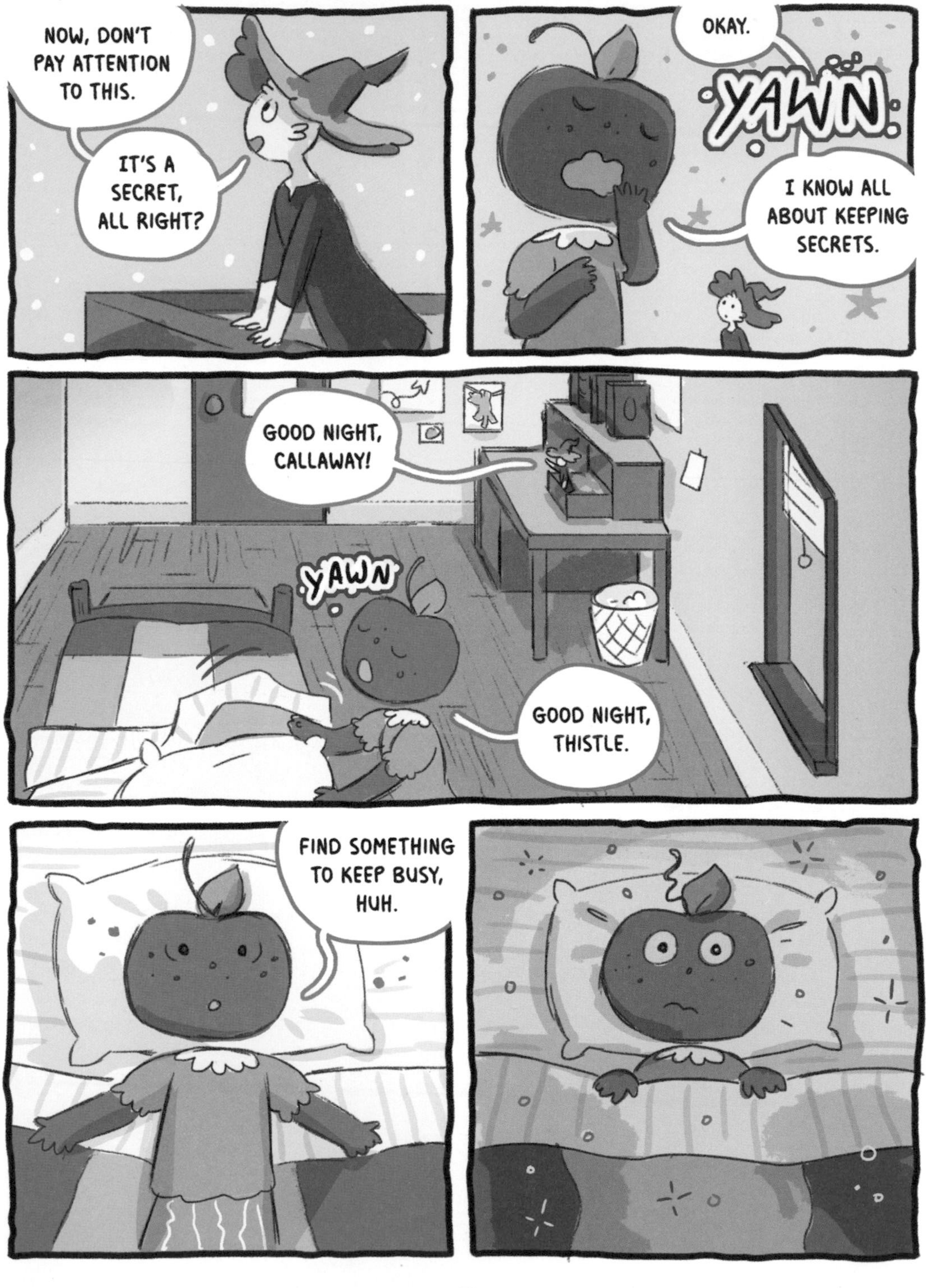
NOW, DON'T PAY ATTENTION TO THIS.
IT'S A SECRET, ALL RIGHT?
OKAY.
YAWN
I KNOW ALL ABOUT KEEPING SECRETS.
GOOD NIGHT, CALLAWAY!
YAWN
GOOD NIGHT, THISTLE.
FIND SOMETHING TO KEEP BUSY, HUH.

CHAPTER 3

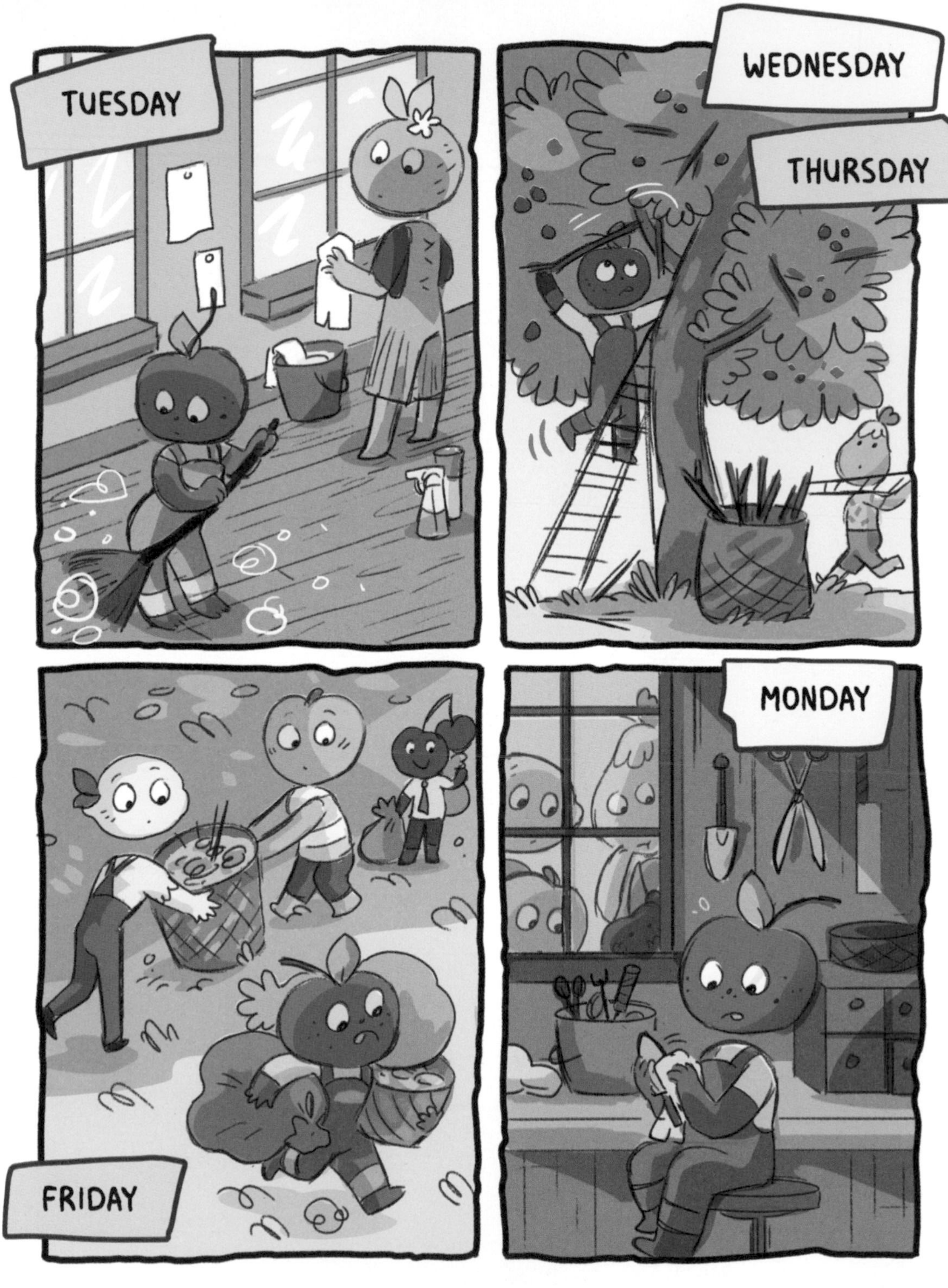
TUESDAY
WEDNESDAY
THURSDAY
FRIDAY
MONDAY

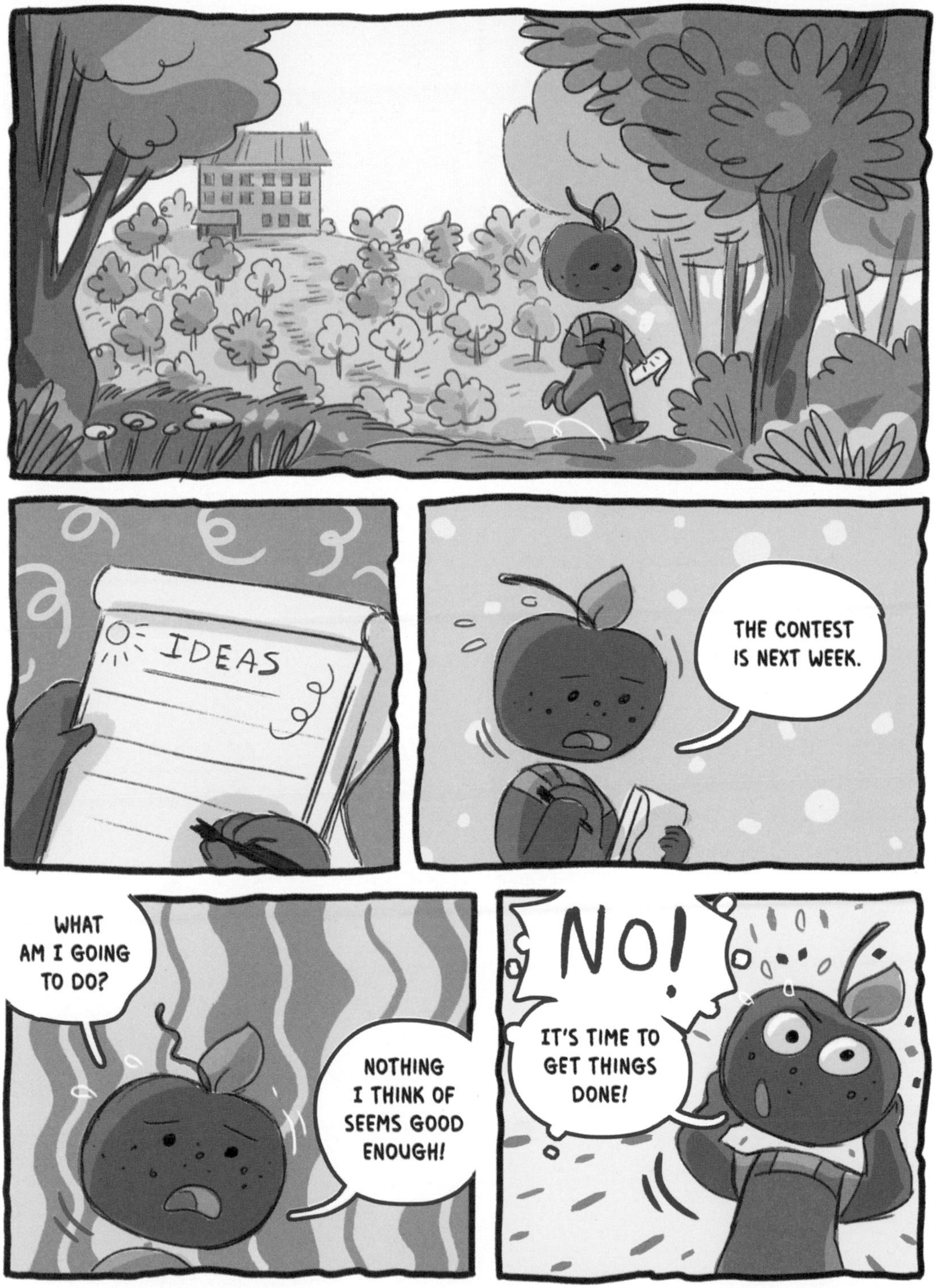
IDEAS
THE CONTEST IS NEXT WEEK.
WHAT AM I GOING TO DO?
NOTHING I THINK OF SEEMS GOOD ENOUGH!
NO!
IT'S TIME TO GET THINGS DONE!

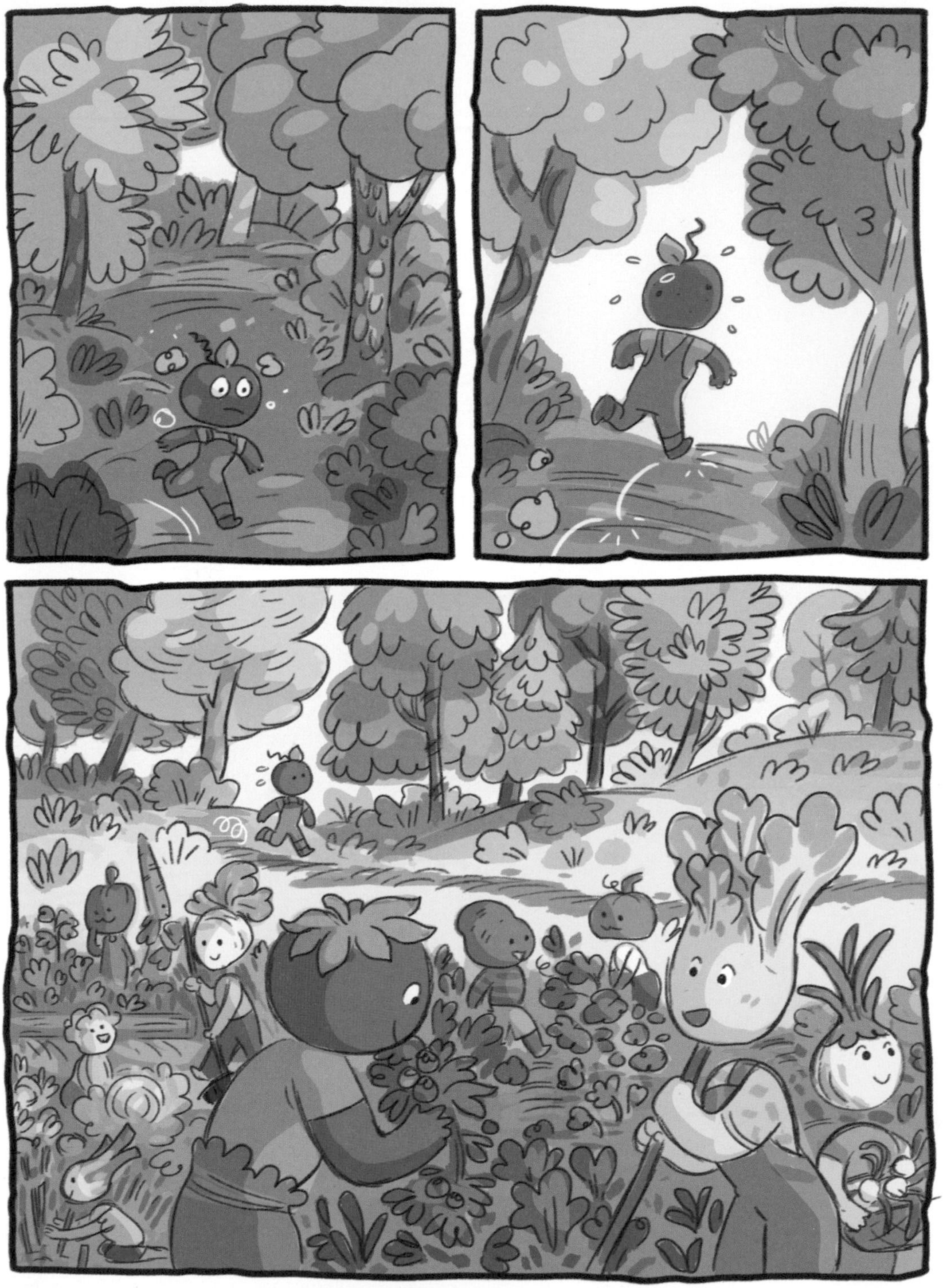

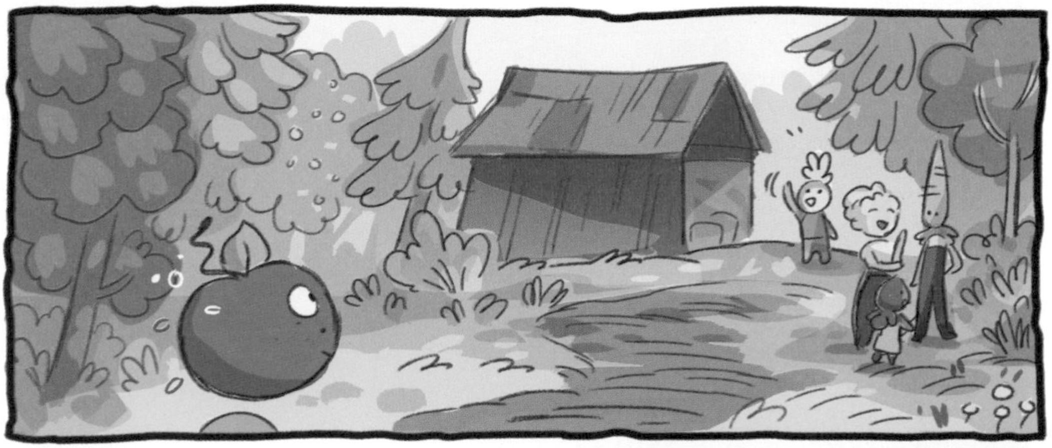

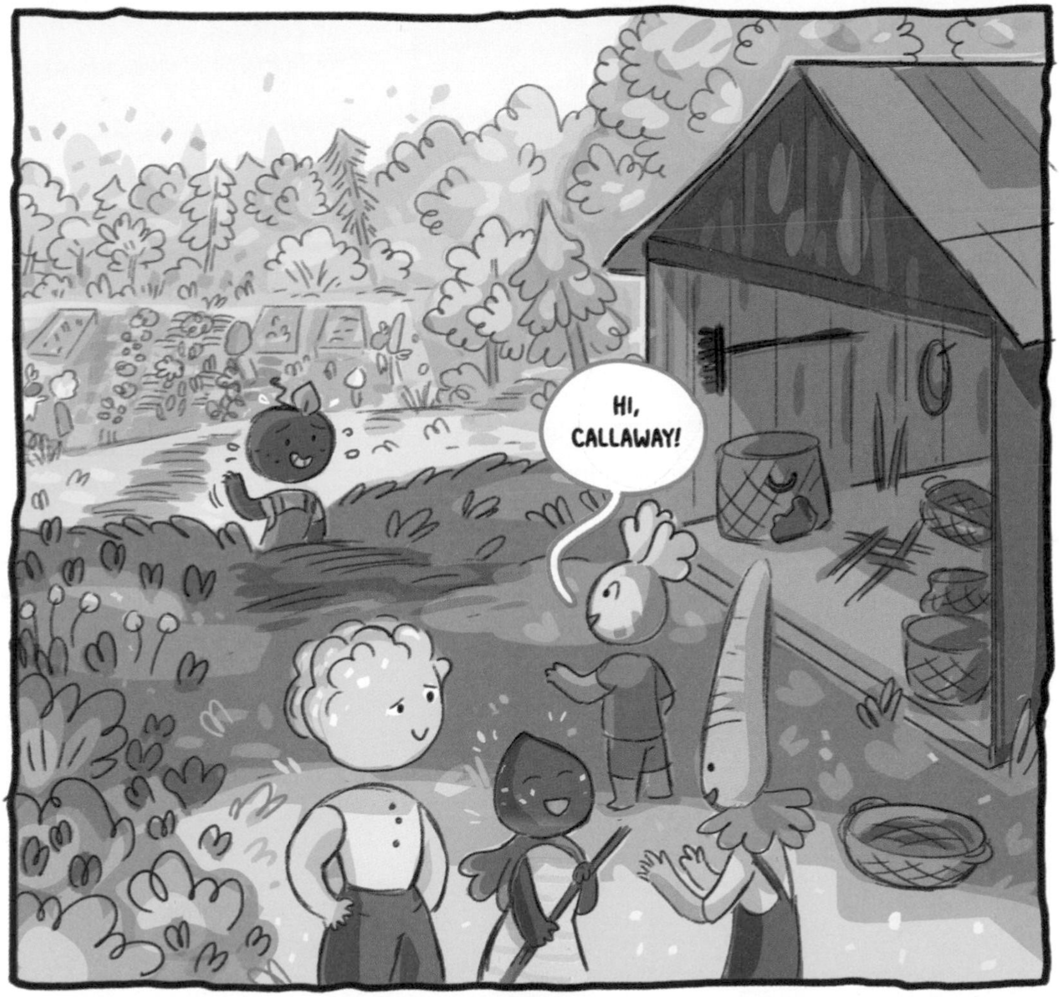
HI, CALLAWAY!

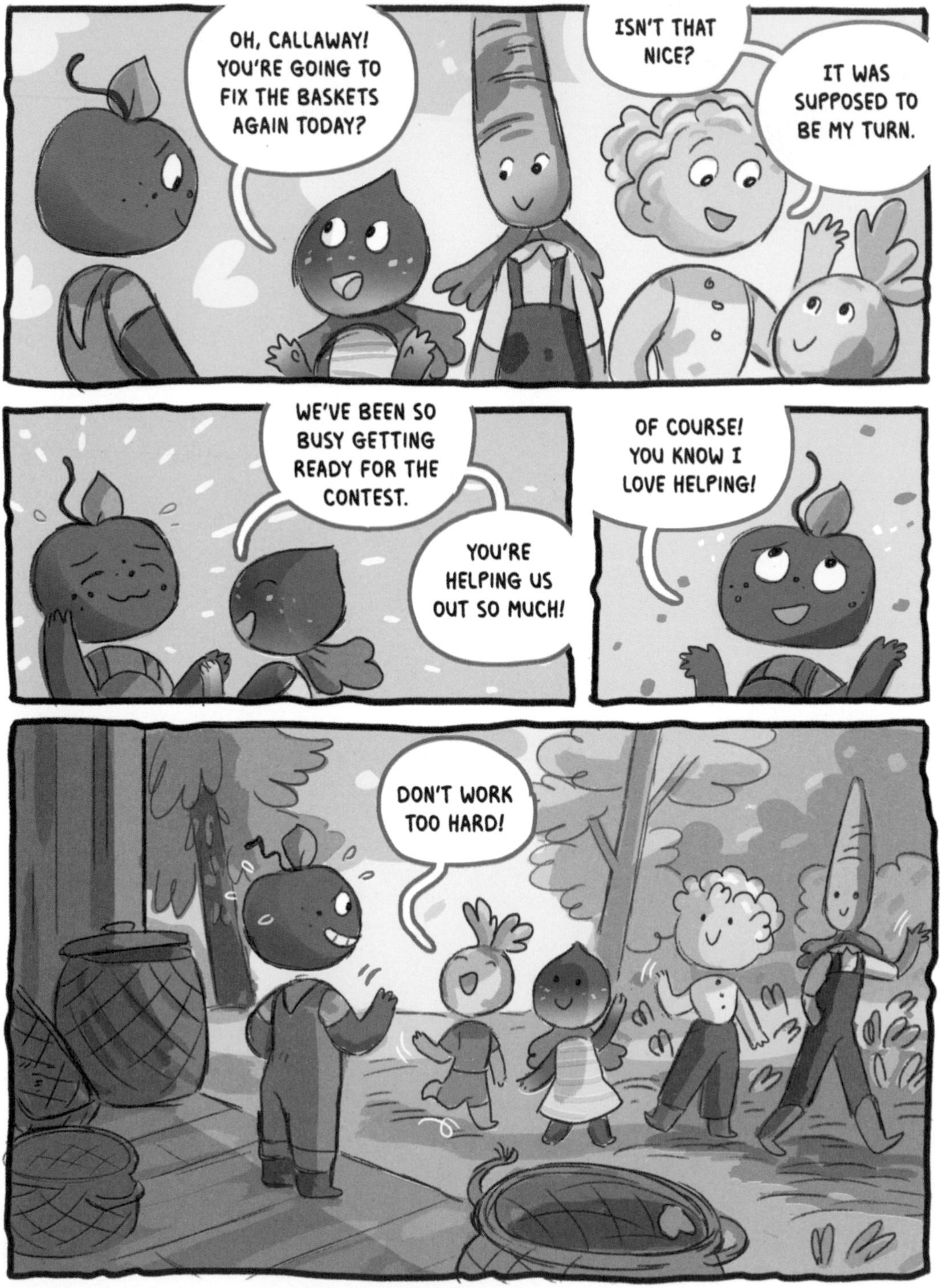
OH, CALLAWAY! YOU'RE GOING TO FIX THE BASKETS AGAIN TODAY?
ISN'T THAT NICE?
IT WAS SUPPOSED TO BE MY TURN.
WE'VE BEEN SO BUSY GETTING READY FOR THE CONTEST.
YOU'RE HELPING US OUT SO MUCH!
OF COURSE! YOU KNOW I LOVE HELPING!
DON'T WORK TOO HARD!

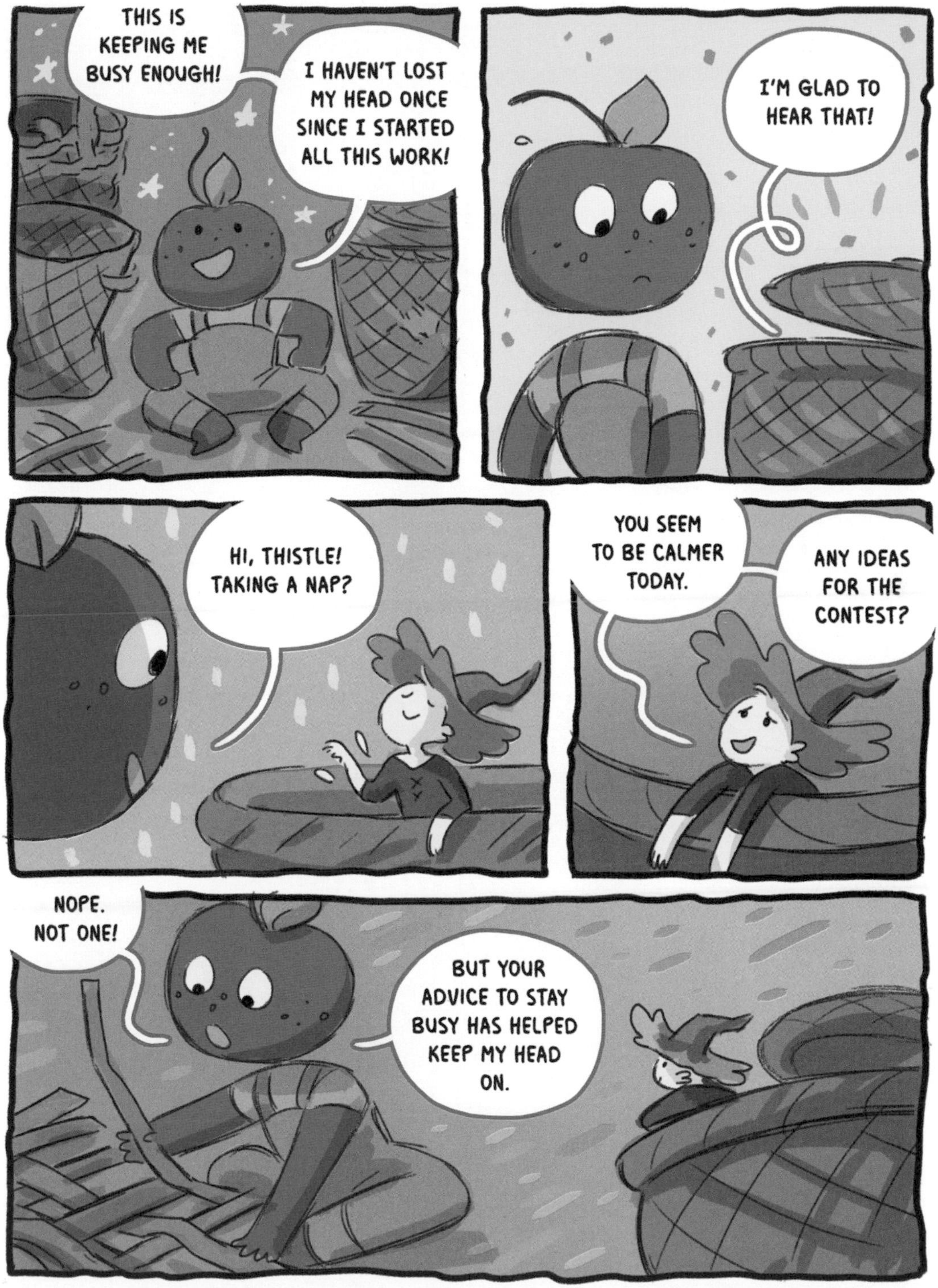
THIS IS KEEPING ME BUSY ENOUGH!
I HAVEN'T LOST MY HEAD ONCE SINCE I STARTED ALL THIS WORK!
I'M GLAD TO HEAR THAT!
HI, THISTLE! TAKING A NAP?
YOU SEEM TO BE CALMER TODAY.
ANY IDEAS FOR THE CONTEST?
NOPE. NOT ONE!
BUT YOUR ADVICE TO STAY BUSY HAS HELPED KEEP MY HEAD ON.

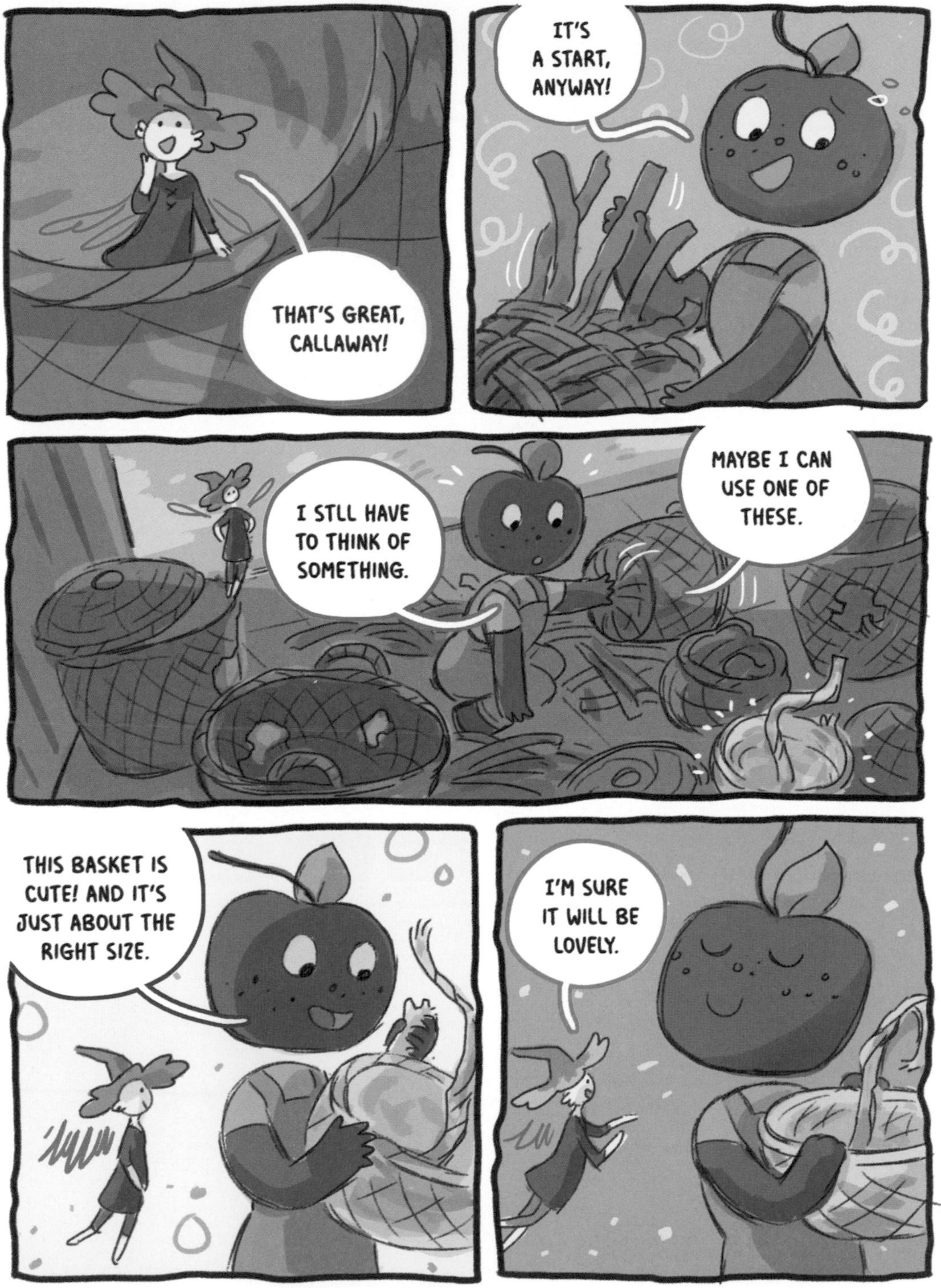
THAT'S GREAT, CALLAWAY!
IT'S A START, ANYWAY!
I STLL HAVE TO THINK OF SOMETHING.
MAYBE I CAN USE ONE OF THESE.
THIS BASKET IS CUTE! AND IT'S JUST ABOUT THE RIGHT SIZE.
I'M SURE IT WILL BE LOVELY.

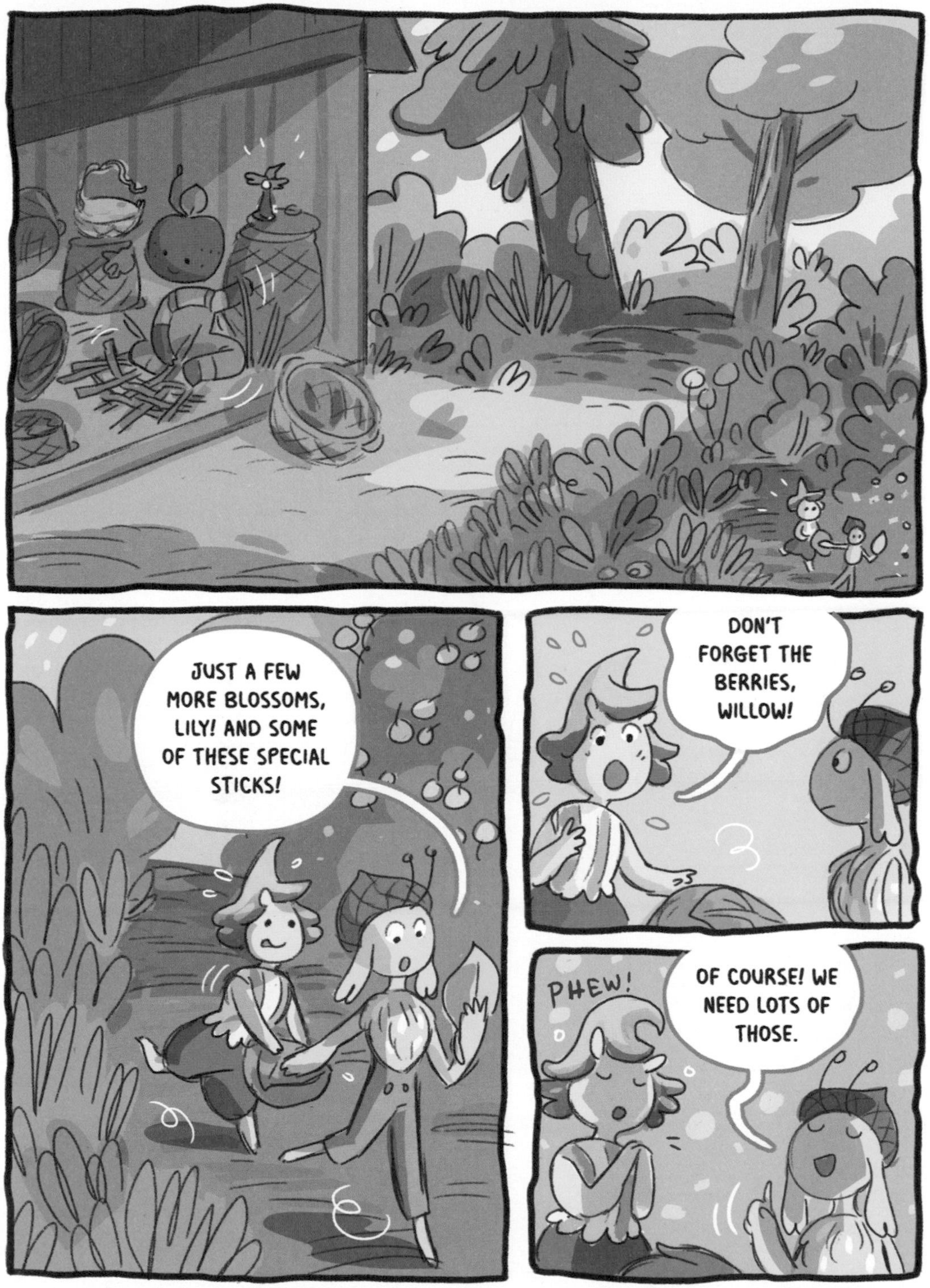
JUST A FEW MORE BLOSSOMS, LILY! AND SOME OF THESE SPECIAL STICKS!
DON'T FORGET THE BERRIES, WILLOW!
PHEW!
OF COURSE! WE NEED LOTS OF THOSE.

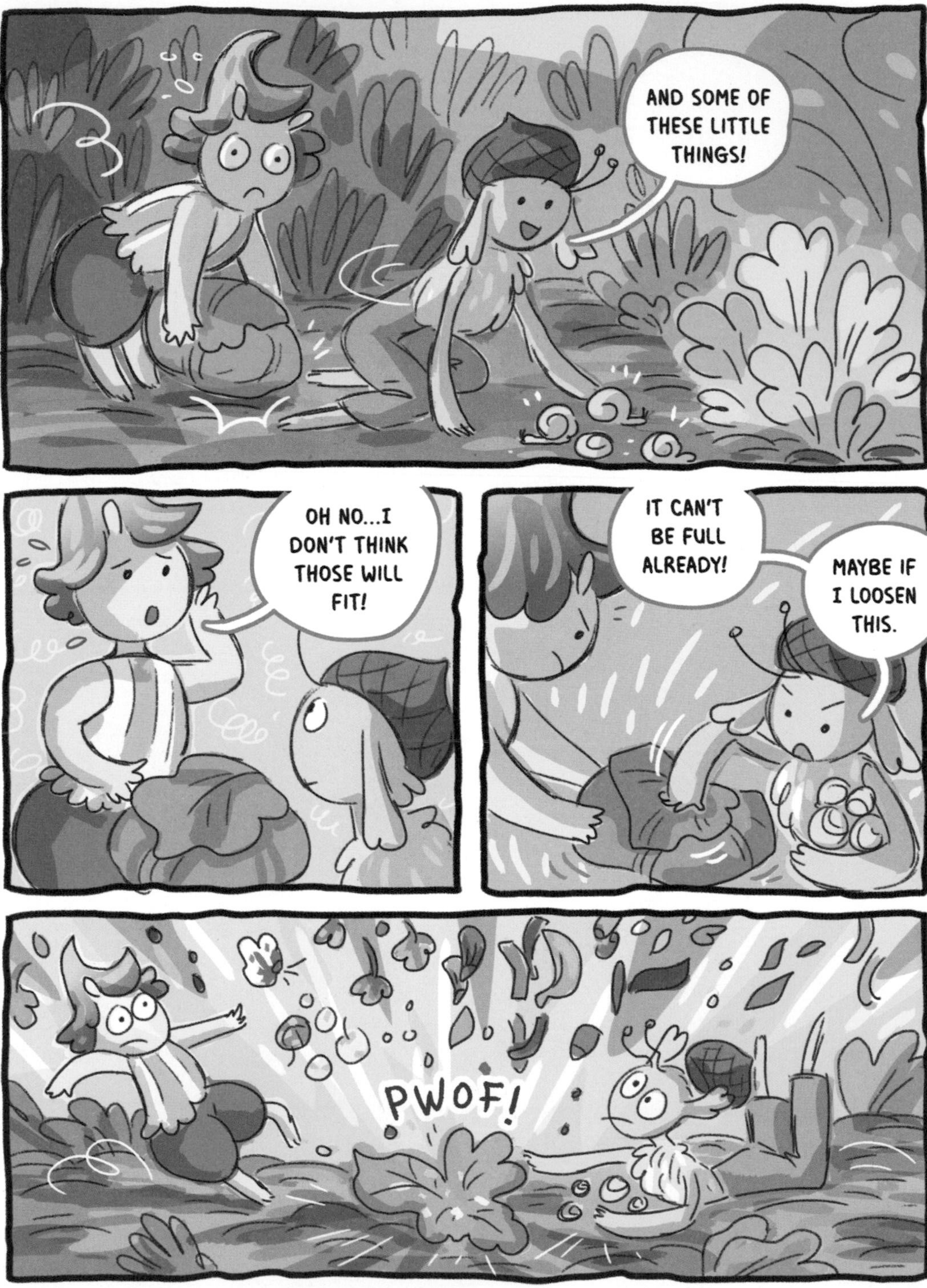
AND SOME OF THESE LITTLE THINGS!
OH NO...I DON'T THINK THOSE WILL FIT!
IT CAN'T BE FULL ALREADY!
MAYBE IF I LOOSEN THIS.
PWOF!

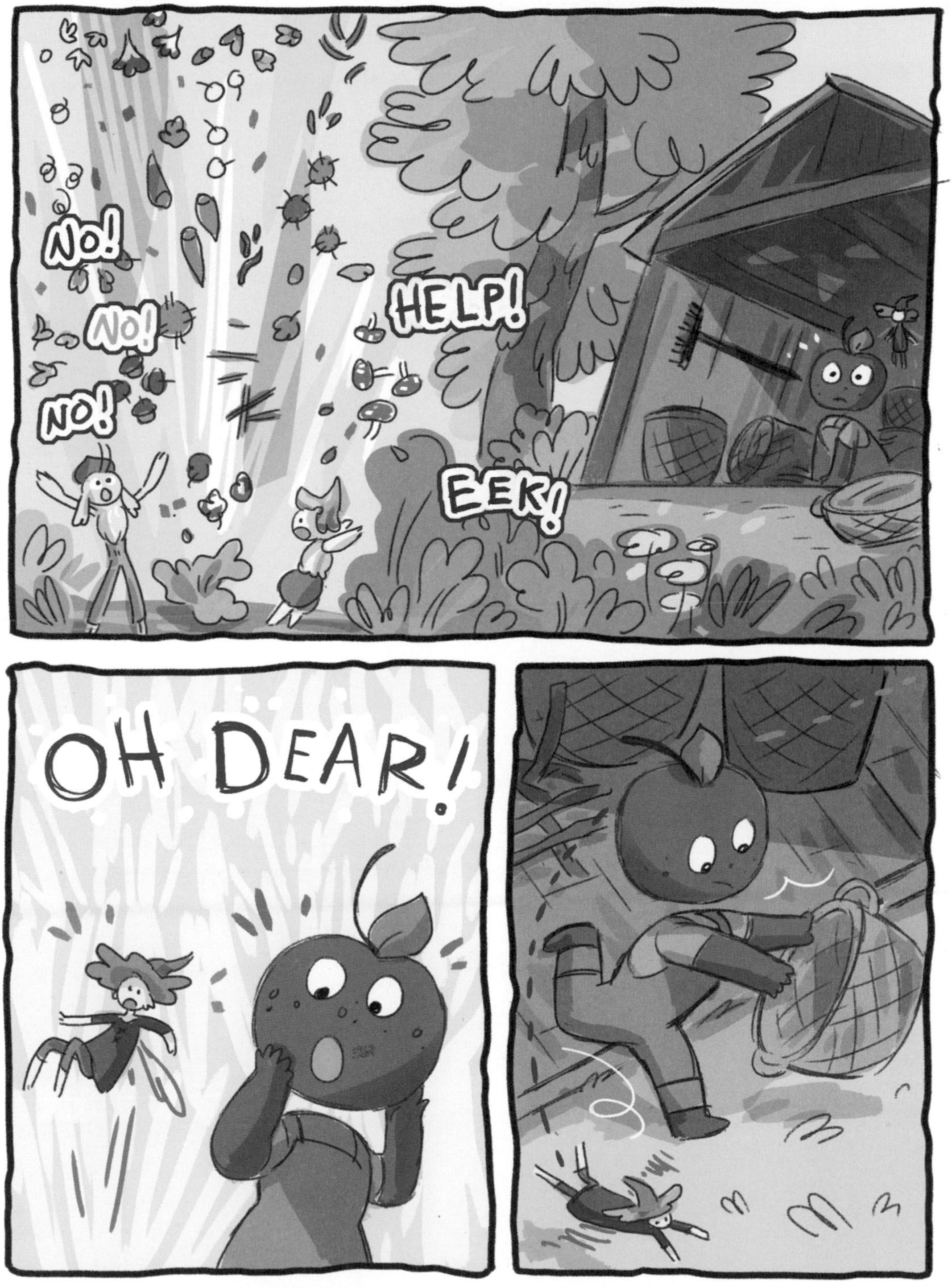

NO!
NO!
NO!
HELP!
EEK!
OH DEAR!

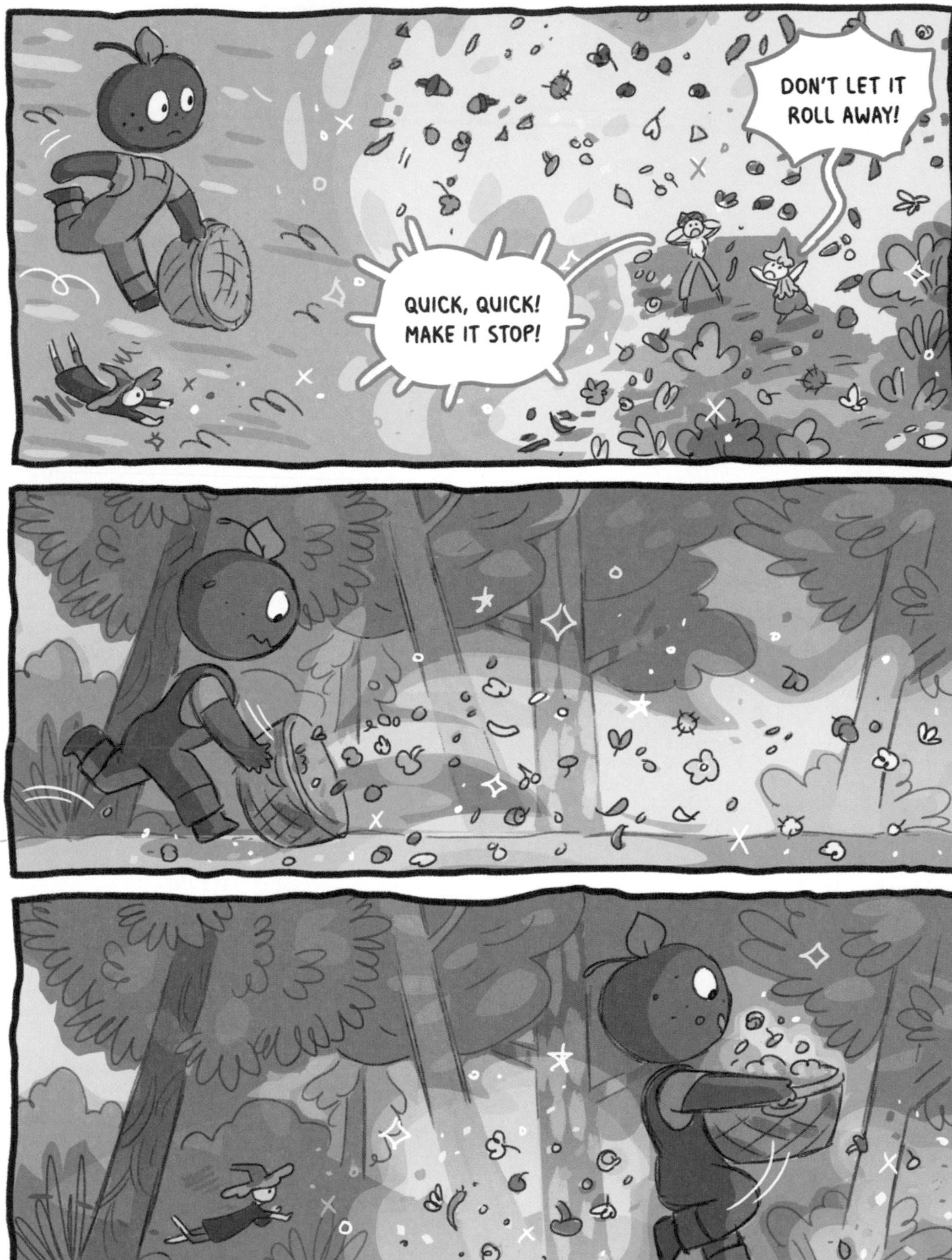
QUICK, QUICK! MAKE IT STOP!
DON'T LET IT ROLL AWAY!

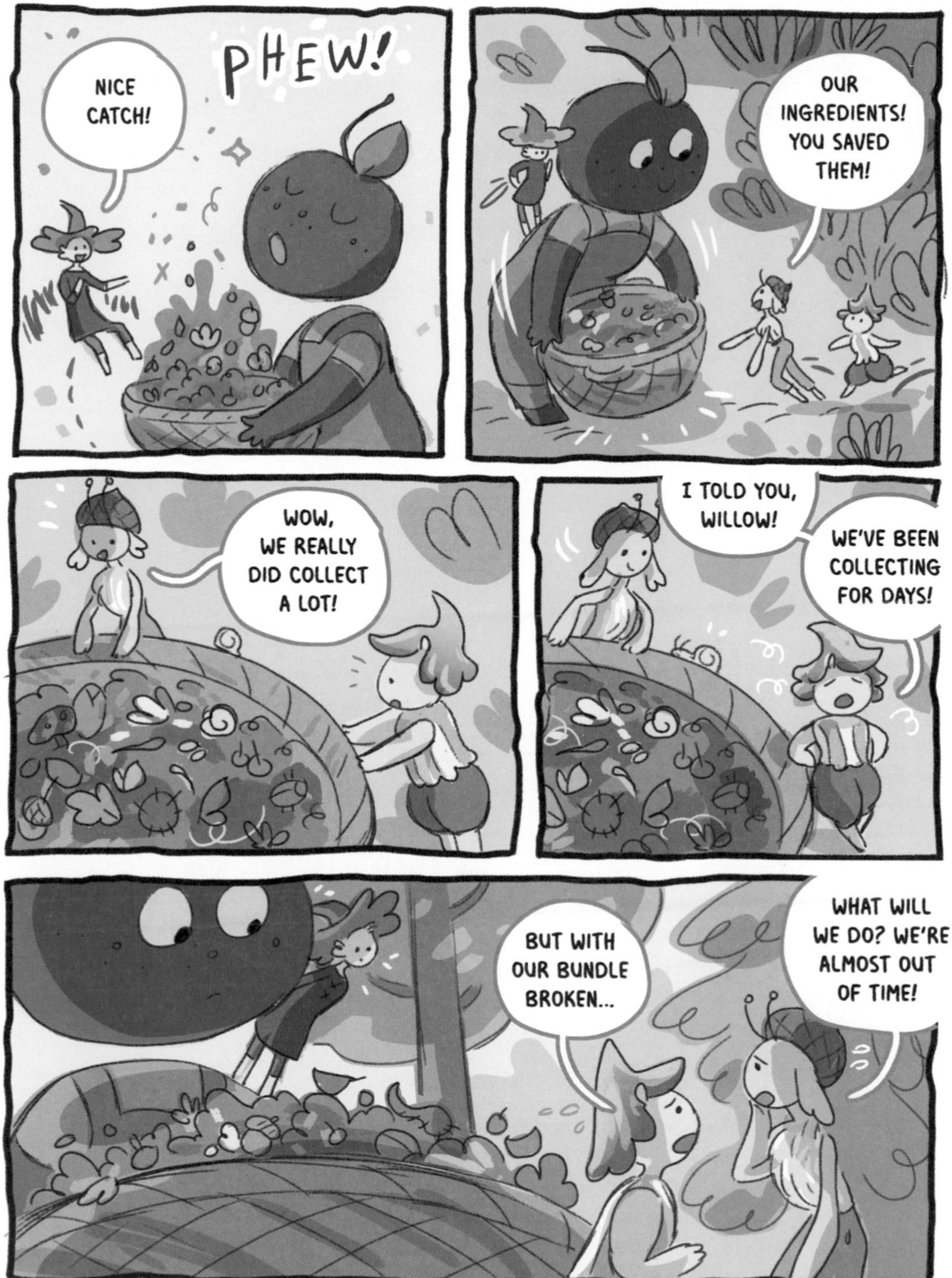
PHEW!
NICE CATCH!
OUR INGREDIENTS! YOU SAVED THEM!
WOW, WE REALLY DID COLLECT A LOT!
I TOLD YOU, WILLOW!
WE'VE BEEN COLLECTING FOR DAYS!
BUT WITH OUR BUNDLE BROKEN...
WHAT WILL WE DO? WE'RE ALMOST OUT OF TIME!

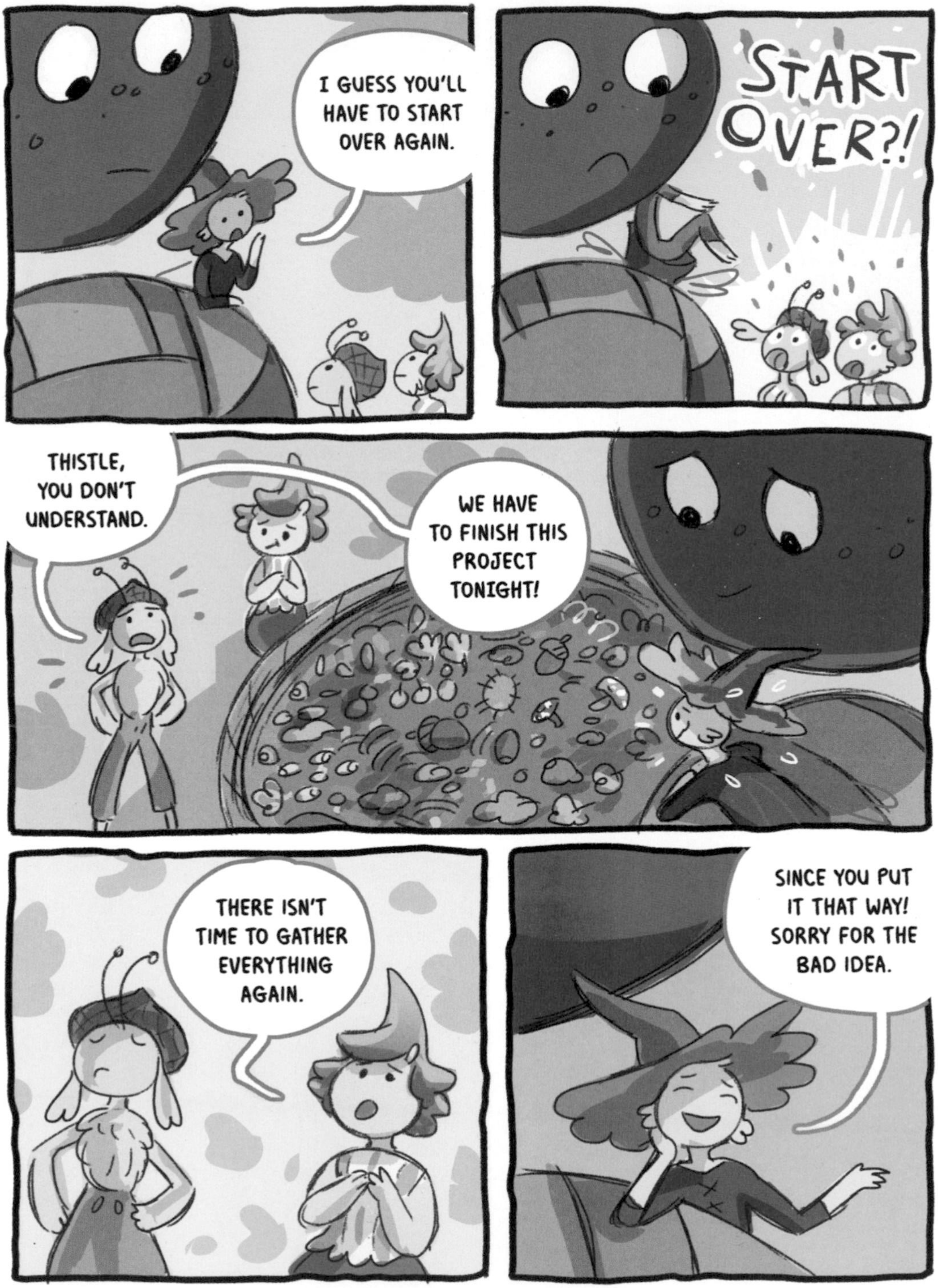
I GUESS YOU'LL HAVE TO START OVER AGAIN.
START OVER?!
THISTLE, YOU DON'T UNDERSTAND.
WE HAVE TO FINISH THIS PROJECT TONIGHT!
THERE ISN'T TIME TO GATHER EVERYTHING AGAIN.
SINCE YOU PUT IT THAT WAY! SORRY FOR THE BAD IDEA.

72

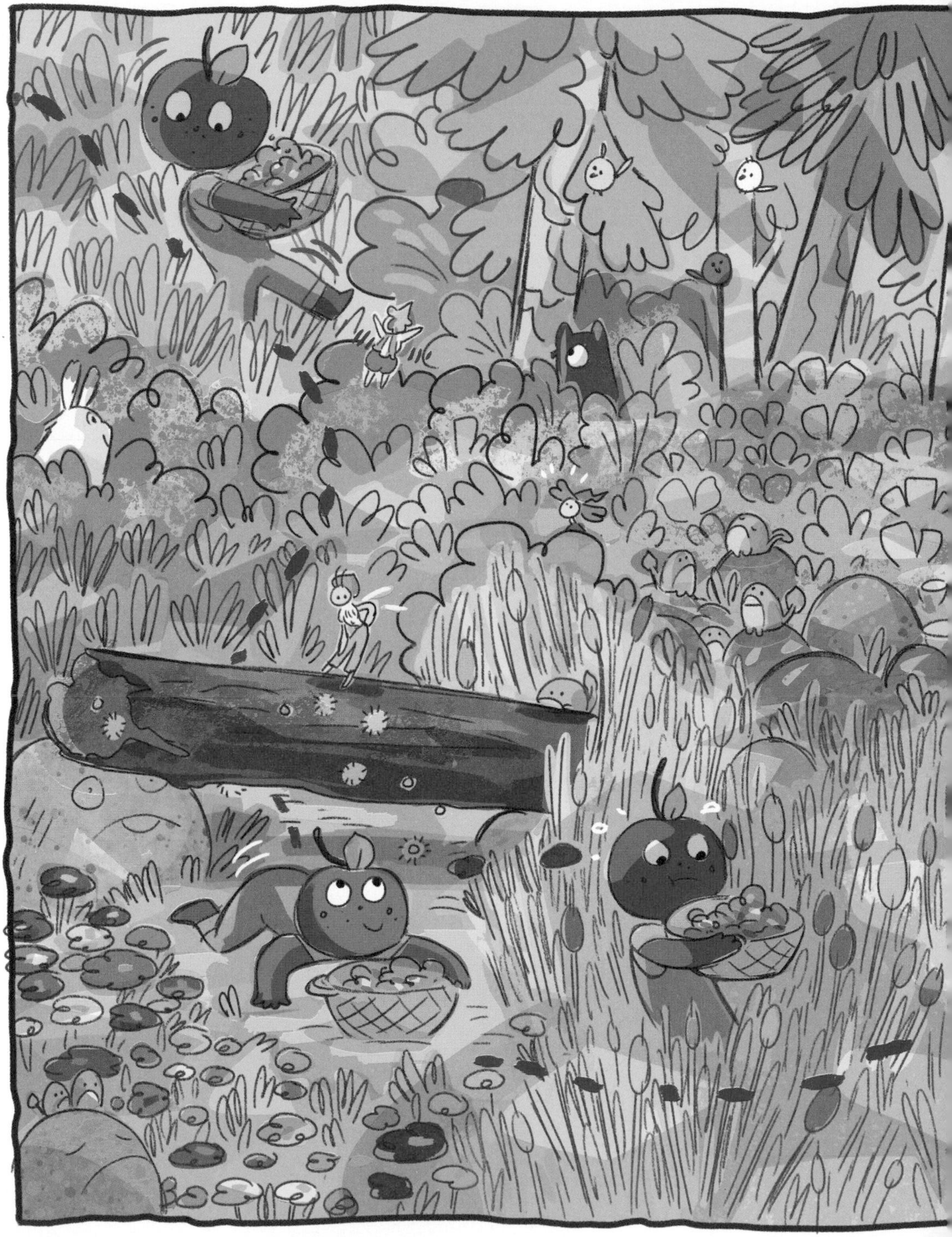

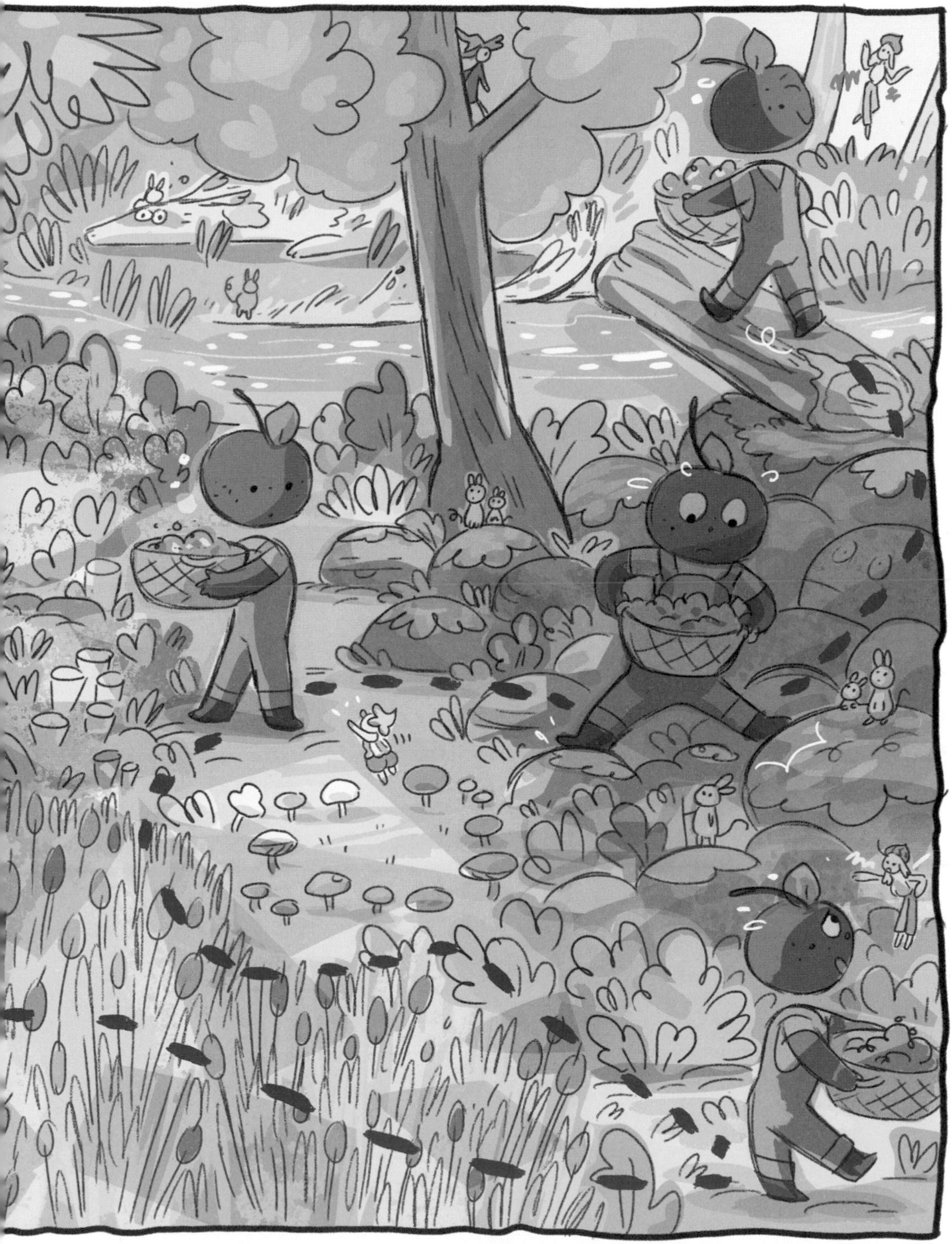

CHAPTER 4

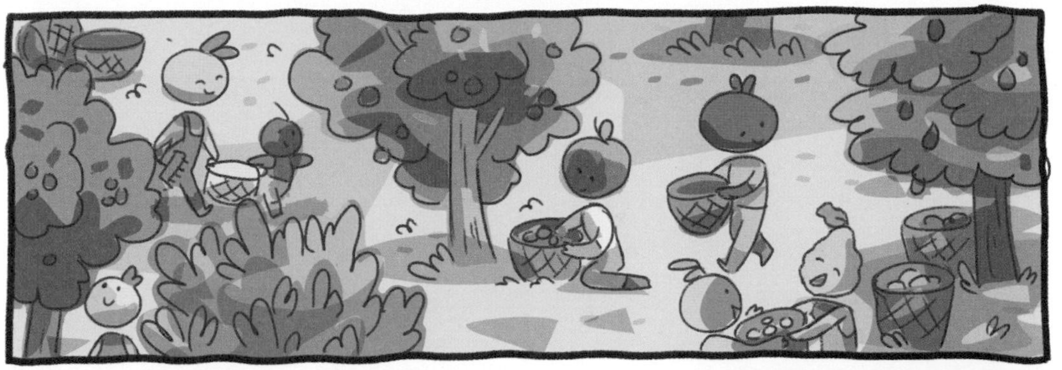

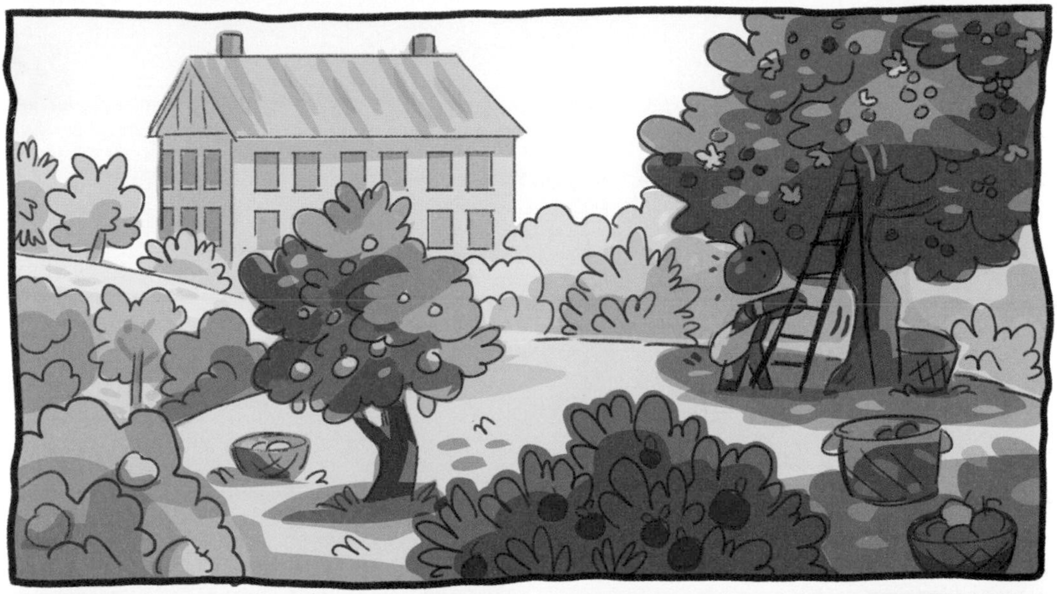

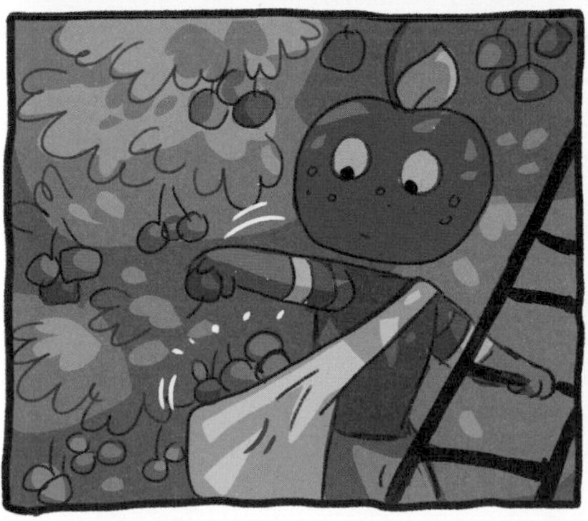

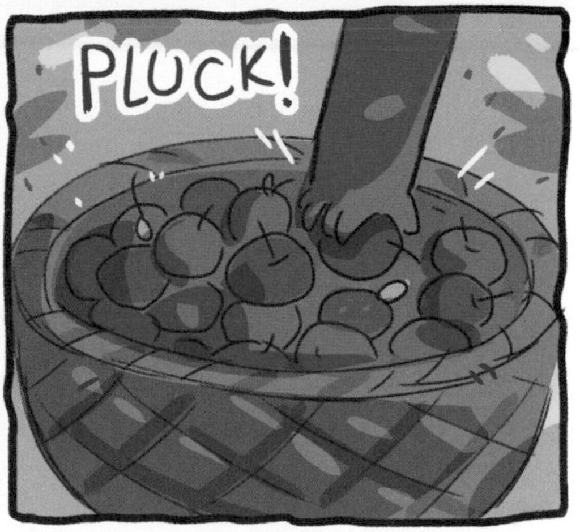
PLUCK!

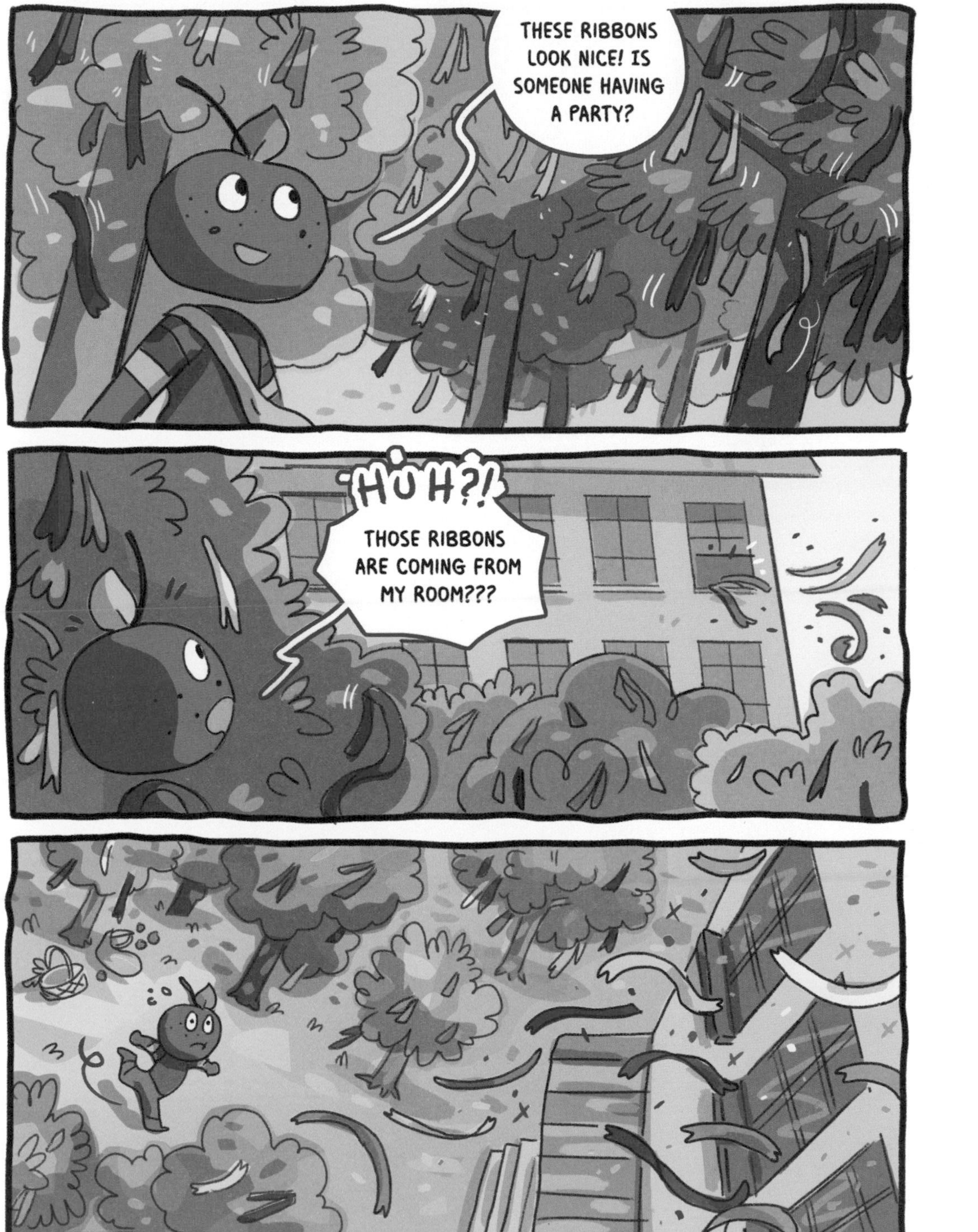
THESE RIBBONS LOOK NICE! IS SOMEONE HAVING A PARTY?
HUH?!
THOSE RIBBONS ARE COMING FROM MY ROOM???

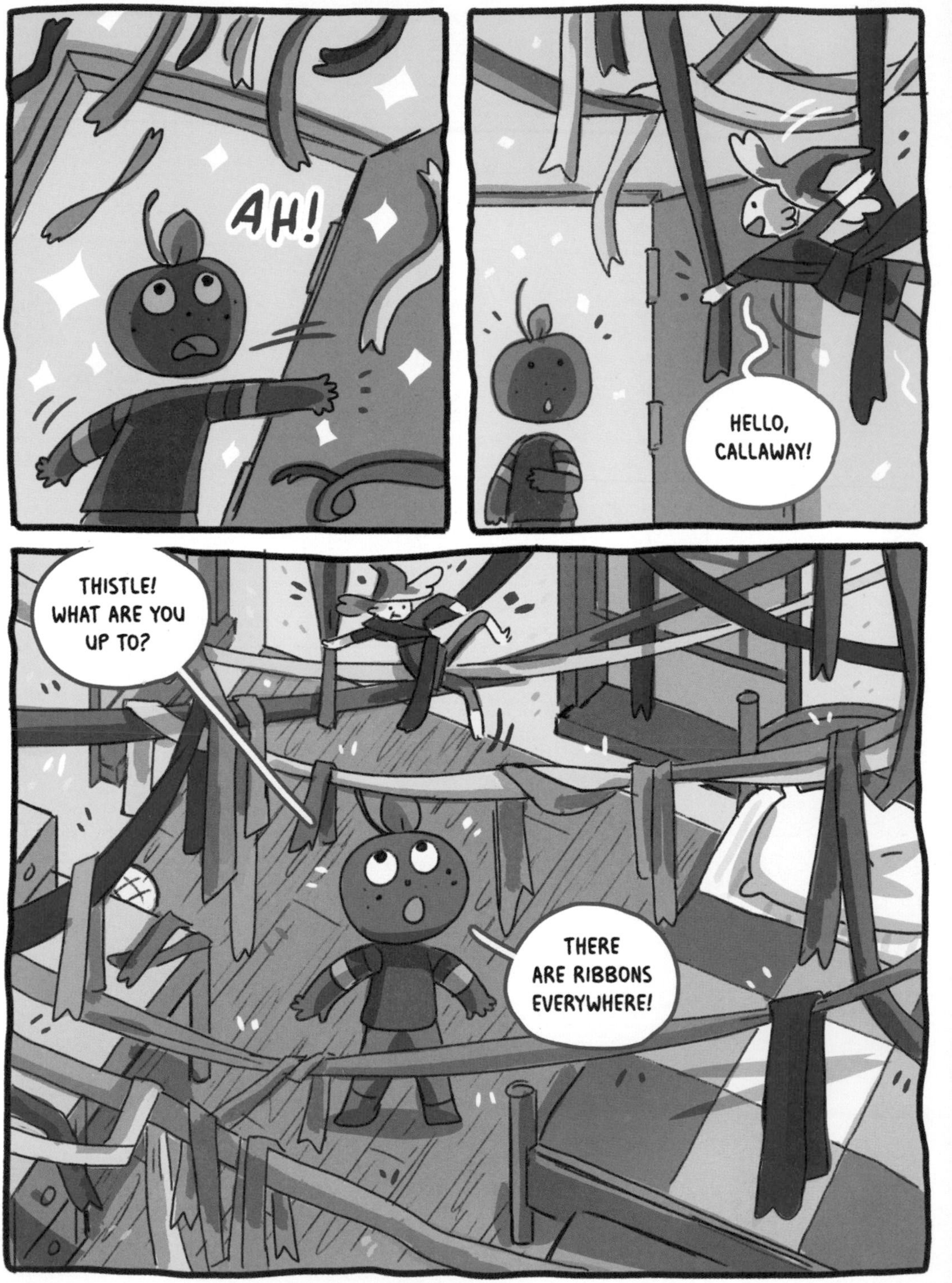
AH!
HELLO, CALLAWAY!
THISTLE! WHAT ARE YOU UP TO?
THERE ARE RIBBONS EVERYWHERE!

91

92

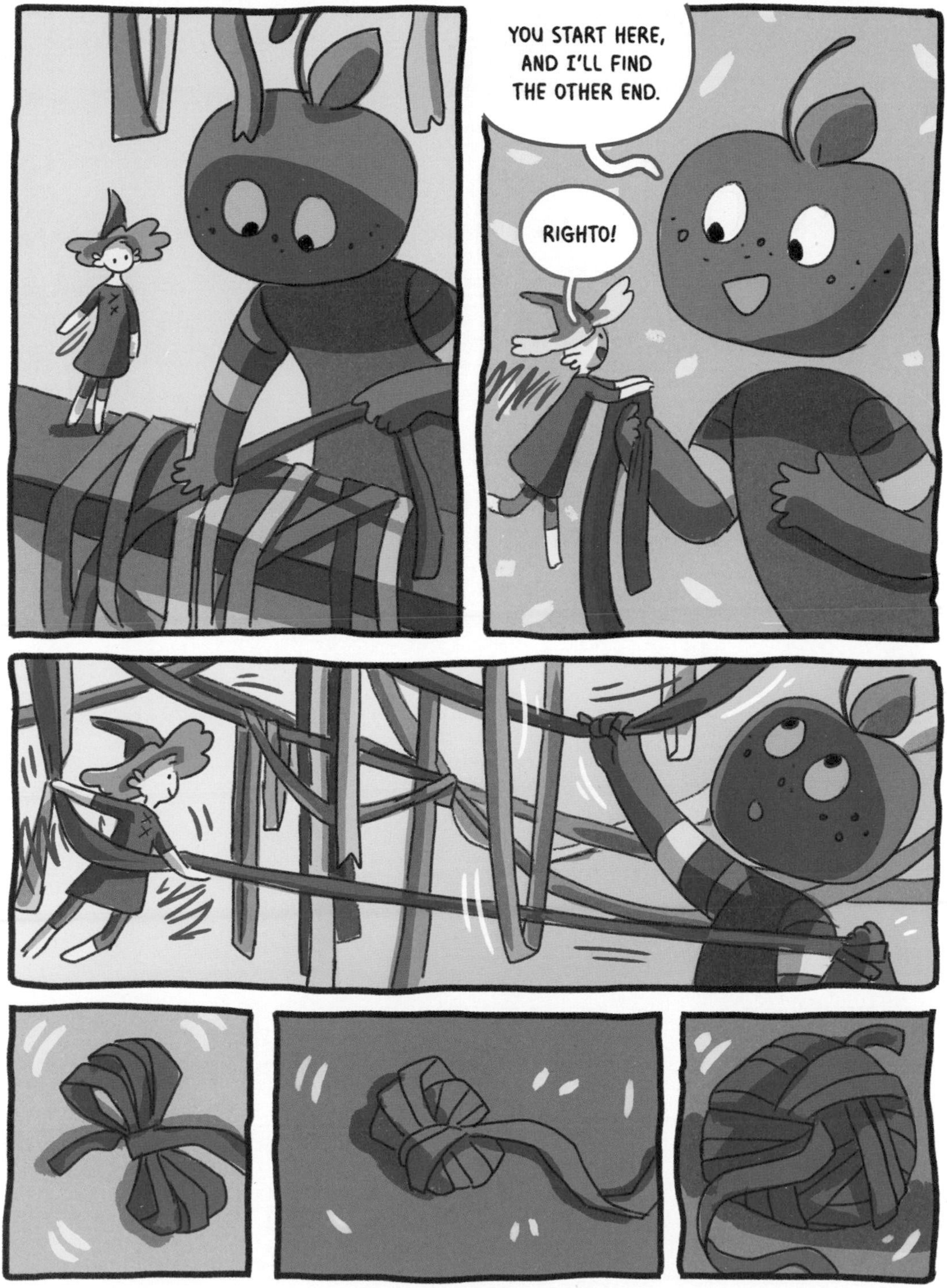
YOU START HERE,
AND I'LL FIND
THE OTHER END.
RIGHTO!

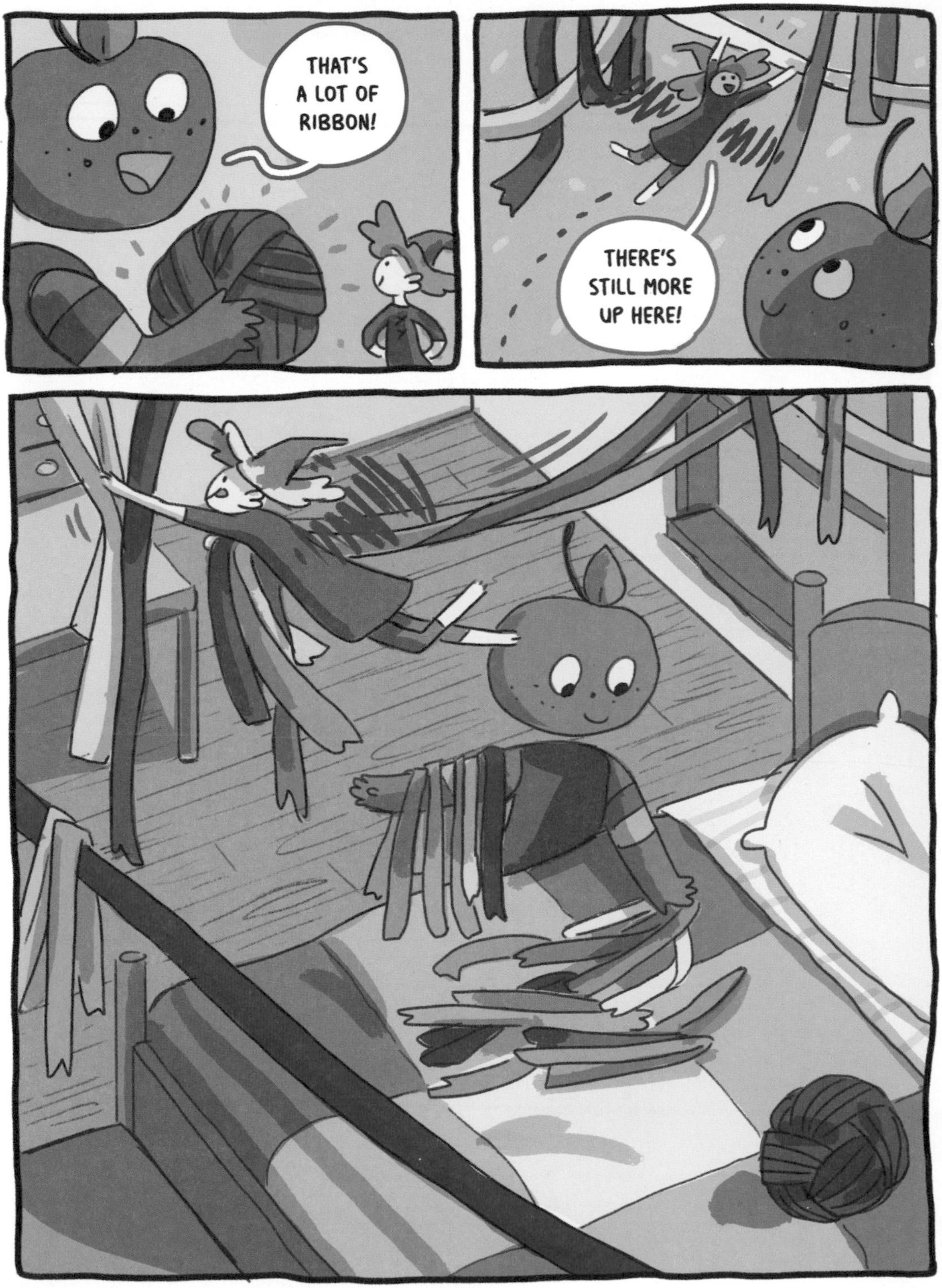
THAT'S A LOT OF RIBBON!
THERE'S STILL MORE UP HERE!

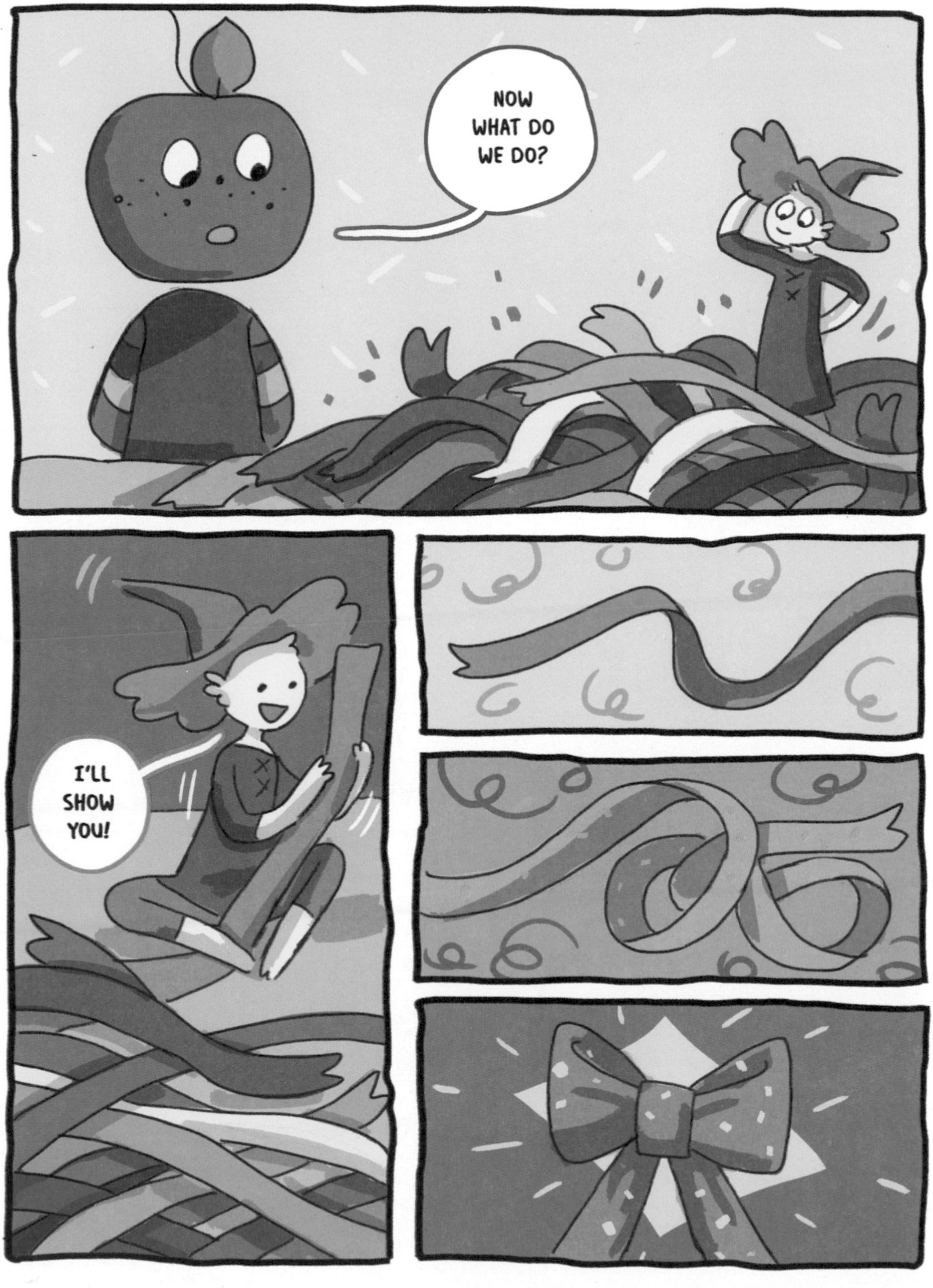
NOW WHAT DO WE DO?
I'LL SHOW YOU!

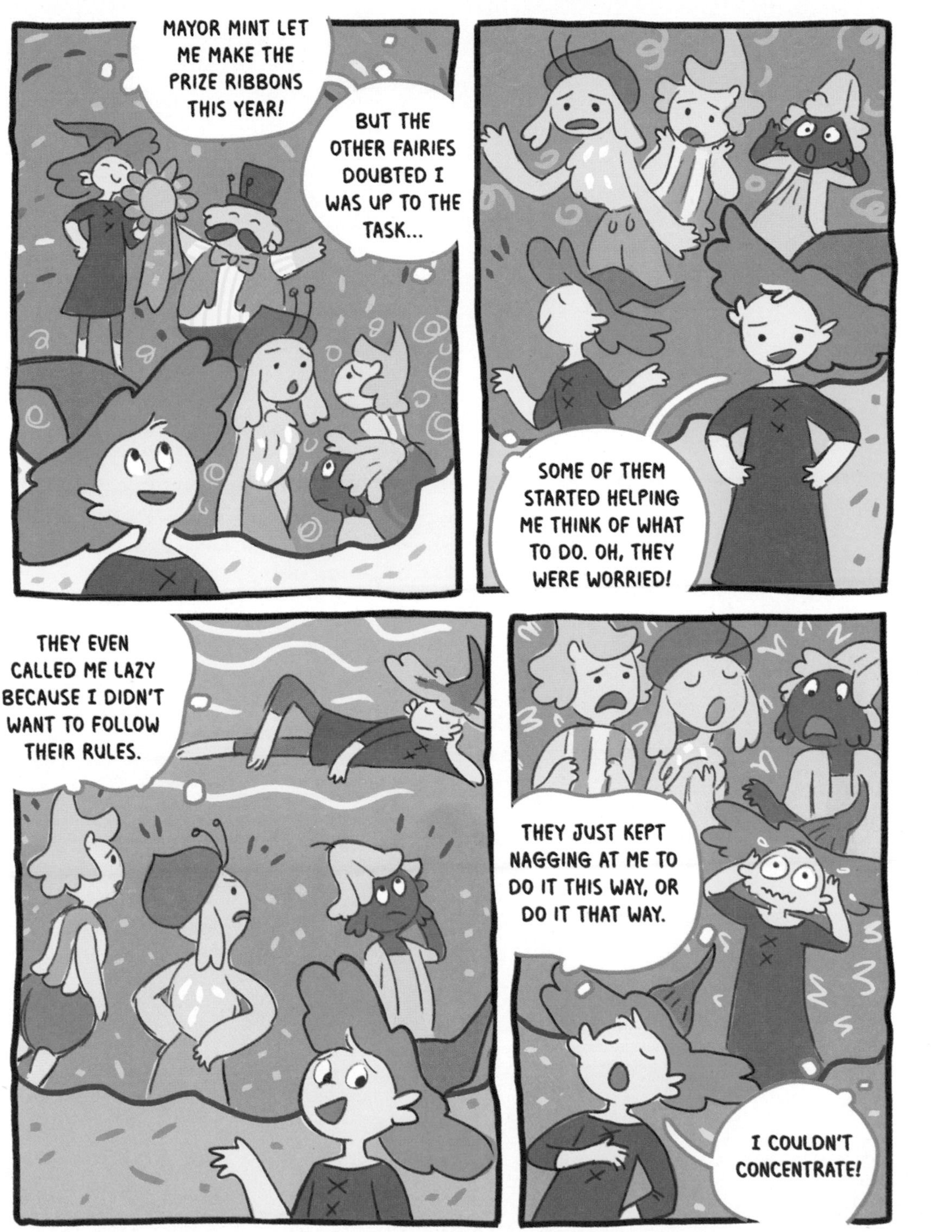
MAYOR MINT LET ME MAKE THE PRIZE RIBBONS THIS YEAR!
BUT THE OTHER FAIRIES DOUBTED I WAS UP TO THE TASK...
SOME OF THEM STARTED HELPING ME THINK OF WHAT TO DO. OH, THEY WERE WORRIED!
THEY EVEN CALLED ME LAZY BECAUSE I DIDN'T WANT TO FOLLOW THEIR RULES.
THEY JUST KEPT NAGGING AT ME TO DO IT THIS WAY, OR DO IT THAT WAY.
I COULDN'T CONCENTRATE!

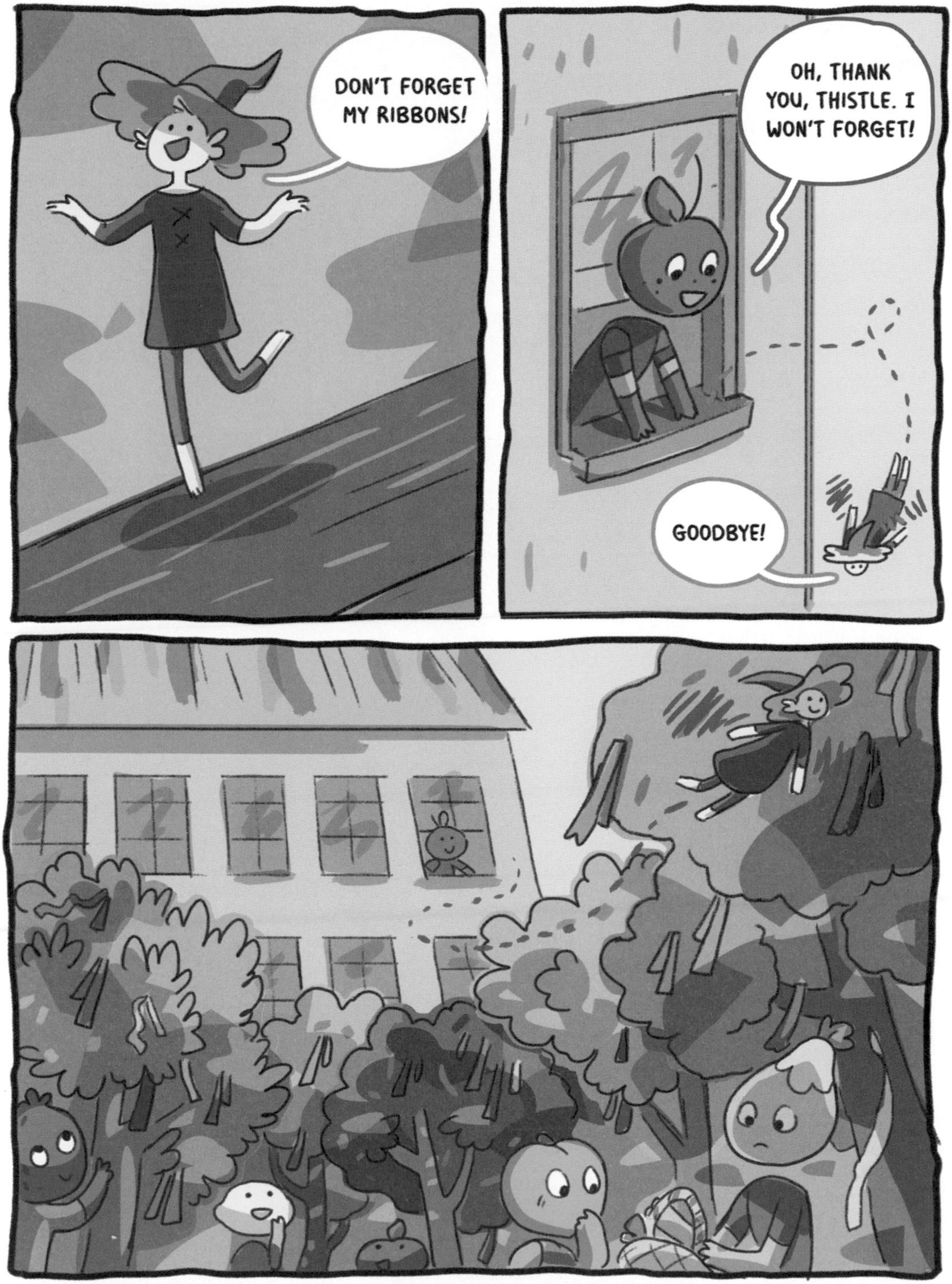
DON'T FORGET MY RIBBONS!
OH, THANK YOU, THISTLE. I WON'T FORGET!
GOODBYE!

CHAPTER 5

108

109

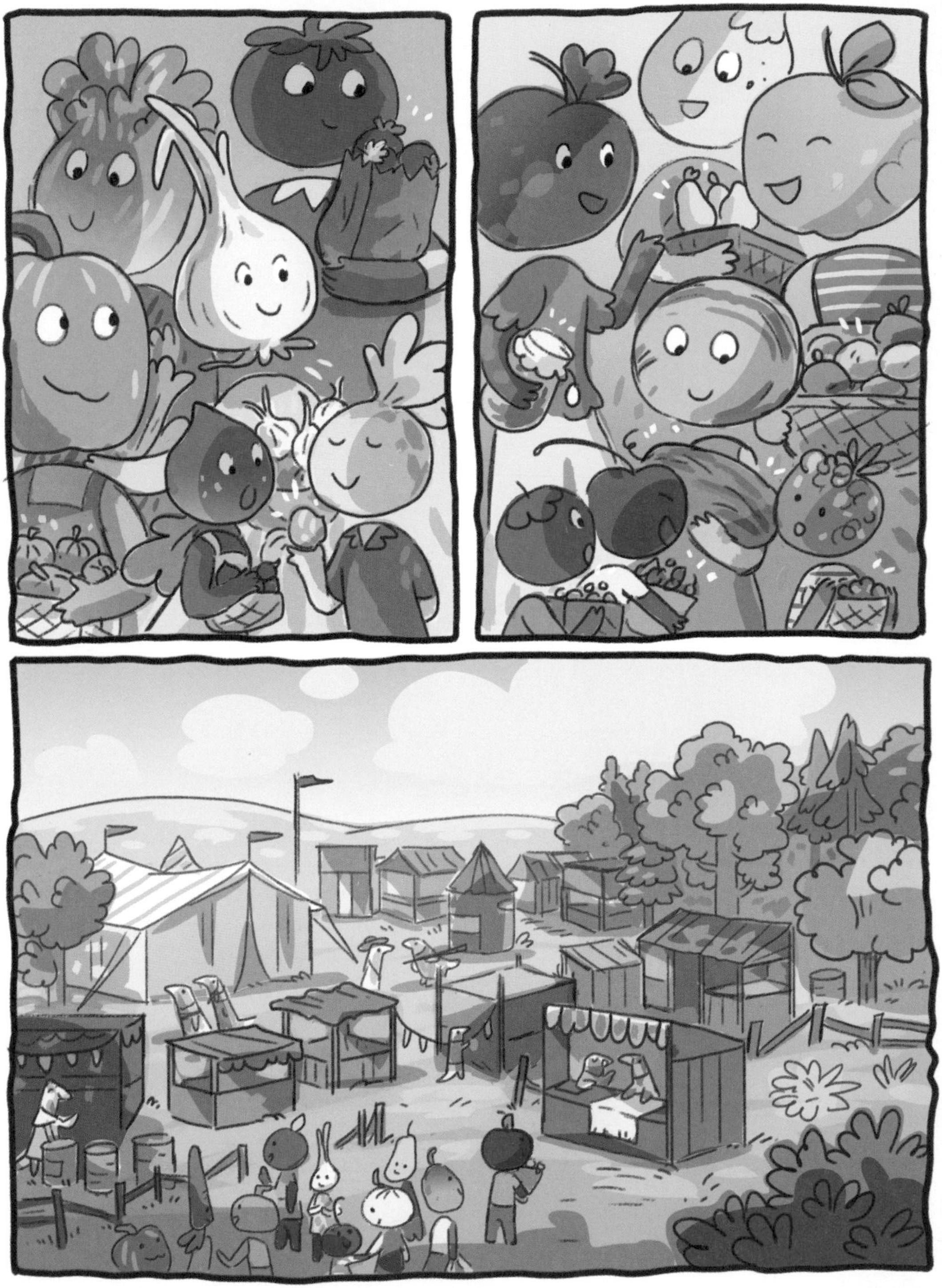

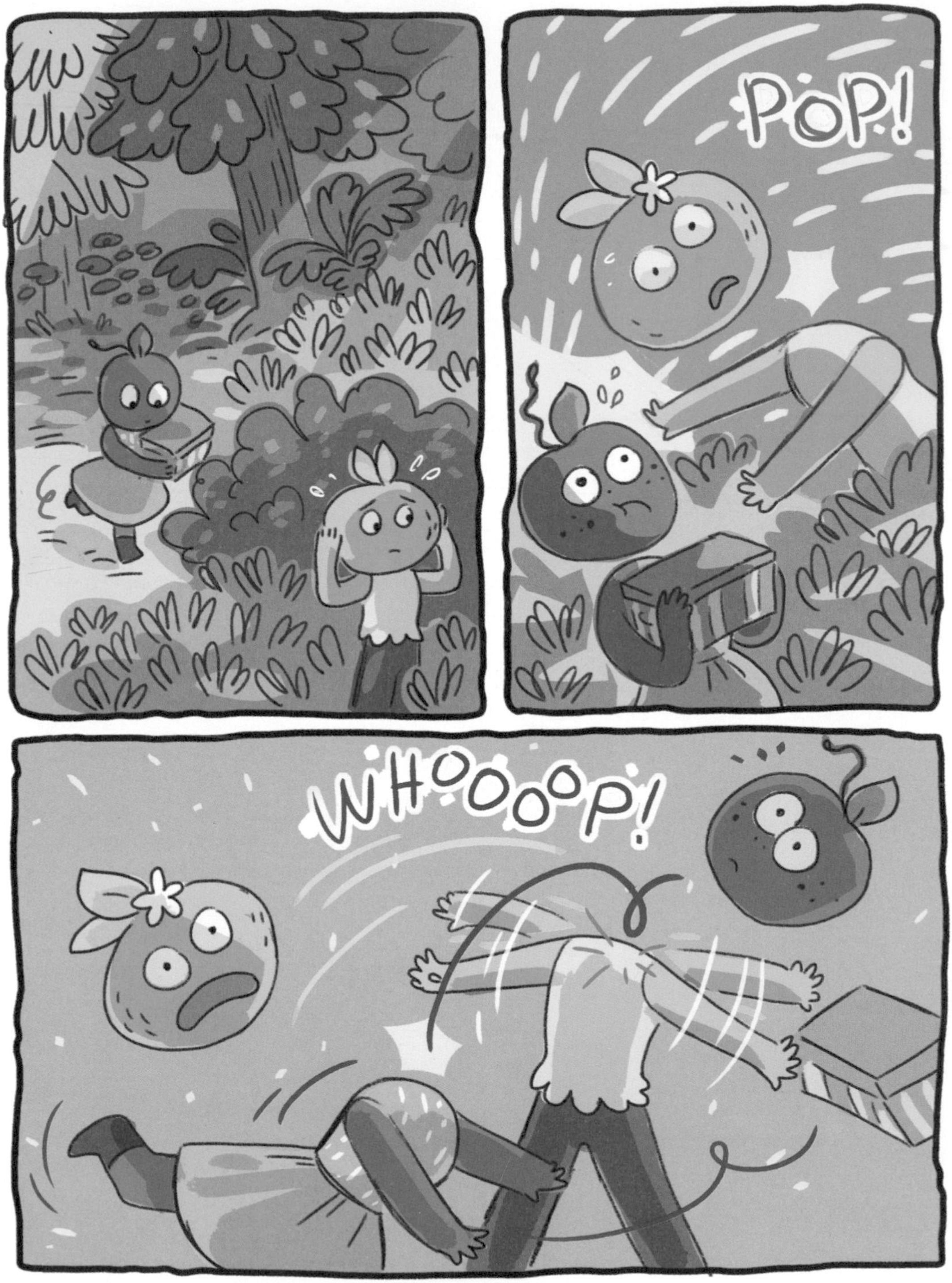
POP!
WHOOOOP!

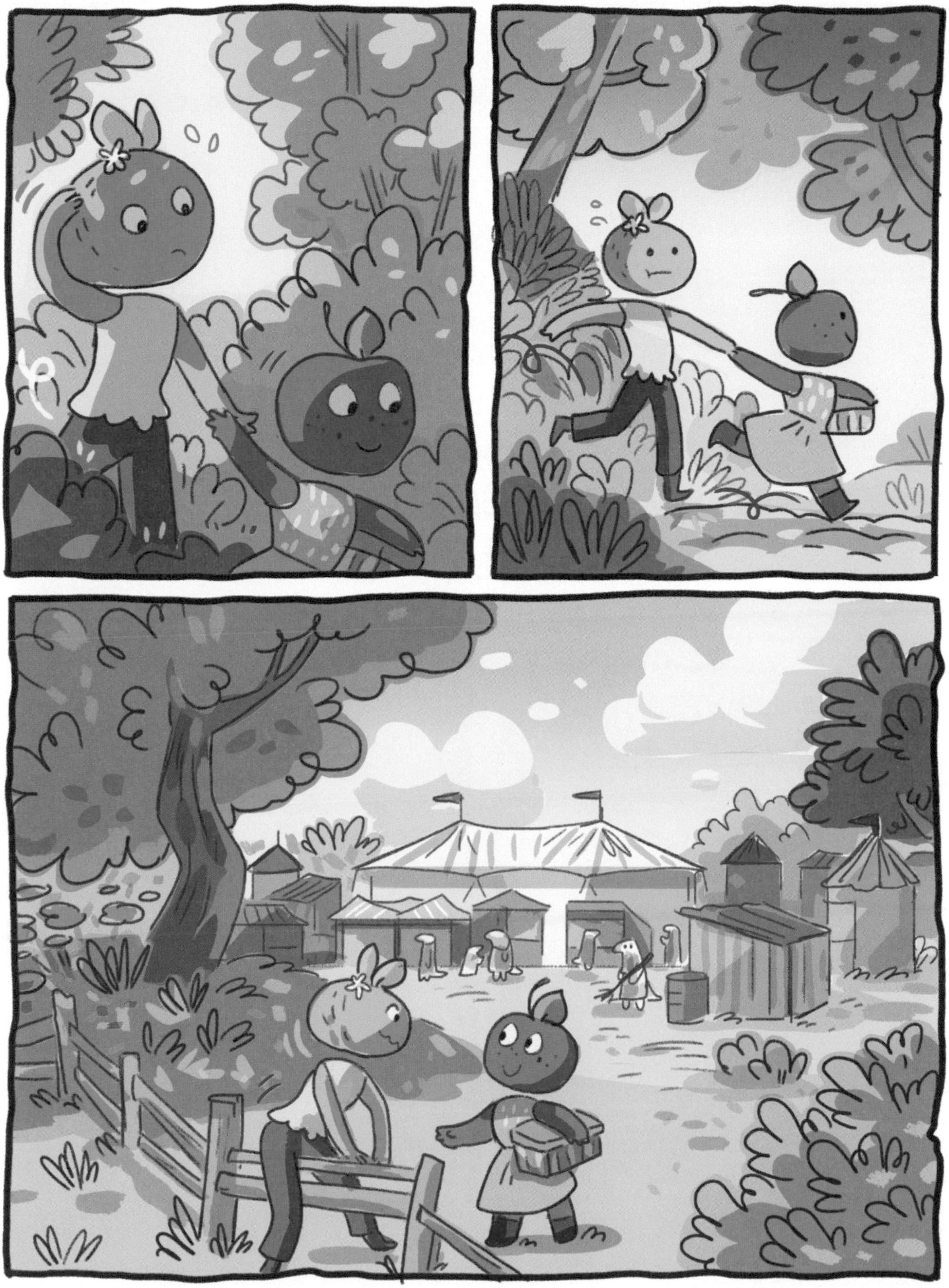

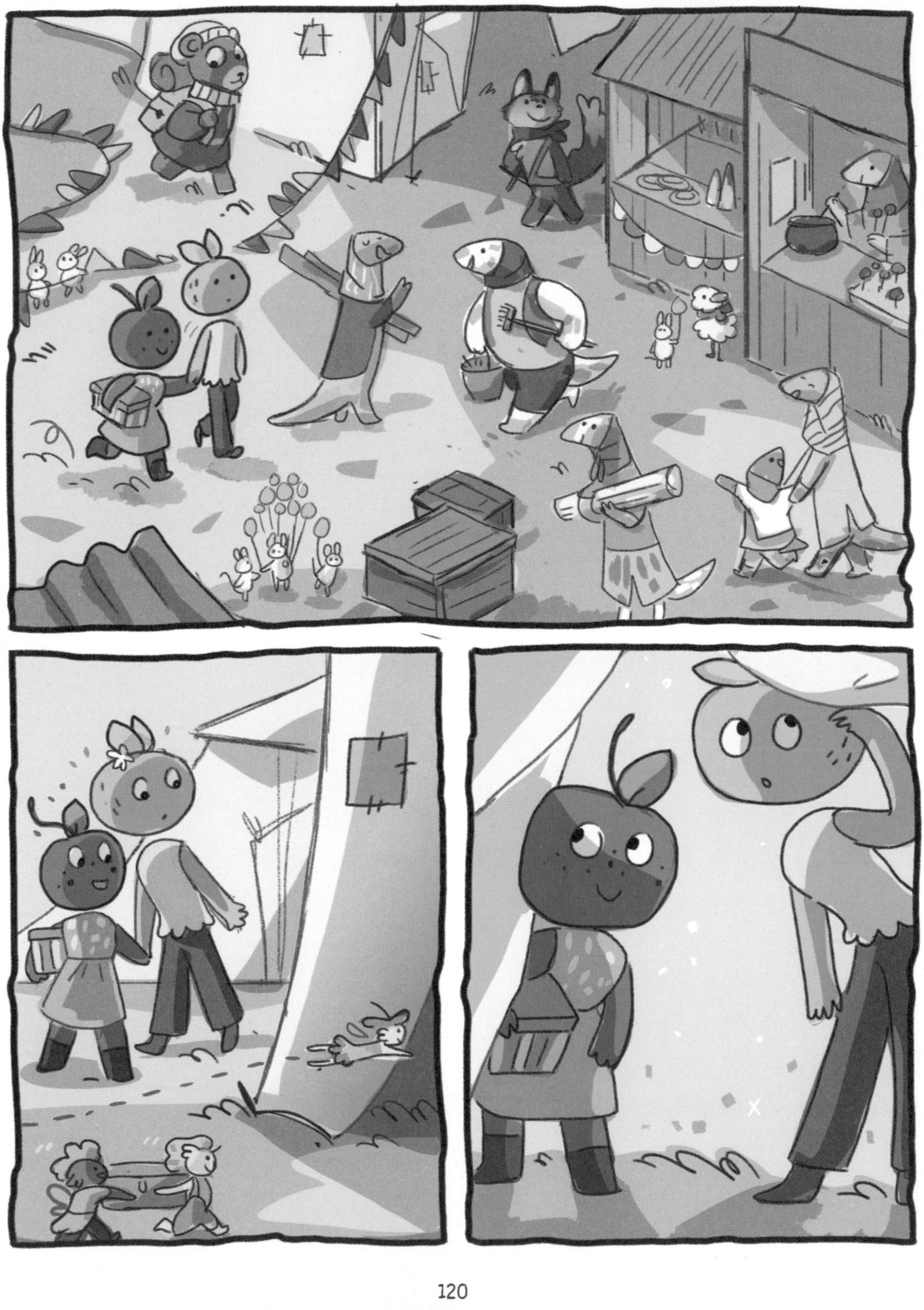

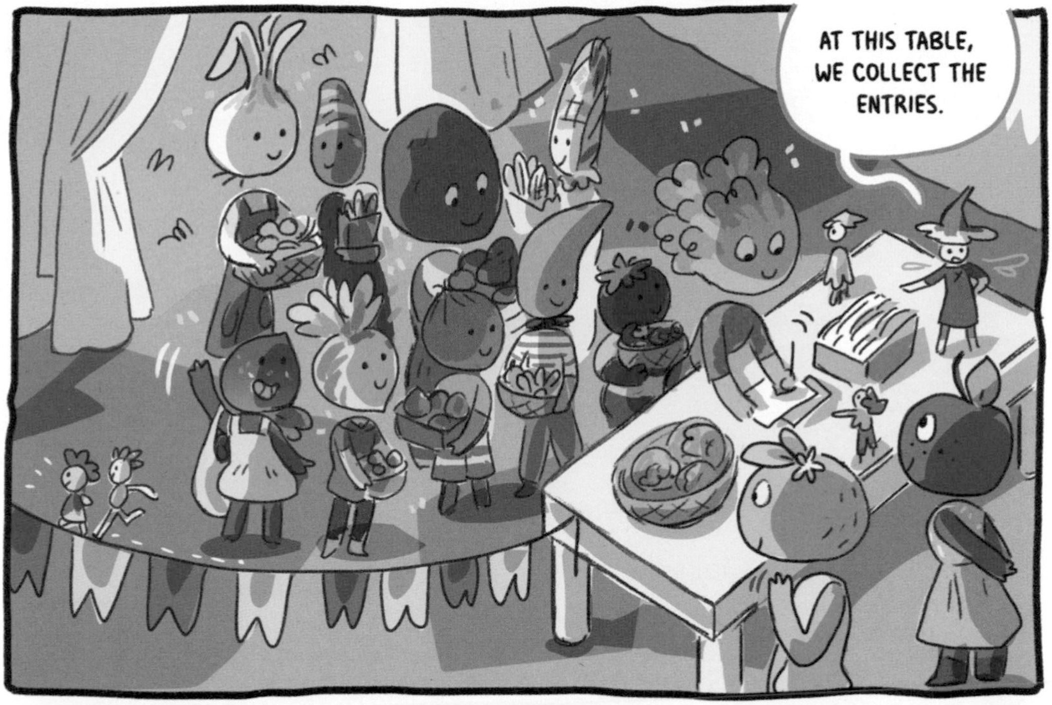
AT THIS TABLE, WE COLLECT THE ENTRIES.

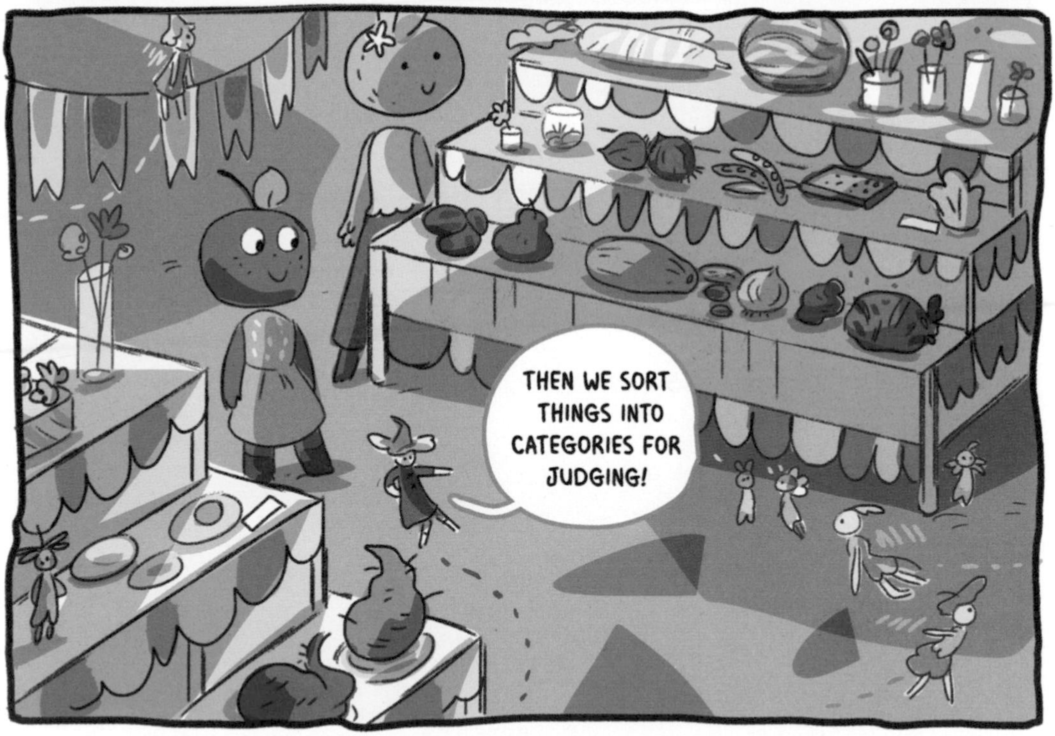
THEN WE SORT THINGS INTO CATEGORIES FOR JUDGING!

131

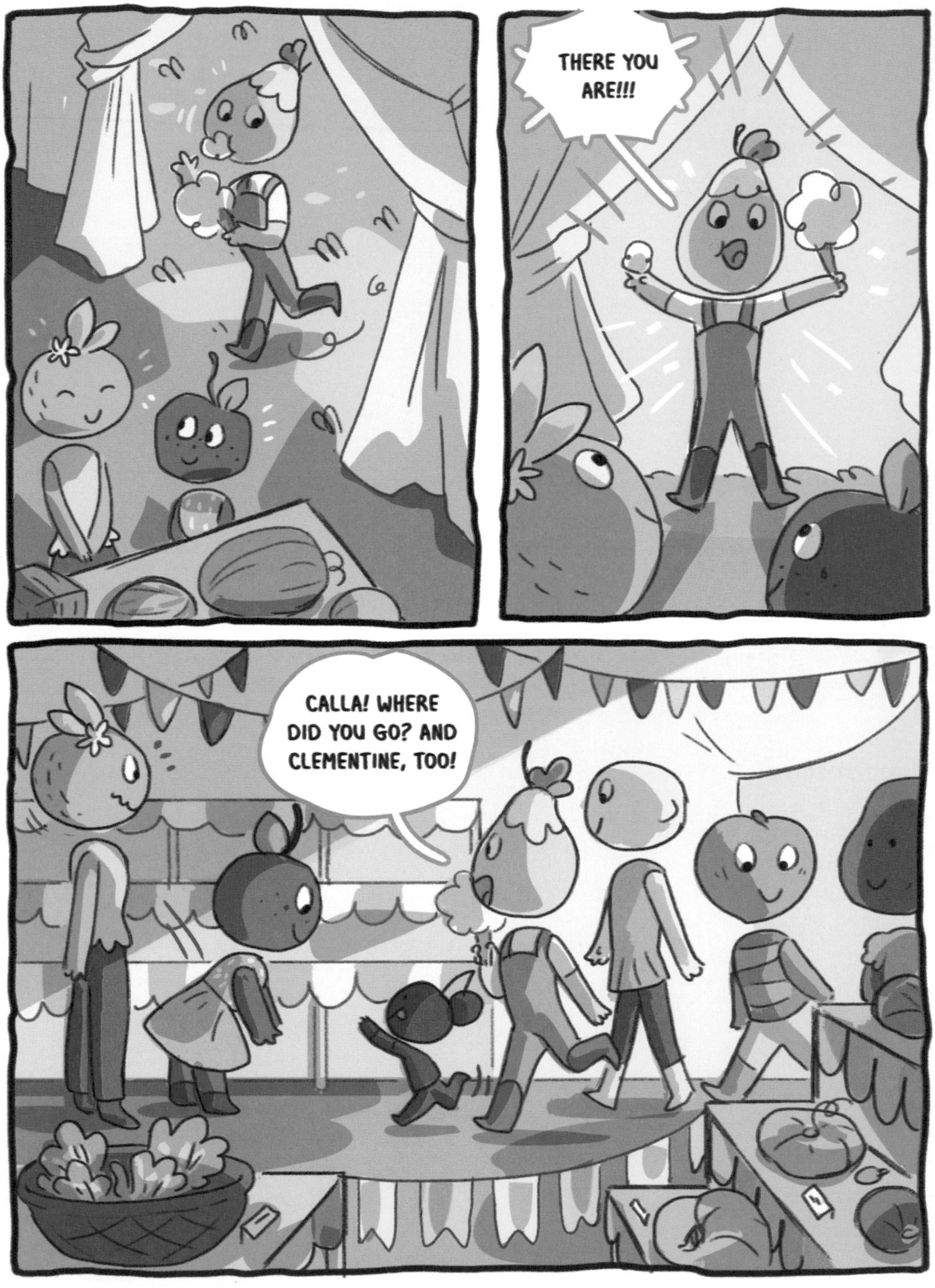
THERE YOU ARE!!!
CALLA! WHERE DID YOU GO? AND CLEMENTINE, TOO!

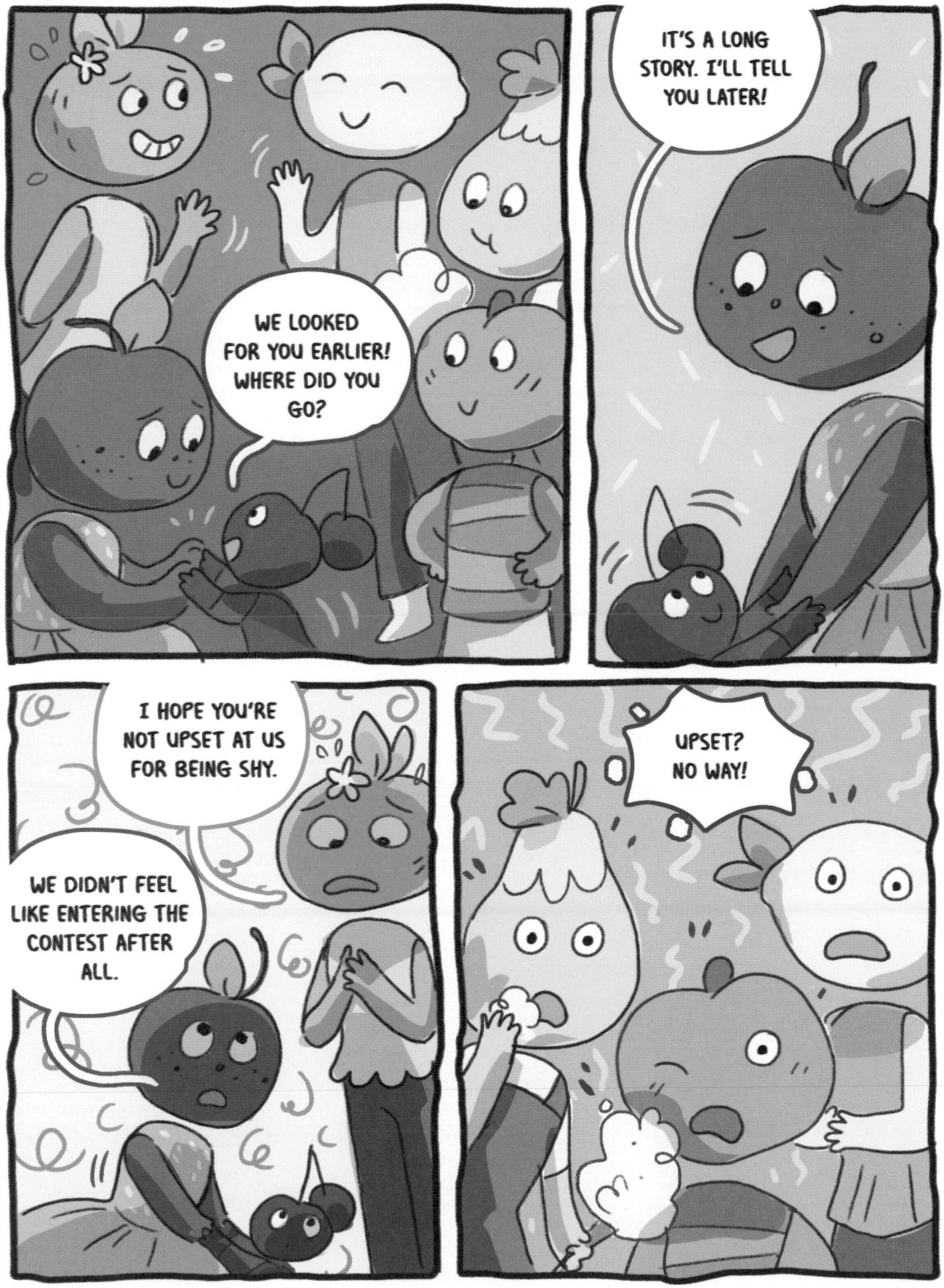
WE LOOKED FOR YOU EARLIER! WHERE DID YOU GO?
IT'S A LONG STORY. I'LL TELL YOU LATER!
I HOPE YOU'RE NOT UPSET AT US FOR BEING SHY.
WE DIDN'T FEEL LIKE ENTERING THE CONTEST AFTER ALL.
UPSET? NO WAY!

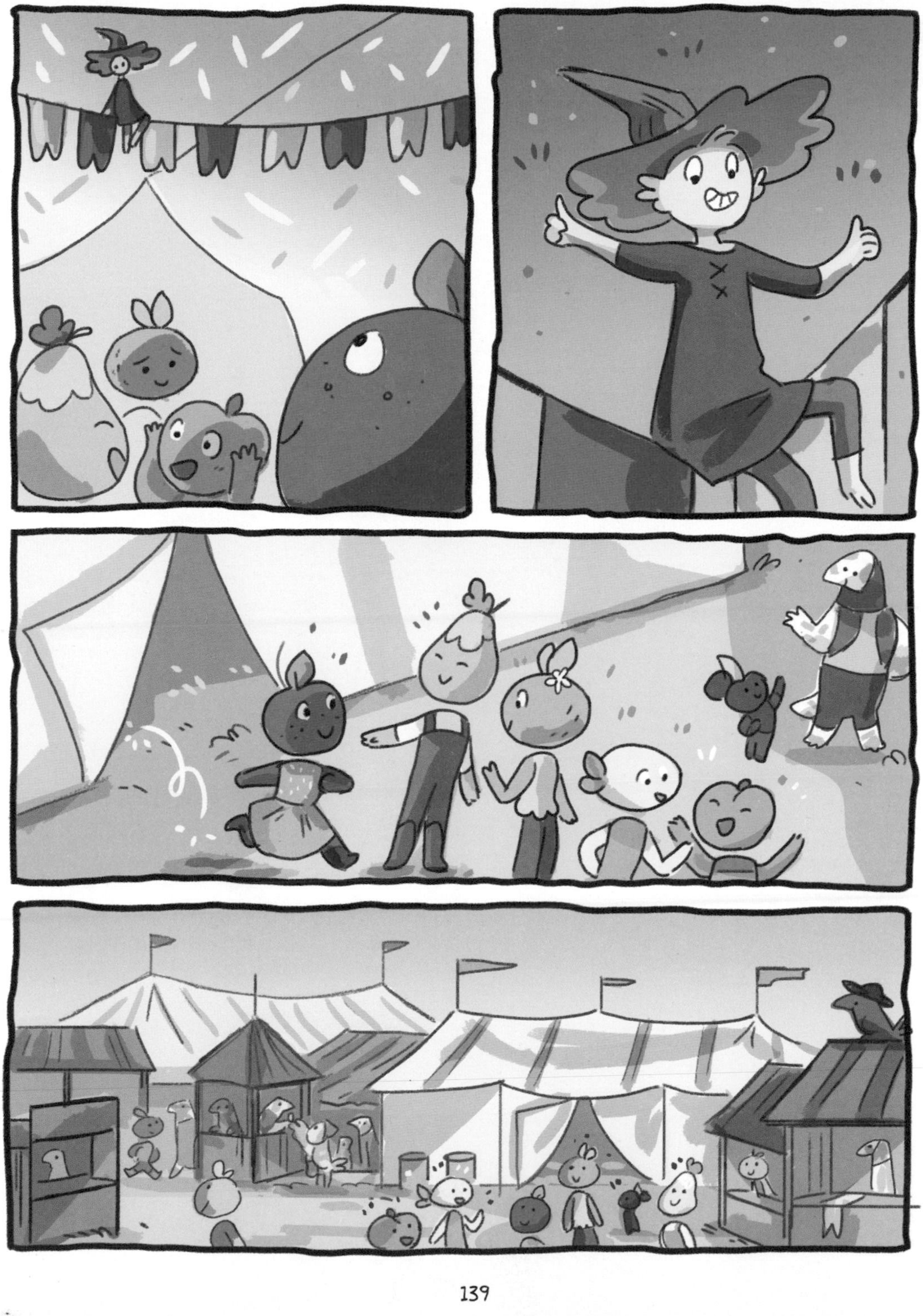

CHAPTER 6

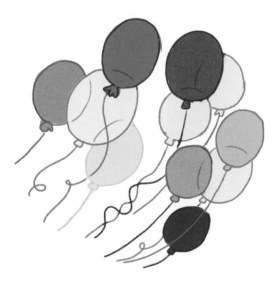

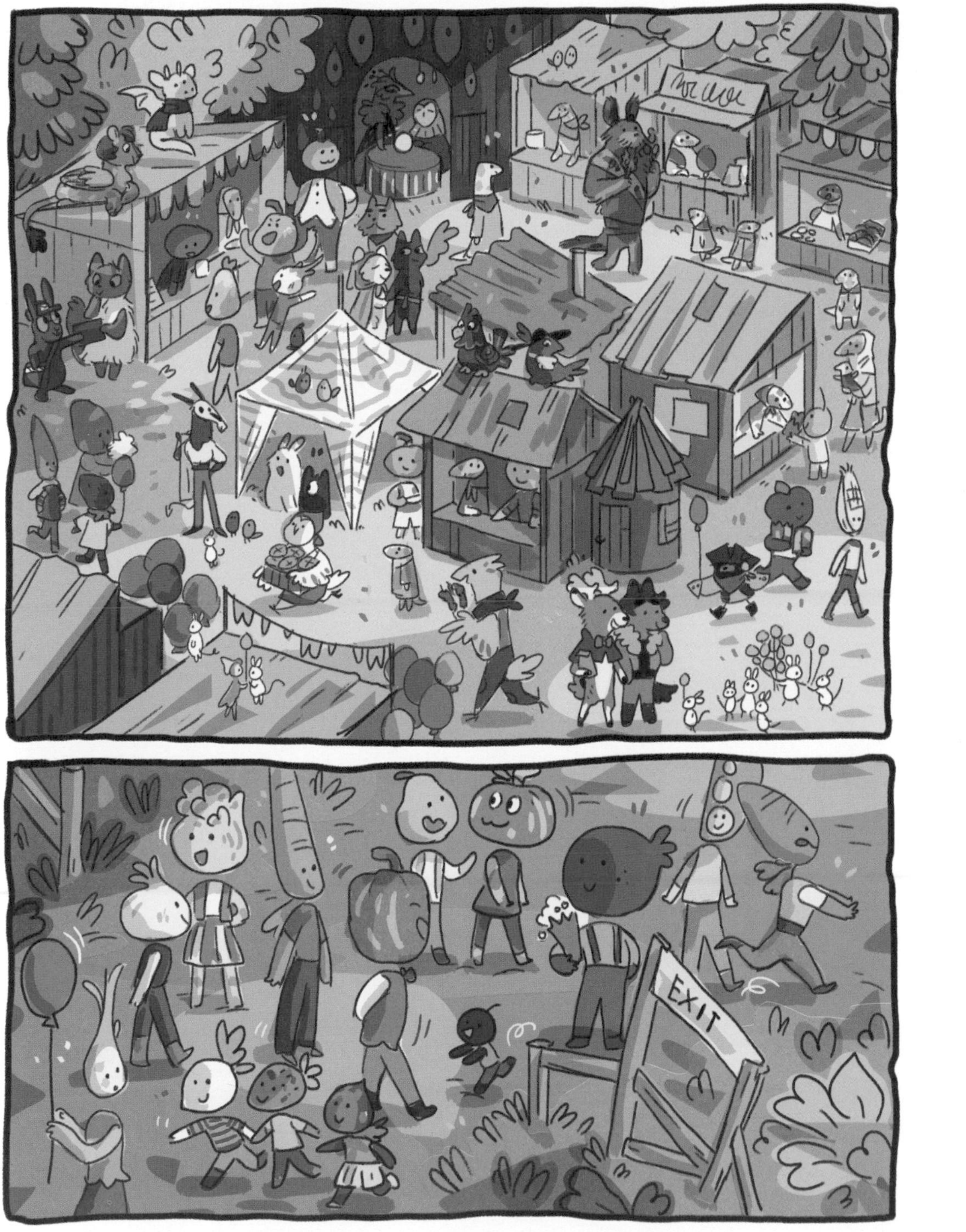
EXIT

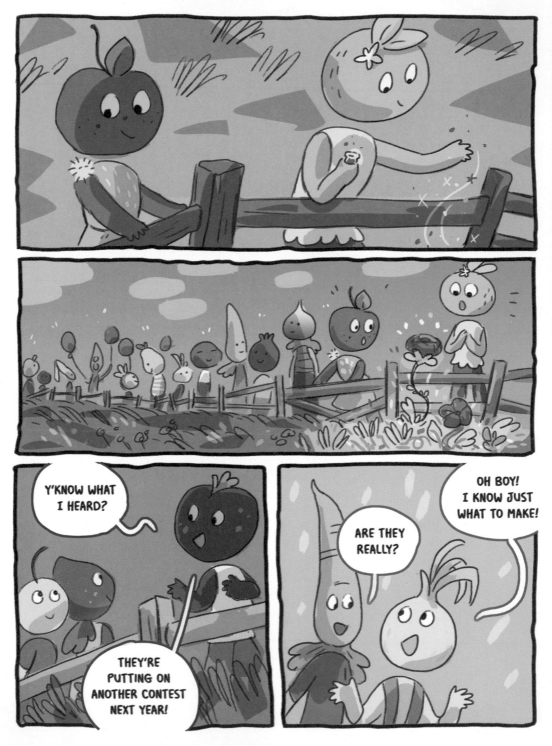

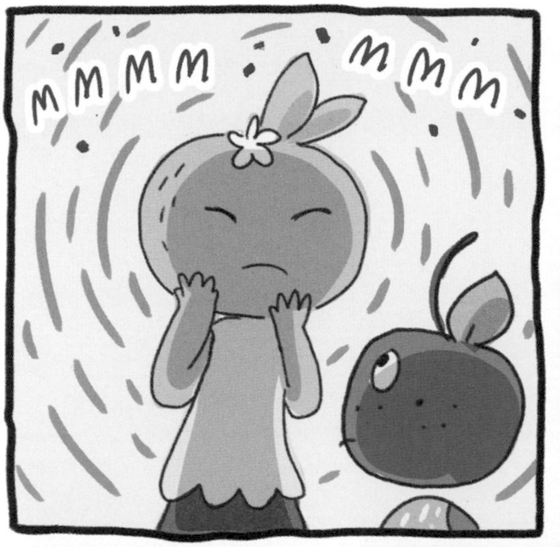
MMMM MMMM

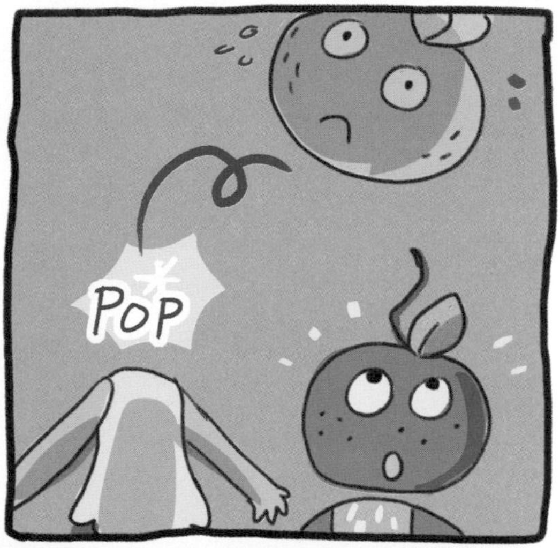
POP

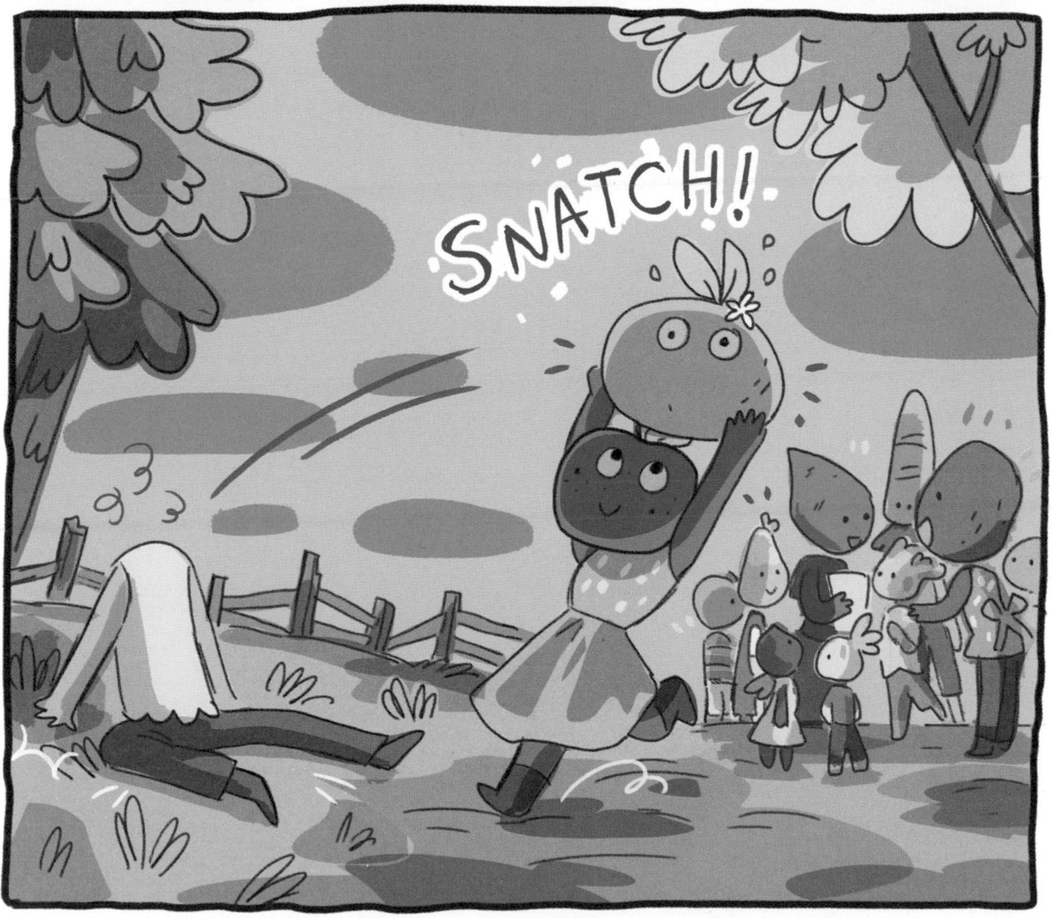
SNATCH!

148

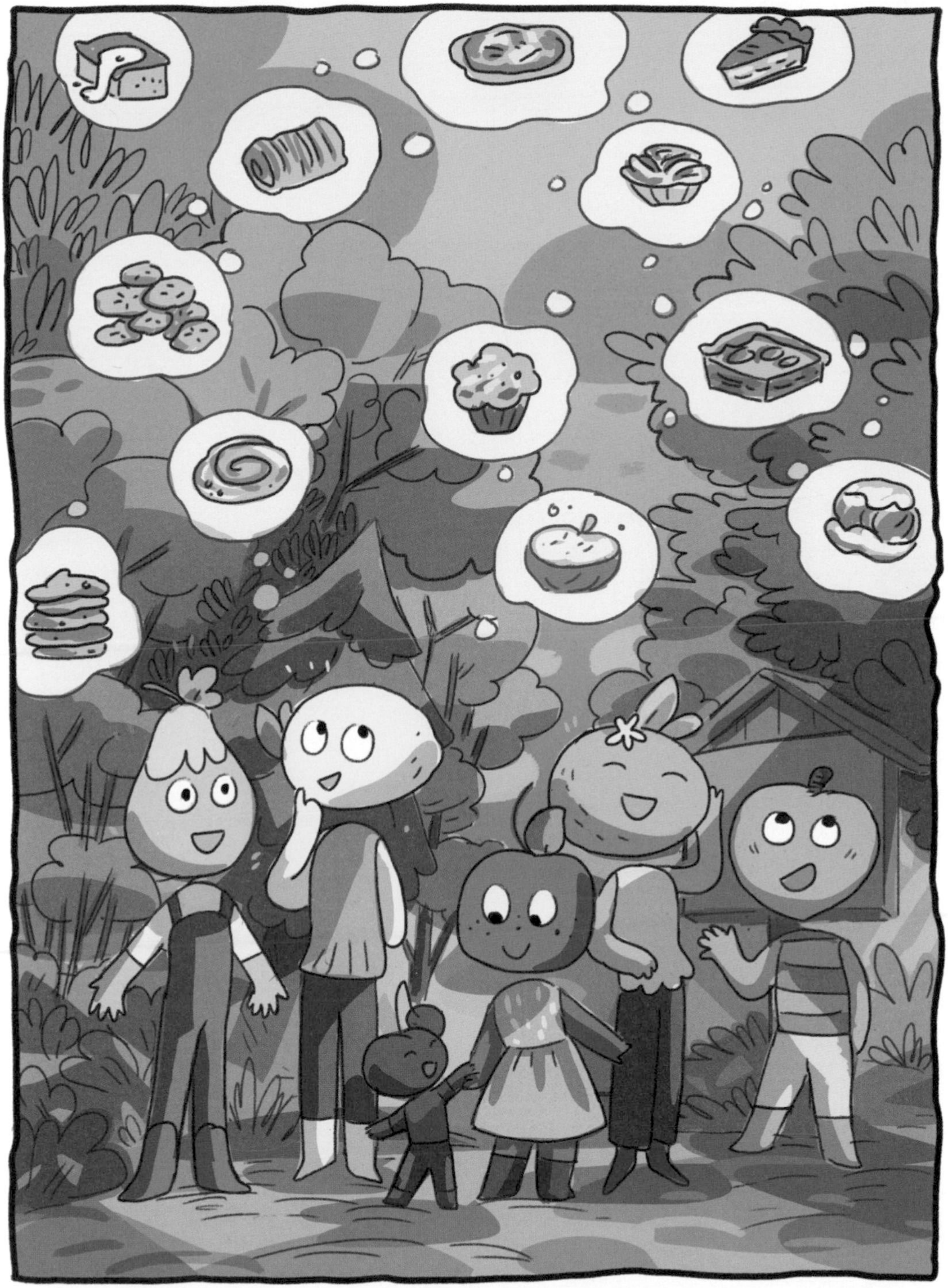

aw·ful·ize (off-uh-līz) v.: to imagine (something) to be as bad as it can possibly be

HAVE YOU EVER HEARD OF "AWFULIZING"? IT WAS A NEW WORD TO ME, THOUGH THE DEFINITION IS FAMILIAR. I SPENT A LOT OF TIME WITH THIS SPECIFIC FORM OF WORRY AS A KID, AND I OFTEN FOUND MYSELF IN CALLAWAY'S SHOES: DRAGGED ALONG BY THE EXCITEMENT OF OTHERS, BUT TOO SHY TO TALK ABOUT THE ANXIOUS WHAT-IFS BUBBLING INSIDE ME. I THINK THAT'S A FAIRLY UNIVERSAL KID THING, AND IT'S AN ADULT THING, TOO.

NOWADAYS, I'M MORE HONEST ABOUT MY LIMITS. I DEFINITELY STILL FEEL ANXIOUS ABOUT SOME THINGS, BUT IT'S AN EFFORT TO CHANGE MY INTERNAL DIALOGUE. I NEVER KNEW ANYONE WHO CHALLENGED MY THOUGHT PATTERNS QUITE LIKE THISTLE DOES FOR CALLAWAY . . . BUT I KNEW A LOT OF KIDS LIKE CLEMENTINE! AND I WAS ONE OF THOSE KIDS, TOO. I HOPE READERS WILL FIND SOME INSPIRATION IN CALLAWAY'S STORY, AND PERHAPS SEE SOMETHING OF THEMSELVES IN THE WAY SHE NAVIGATES HER WORRIES.

CRABAPPLE TROUBLE IS FINISHED AT LAST . . . AND I HAVE A LOT OF PEOPLE TO THANK!

A HUGE THANK YOU TO MOM AND DAD, WHO WERE GENEROUS, PATIENT, AND KIND WHILE I WORKED ON MY FIRST BOOK. I KNOW WE'RE A FAMILY THAT'S USED TO SHARING EVERYTHING, SO IT'S HARD THAT THINGS LIKE THIS ARE BETTER DONE IN SECRET . . . BUT THANK YOU FOR AT LEAST TRYING NOT TO BE TOO NOSY WHILE I WORKED!

HIGH FIVES TO MY THREE FAVORITE BROTHERS, BEN, JACOB, AND COLIN, WHO WERE NOTHING BUT ENCOURAGING THROUGH THE WHOLE PROCESS. THANKS SO MUCH FOR KEEPING ME ON TASK WITH CHOICE MEMES, AND SIBLING ADVICE SHARED OVER COFFEE AND GAMES.

SUPER BIG THANKS TO GINA, WHITNEY, AND PATRICK—MY AWESOME CONTACTS AT RHG! I KNEW THAT MAKING A BOOK WOULD BE A TEAM EFFORT, BUT I NEVER IMAGINED I'D HAVE SUCH SUPPORTIVE, KNOWLEDGEABLE, AND PLAYFUL TEAMMATES. I'M SO GRATEFUL TO HAVE HAD YOUR GUIDANCE ALONG THE WAY. THANK YOU FOR MAKING THE PROCESS SO MUCH FUN AND FOR HELPING ME CRAFT A STORY I'M SO EXCITED TO SHARE!

ALSO THANK YOU TO THE MANY FRIENDS WHO MAKE UP THE *SECRET TWITTER* SQUAD: ASHEL, BEL, CHOO, CRYPTO, ELI, EMILY, GRACE, JELLY, KATIE, LIZZIE, MIRANDA, RENEE, AND VIV. MY FEED HAS BEEN NOTHING BUT THE FINEST FRESH TAKES, INSIGHT, AND ENCOURAGEMENT AMONG THE CRAZINESS THAT SOCIAL MEDIA HAS BECOME. WE ARE SOMEHOW ALL WORKING TOWARD NEW PASSIONS AND EXCITING OPPORTUNITIES . . . AND IT'S SO AMAZING THAT WE CAN SHARE THAT EXPERIENCE! HEART EMOJIS FOR ALL Y'ALL!

LAST, AN EXTRA SPECIAL THANKS TO BRITT, WHO PUT MY NAME AND PORTFOLIO IN FRONT OF GINA IN THE FIRST PLACE! THIS DOOR WAS ALREADY OPEN, BUT THANKS FOR DROPKICKING ME THROUGH IT!

CHARACTER CREATION

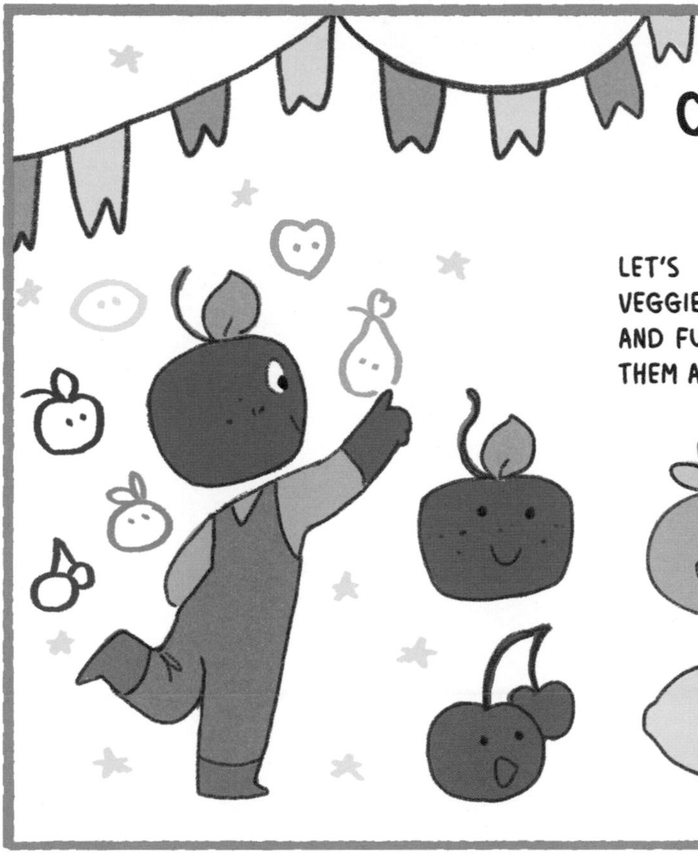

LET'S DRAW SOME FRUIT AND VEGGIE CHARACTERS! IT'S EASY AND FUN ONCE YOU LEARN TO SEE THEM AS SIMPLE SHAPES.

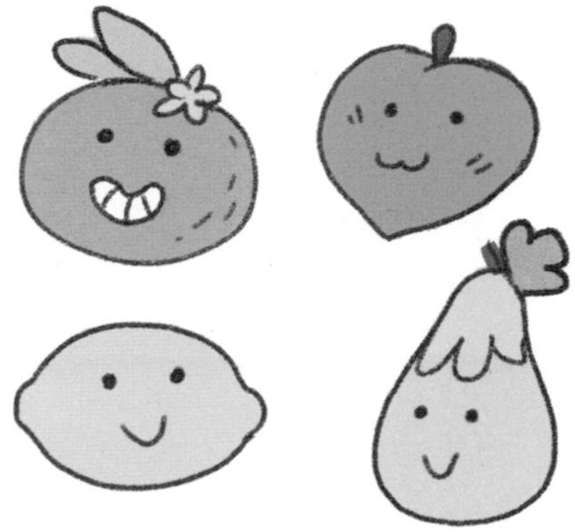

CALLAWAY

CRABAPPLES ARE SHAPED LIKE A SQUARE. CAN YOU THINK OF OTHER FRUITS AND VEGGIES THAT HAVE THIS SHAPE?

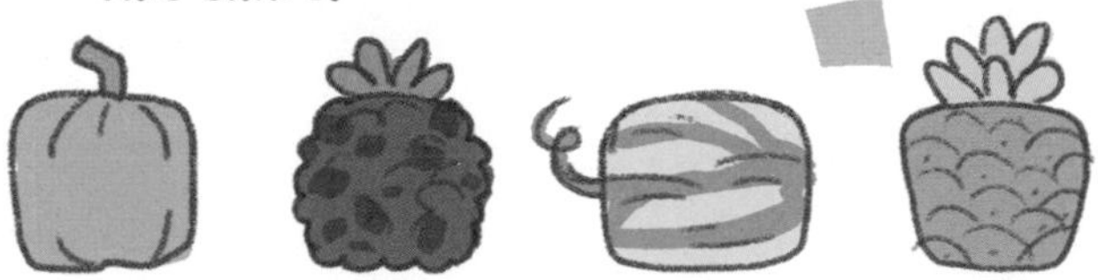

PUMPKIN BLACKBERRY MELON PINEAPPLE

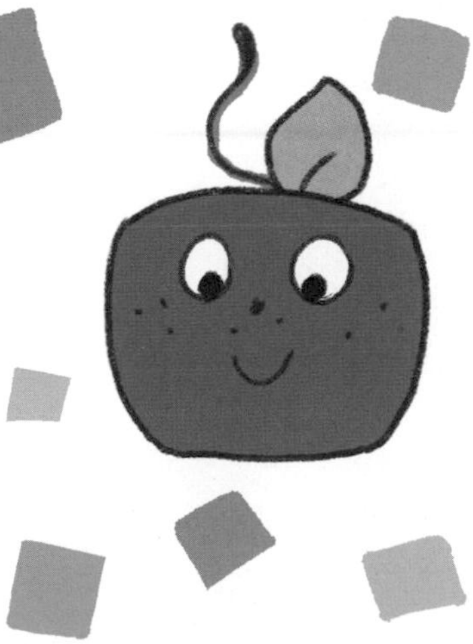

CLEMENTINE AND CITRA

LEMONS AND ORANGES LOOK LIKE CIRCLES AND OVALS. LOTS OF OTHER FRUITS AND VEGGIES ARE SHAPED LIKE THIS, TOO.

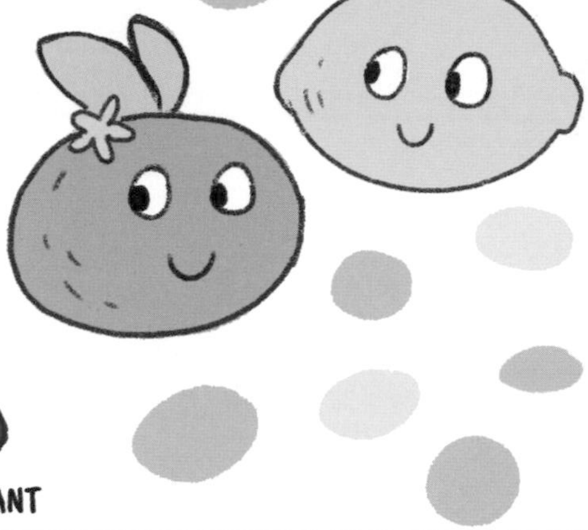

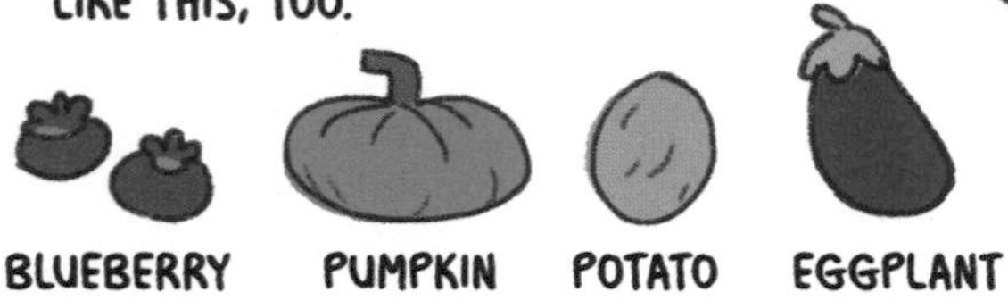
BLUEBERRY
PUMPKIN
POTATO
EGGPLANT

PEACHY AND AVI

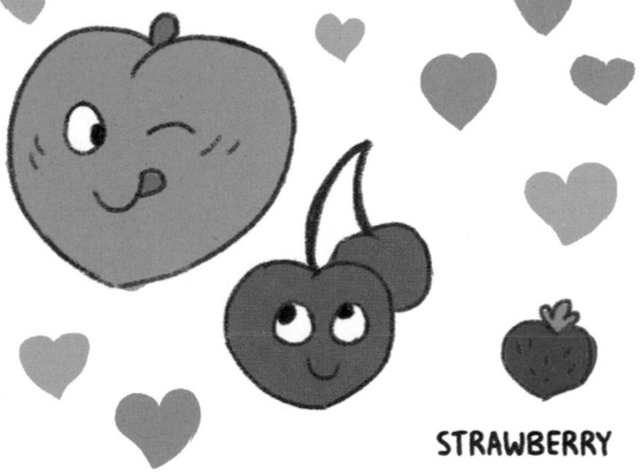

PEACHES AND CHERRIES ARE SHAPED LIKE HEARTS. THIS SHAPE IS A LITTLE SQUASHED SOMETIMES.

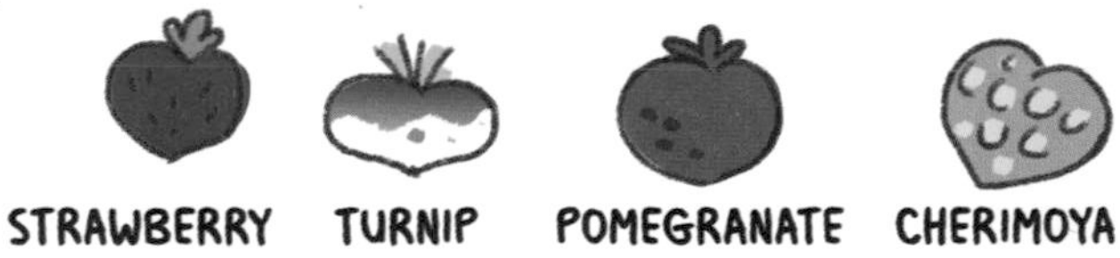
STRAWBERRY
TURNIP
POMEGRANATE
CHERIMOYA

PEARY

PEARS LOOK A LOT LIKE TRIANGLES TO ME. CAN YOU THINK OF OTHER FRUIT AND VEGGIES THAT SHARE THIS SHAPE?

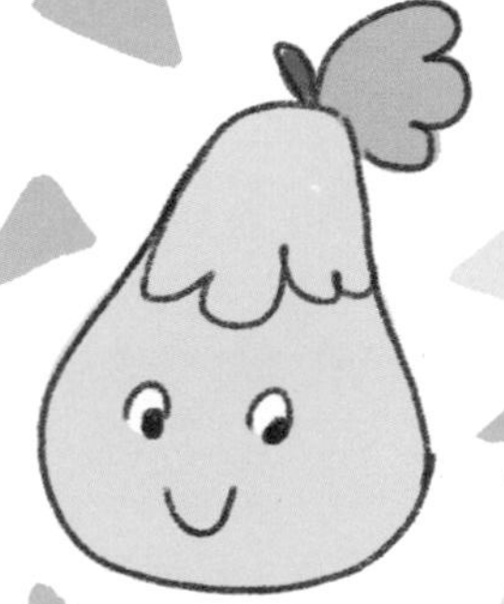

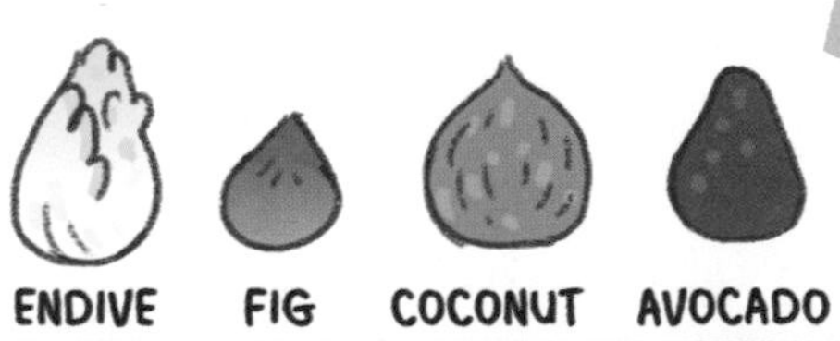
ENDIVE
FIG
COCONUT
AVOCADO

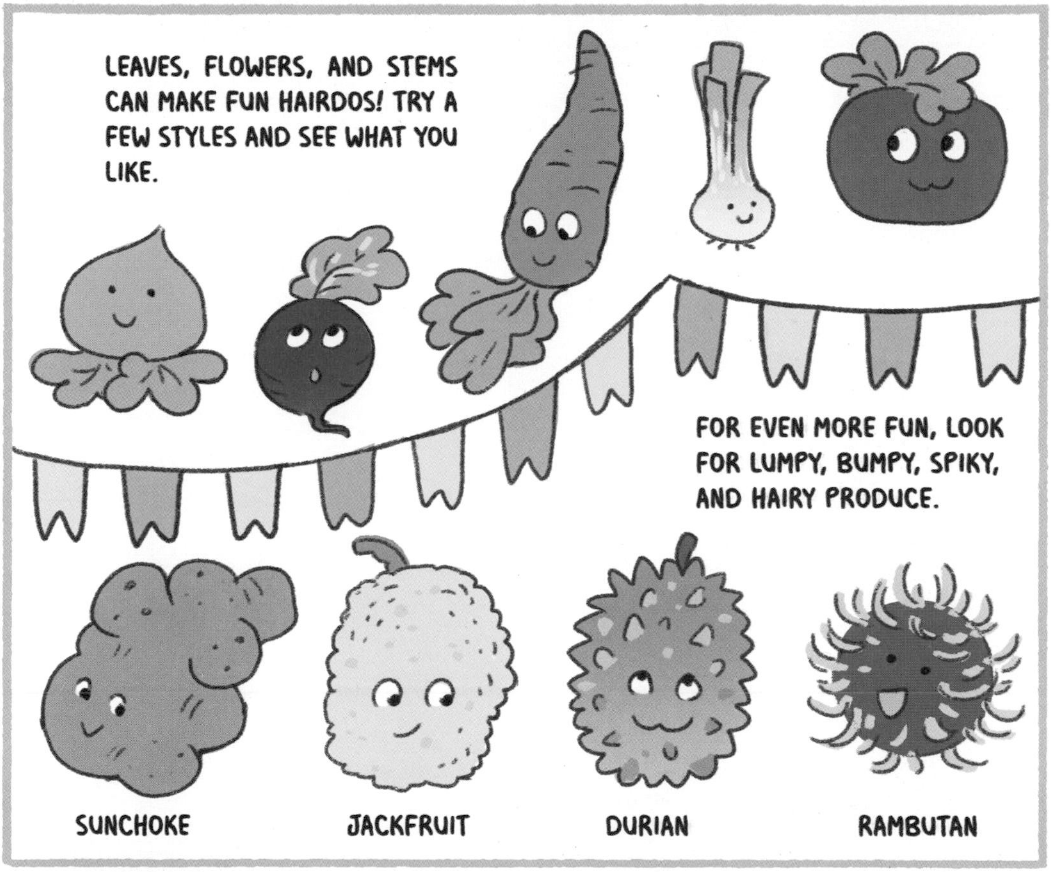
LEAVES, FLOWERS, AND STEMS CAN MAKE FUN HAIRDOS! TRY A FEW STYLES AND SEE WHAT YOU LIKE.
FOR EVEN MORE FUN, LOOK FOR LUMPY, BUMPY, SPIKY, AND HAIRY PRODUCE.
SUNCHOKE
JACKFRUIT
DURIAN
RAMBUTAN

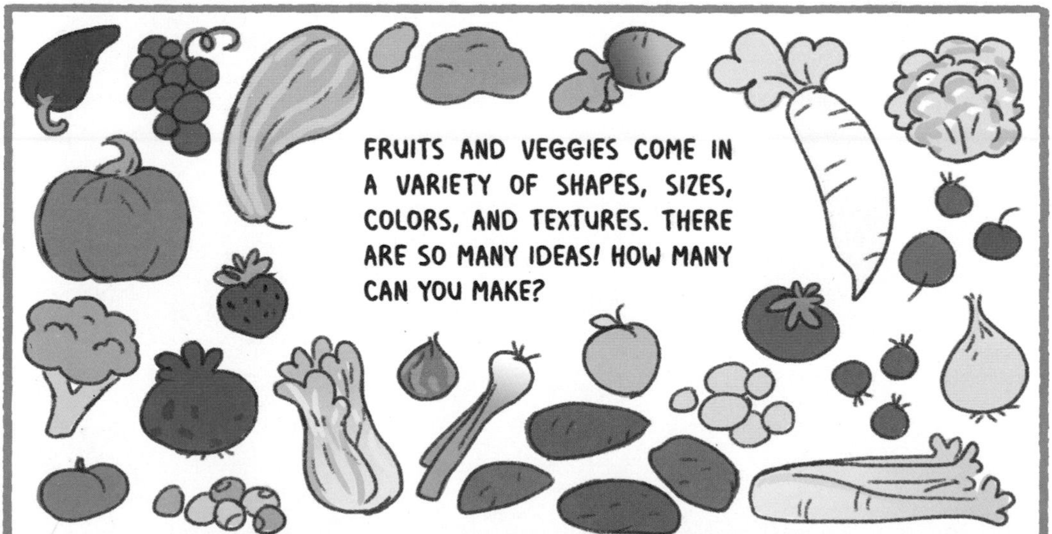
FRUITS AND VEGGIES COME IN A VARIETY OF SHAPES, SIZES, COLORS, AND TEXTURES. THERE ARE SO MANY IDEAS! HOW MANY CAN YOU MAKE?

LET'S DRAW CALLAWAY

1

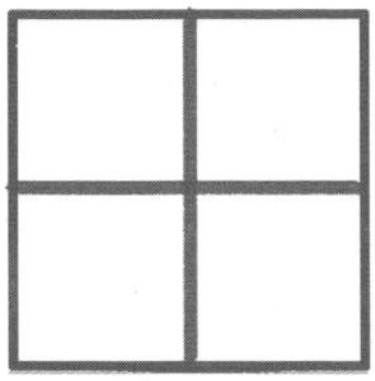

FIRST, LET'S DRAW A SQUARE. NOW LET'S DIVIDE IT INTO EVEN QUARTERS WITH A CROSS DOWN THE MIDDLE.

2

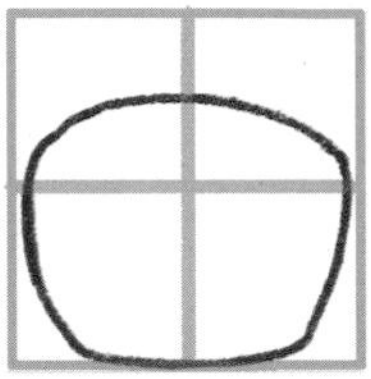

DRAW AN APPLE SHAPE INSIDE THE SQAURE.

3

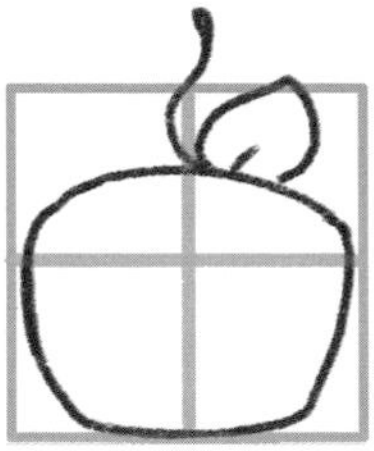

THE LEAF AND STEM START FROM THE MIDDLE OF THE SQUARE.

4

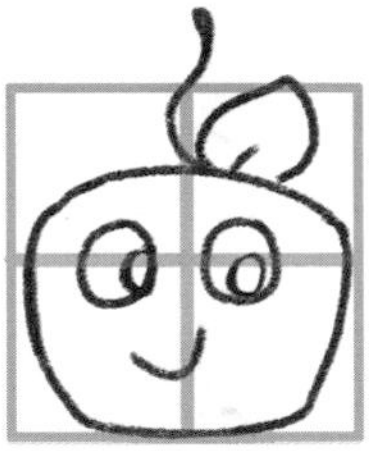

DRAW THE EYES AND MOUTH ALONG THE MIDDLE LINE.

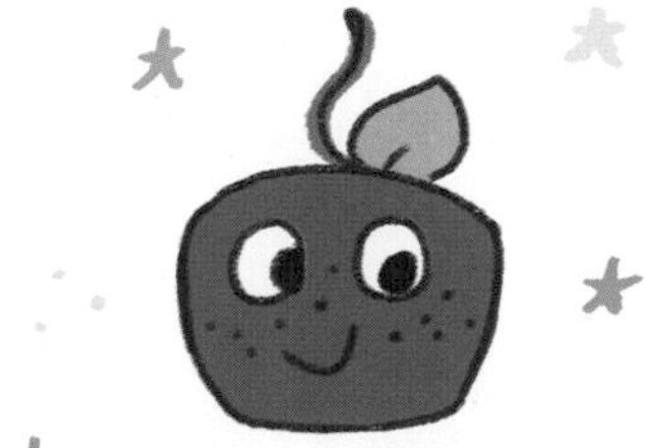

DON'T FORGET HER FRECKLES! NOW ADD SOME COLOR, AND YOU'RE ALL DONE!

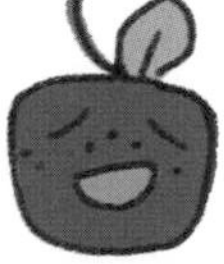

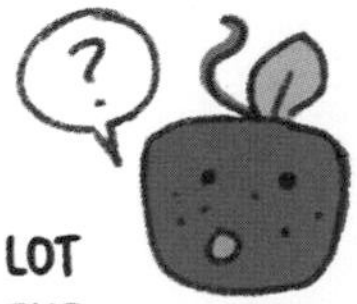
?

CALLAWAY HAS A LOT OF EXPRESSIONS IN THE STORY. WHAT KINDS OF FACES CAN YOU MAKE FOR HER?

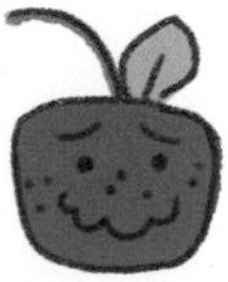

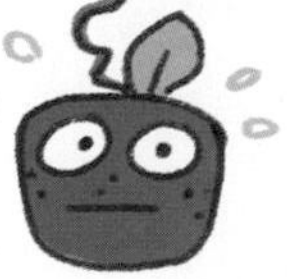

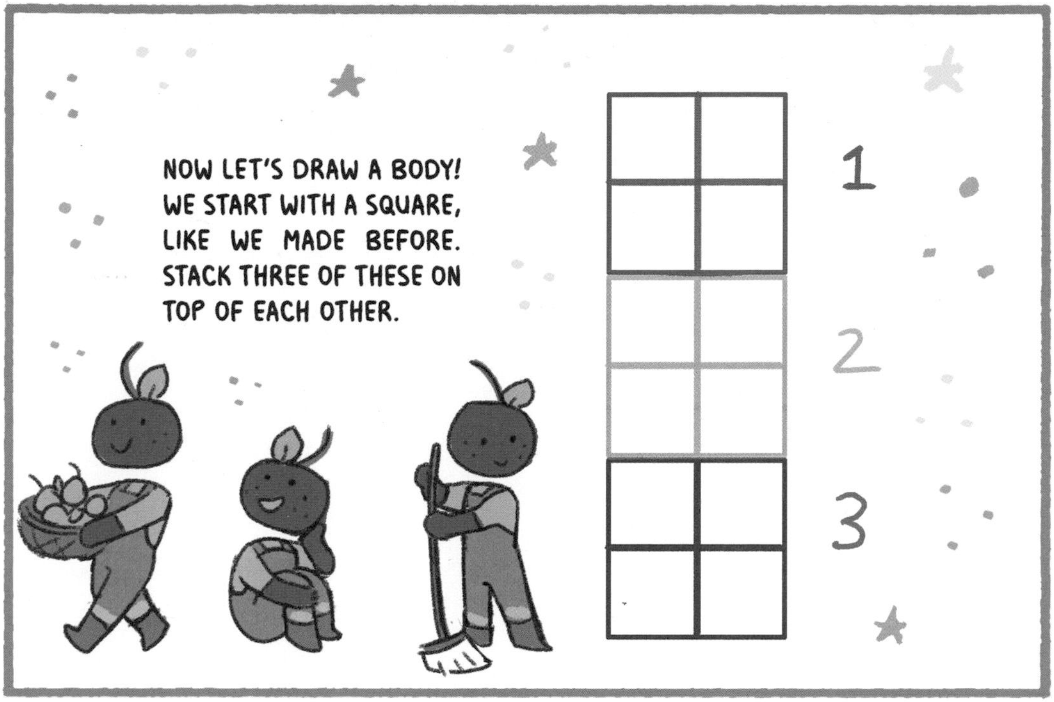
NOW LET'S DRAW A BODY! WE START WITH A SQUARE, LIKE WE MADE BEFORE. STACK THREE OF THESE ON TOP OF EACH OTHER.
1
2
3

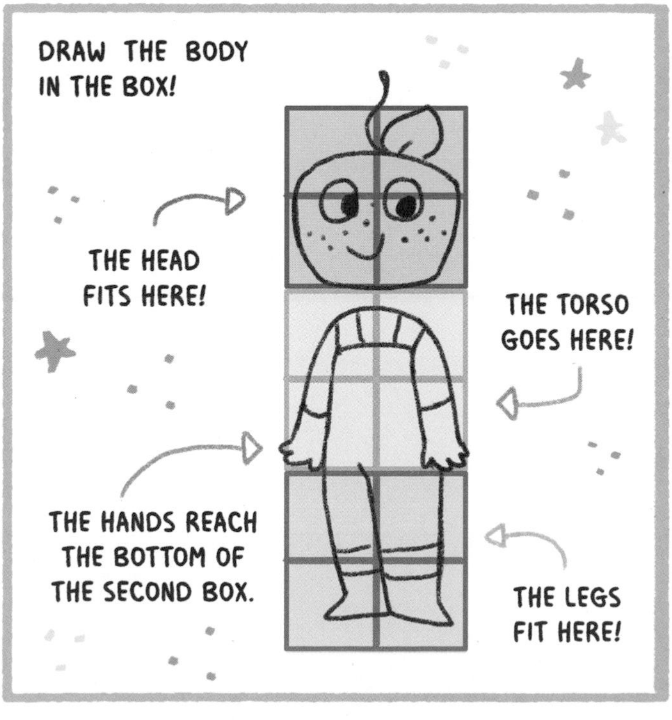
DRAW THE BODY IN THE BOX!
THE HEAD FITS HERE!
THE TORSO GOES HERE!
THE HANDS REACH THE BOTTOM OF THE SECOND BOX.
THE LEGS FIT HERE!

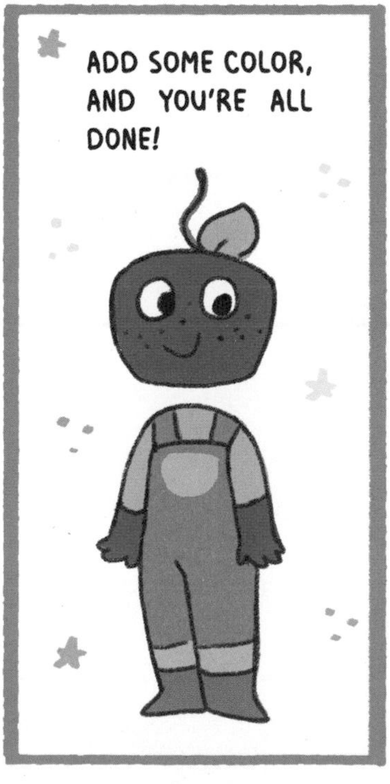
ADD SOME COLOR, AND YOU'RE ALL DONE!

CHARACTER SKETCHES

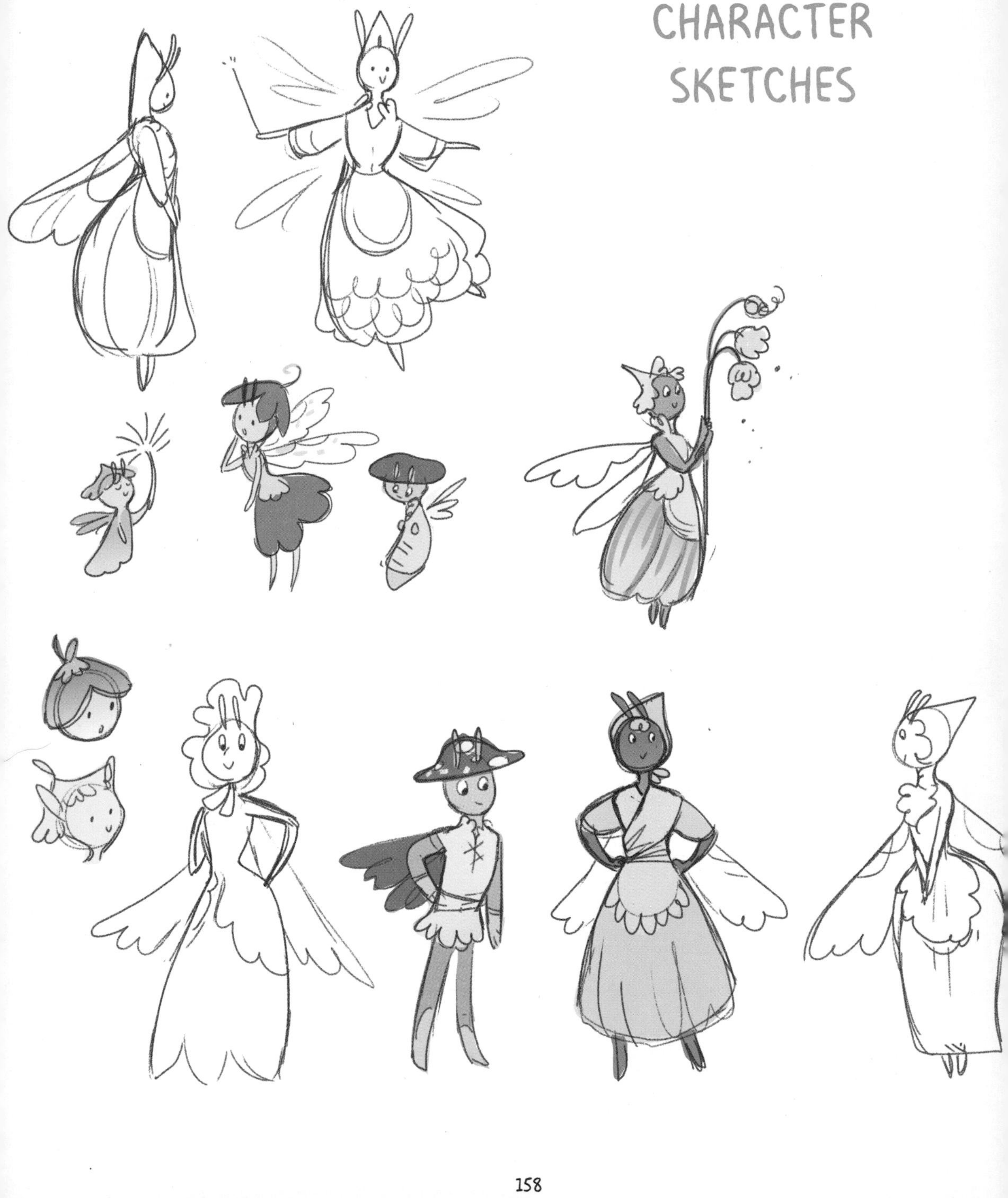

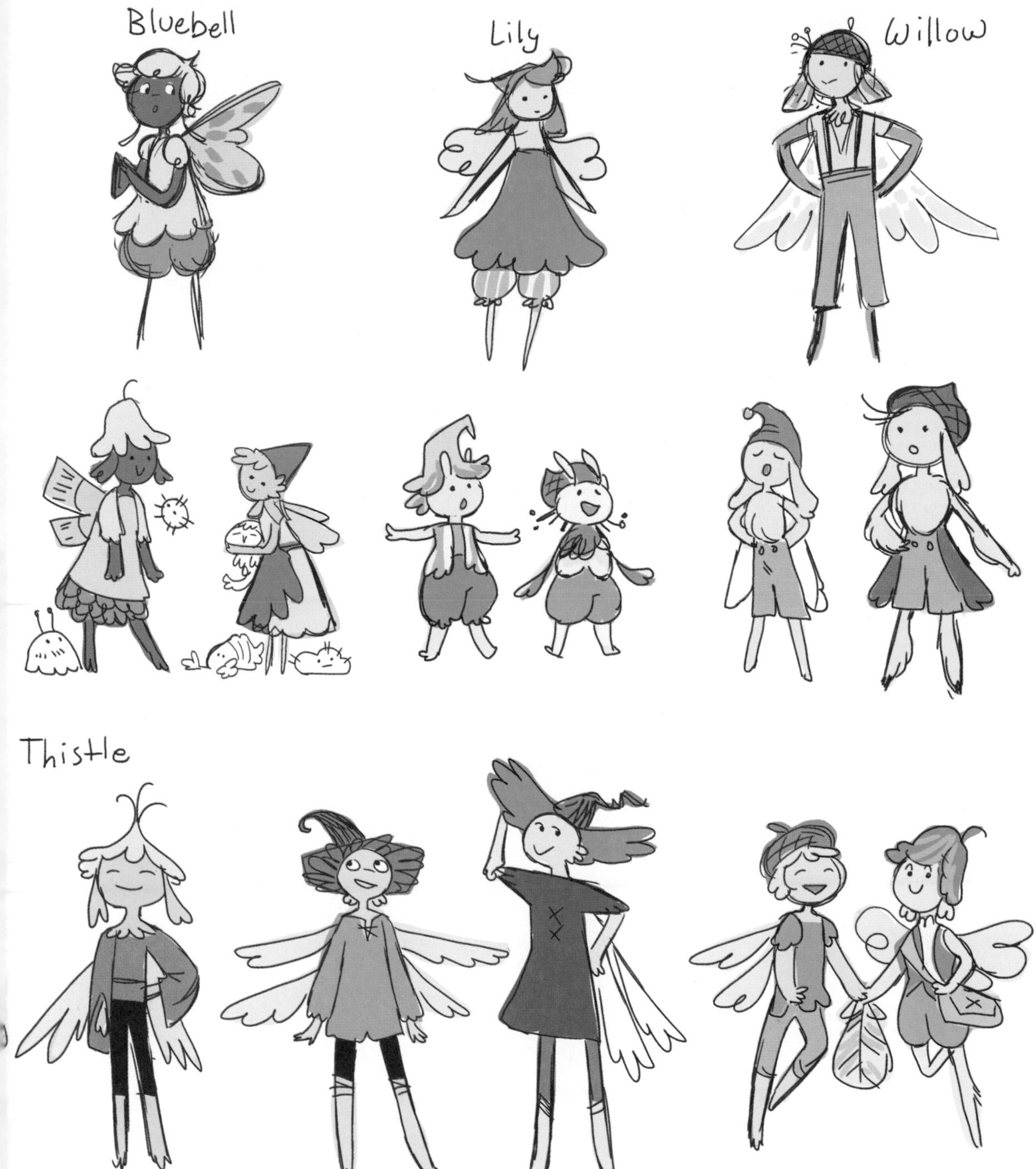
Bluebell
Lily
Willow
Thistle

(EVEN MORE) CHARACTER SKETCHES

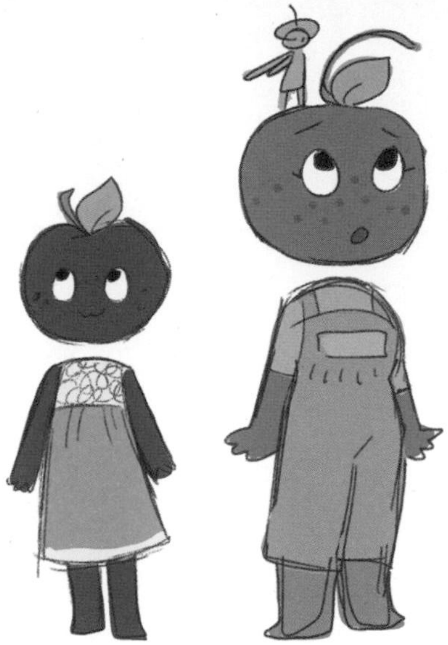

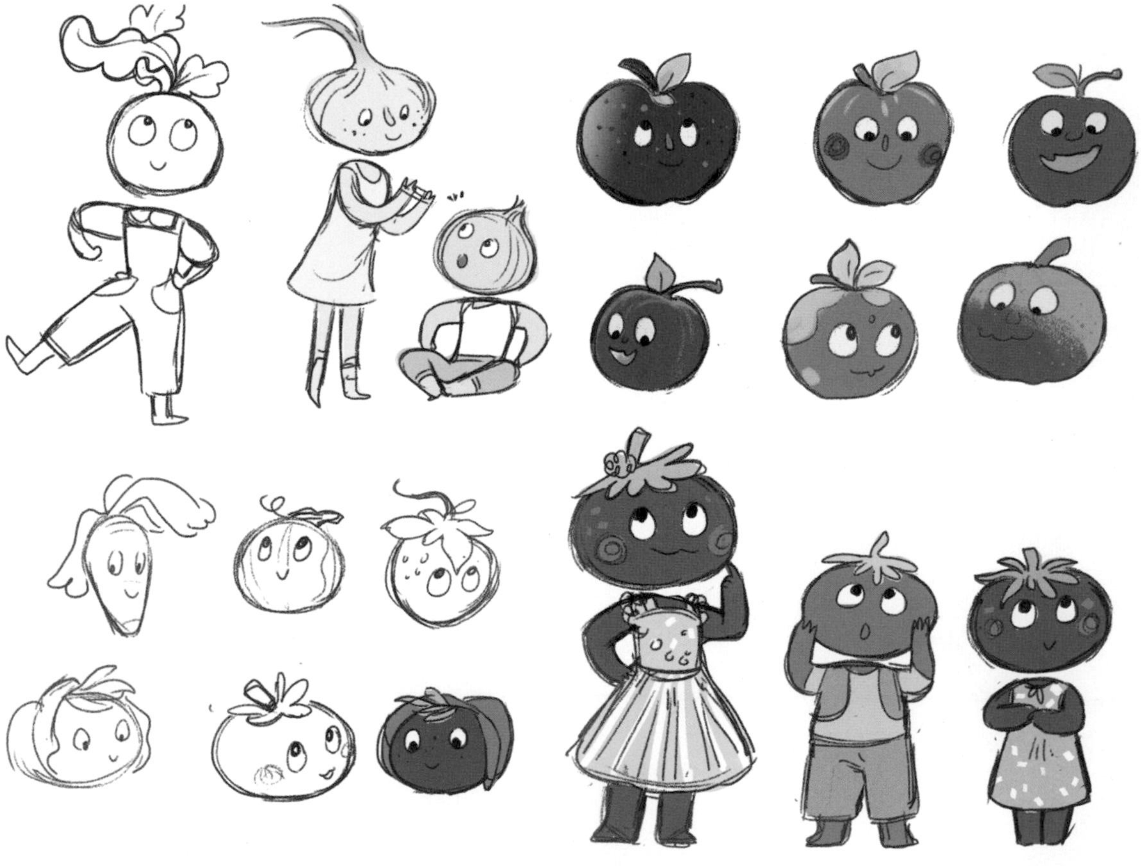

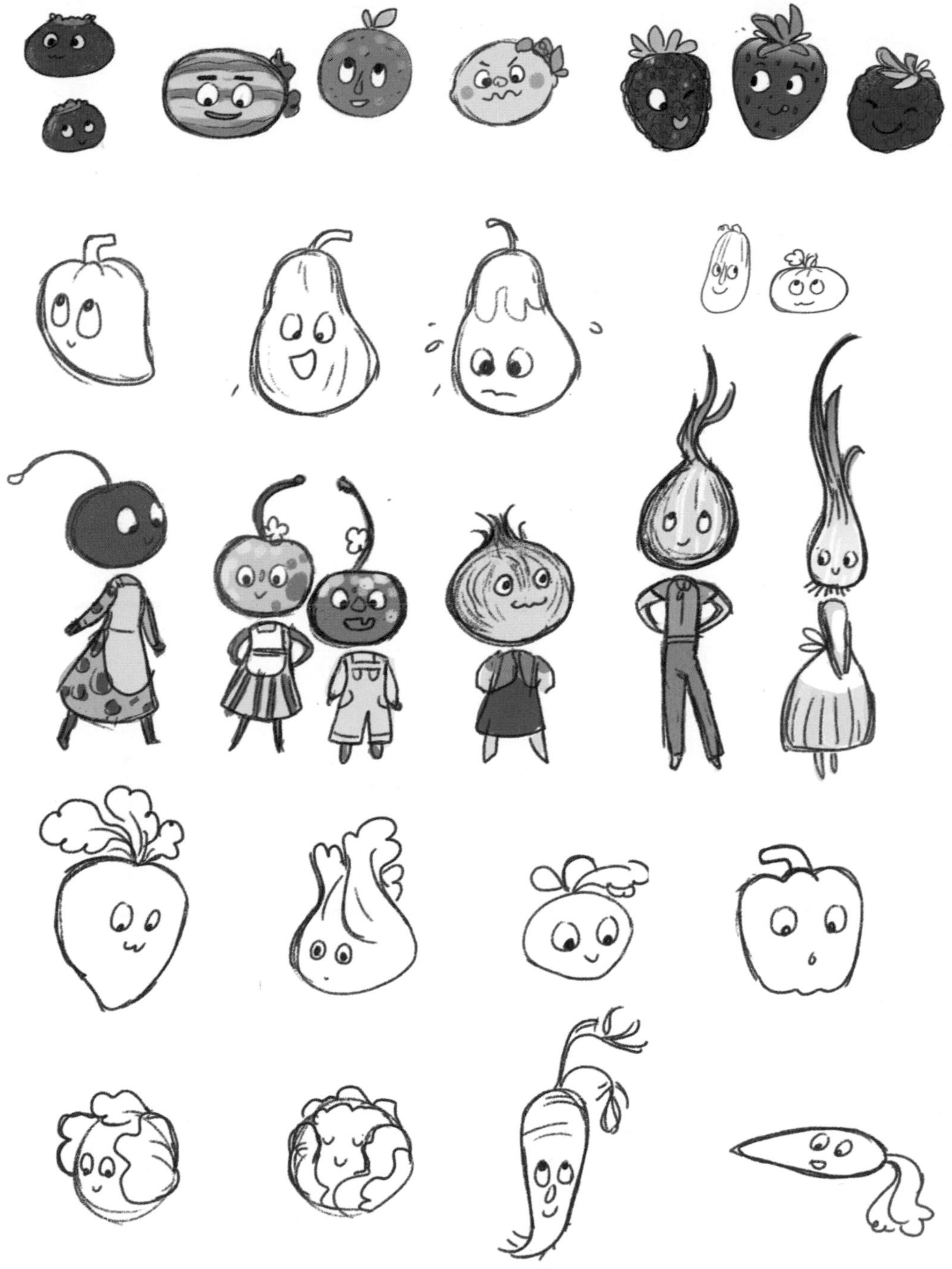

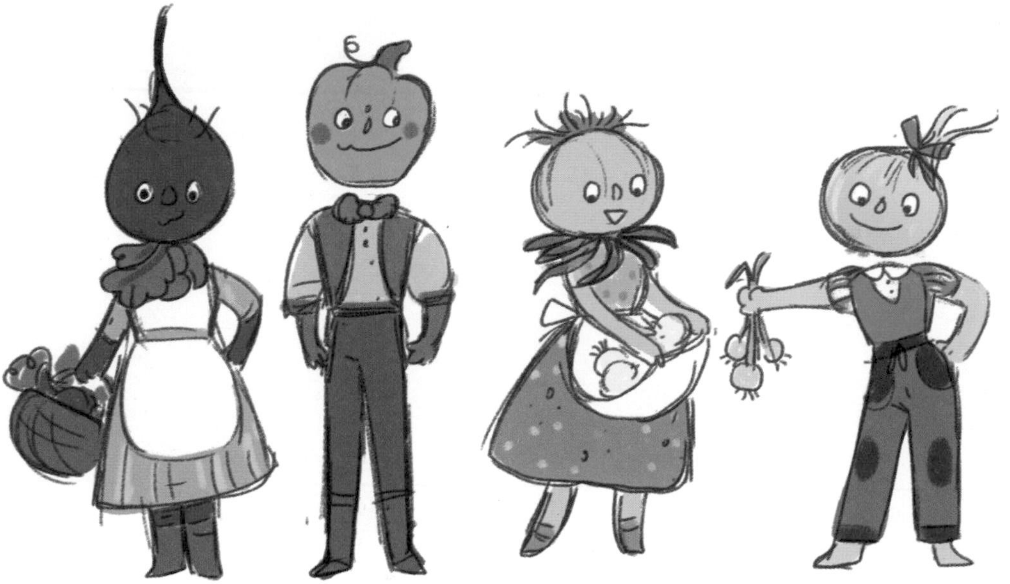

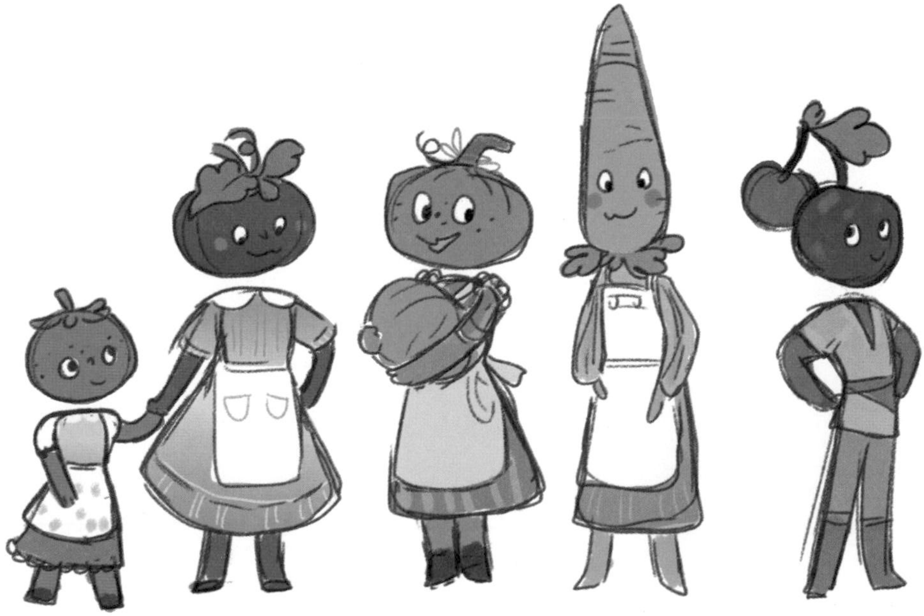

INSPIRATION FOR CRABAPPLE TROUBLE CAME FROM THE SHORT STORY "LUMINA" THAT KAETI COMPLETED IN 2016.

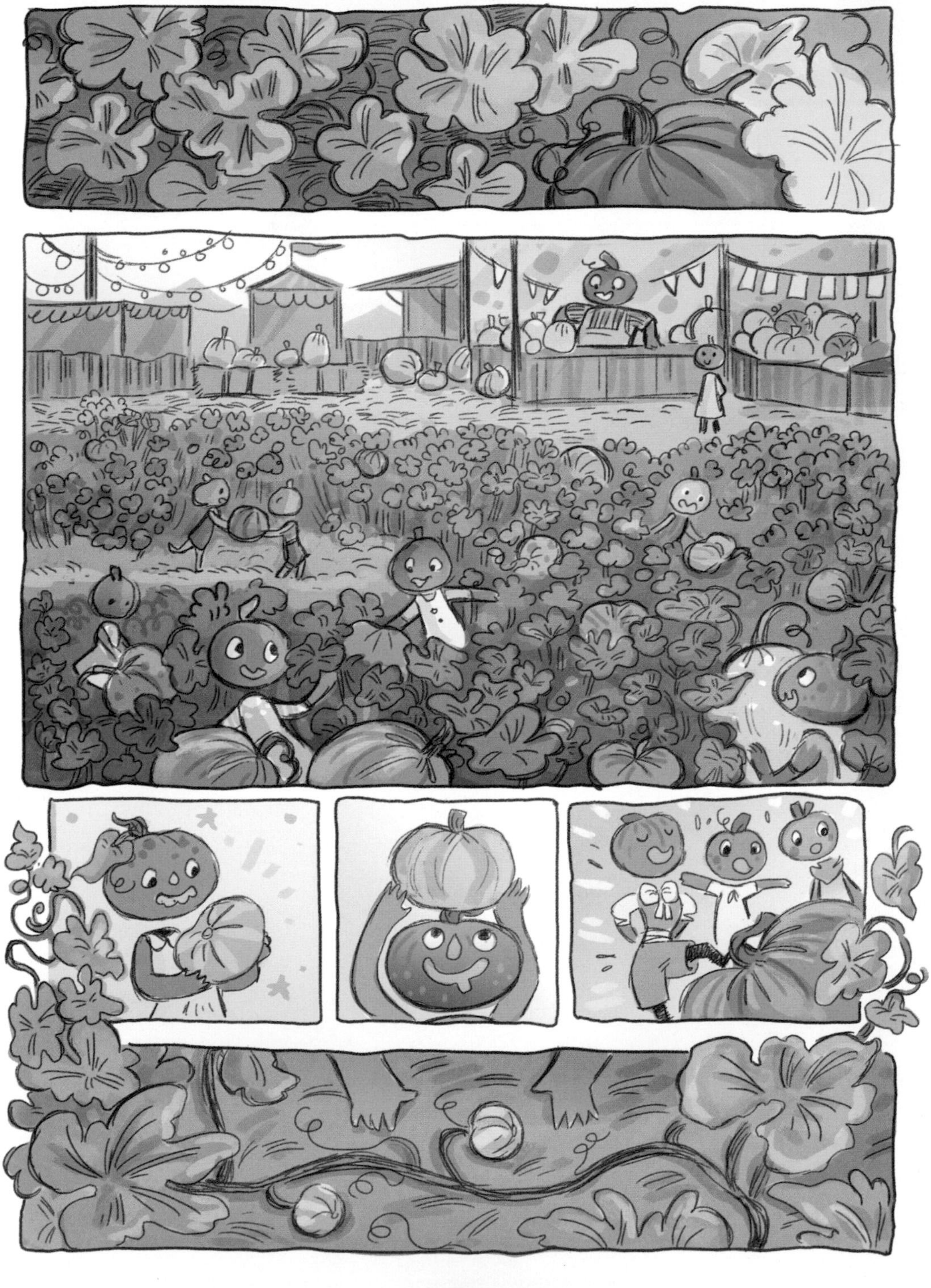

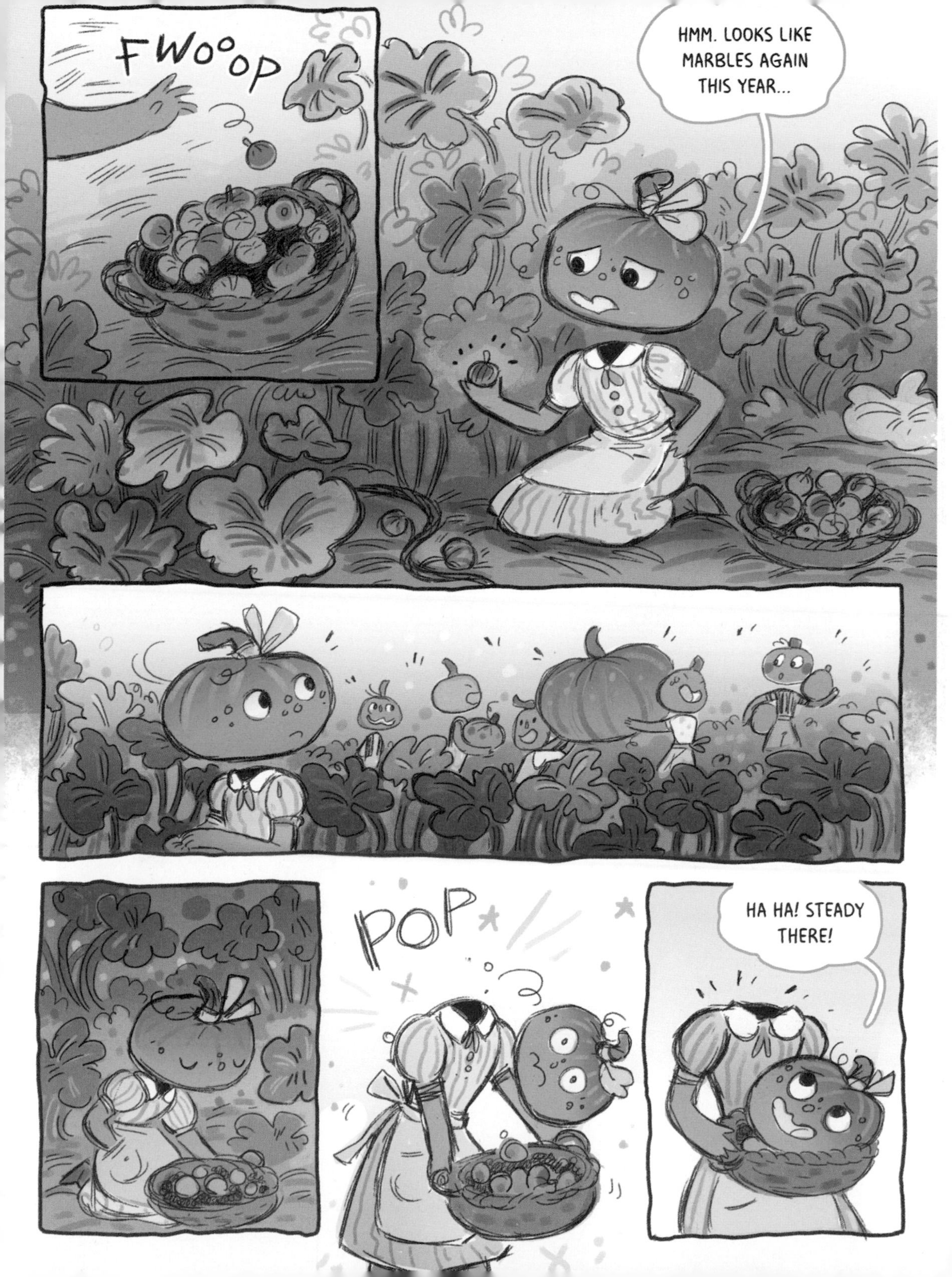
FWOOOP
HMM. LOOKS LIKE MARBLES AGAIN THIS YEAR...
POP
HA HA! STEADY THERE!

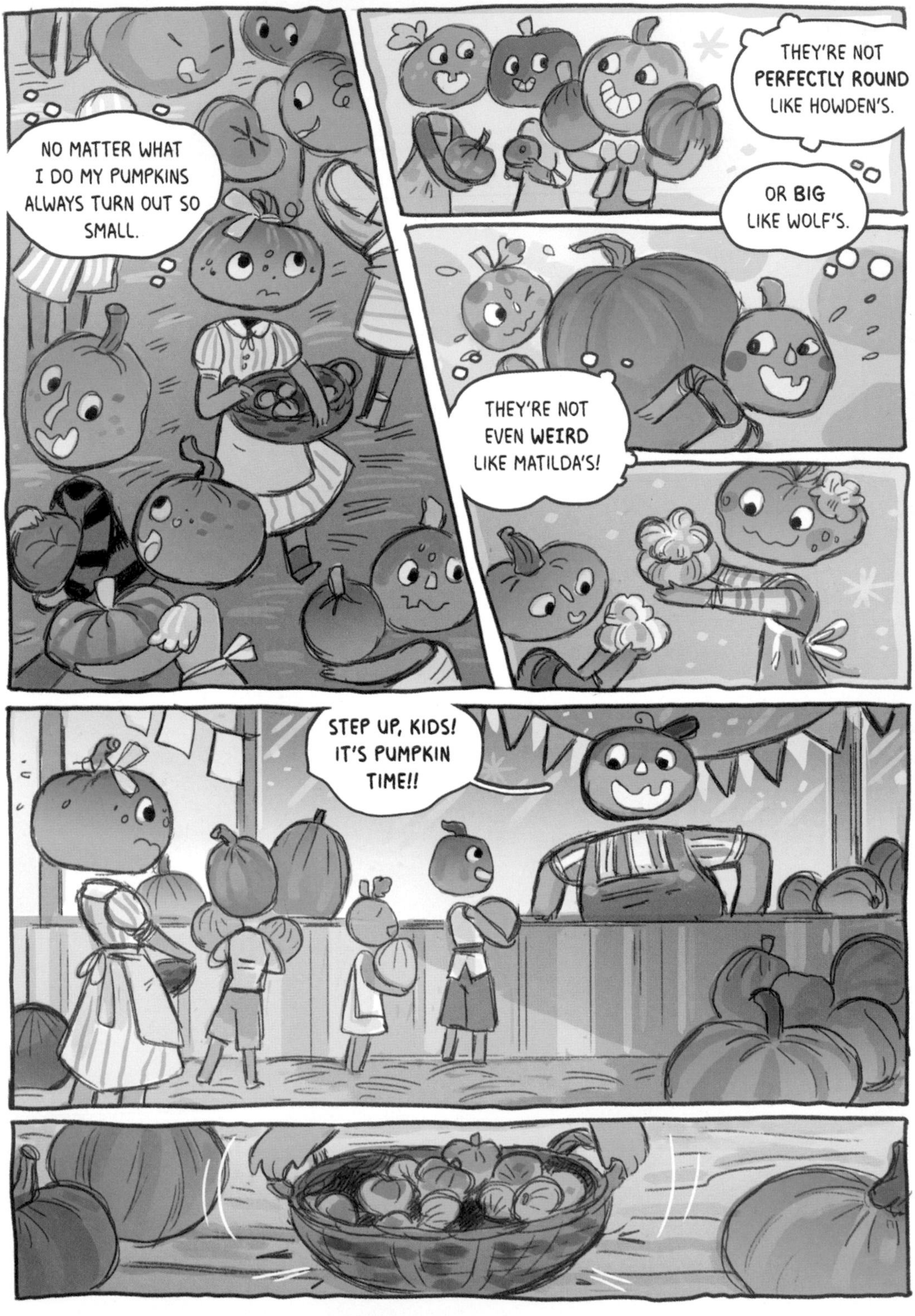
NO MATTER WHAT I DO MY PUMPKINS ALWAYS TURN OUT SO SMALL.
THEY'RE NOT **PERFECTLY ROUND** LIKE HOWDEN'S.
OR **BIG** LIKE WOLF'S.
THEY'RE NOT EVEN **WEIRD** LIKE MATILDA'S!
STEP UP, KIDS! IT'S PUMPKIN TIME!!

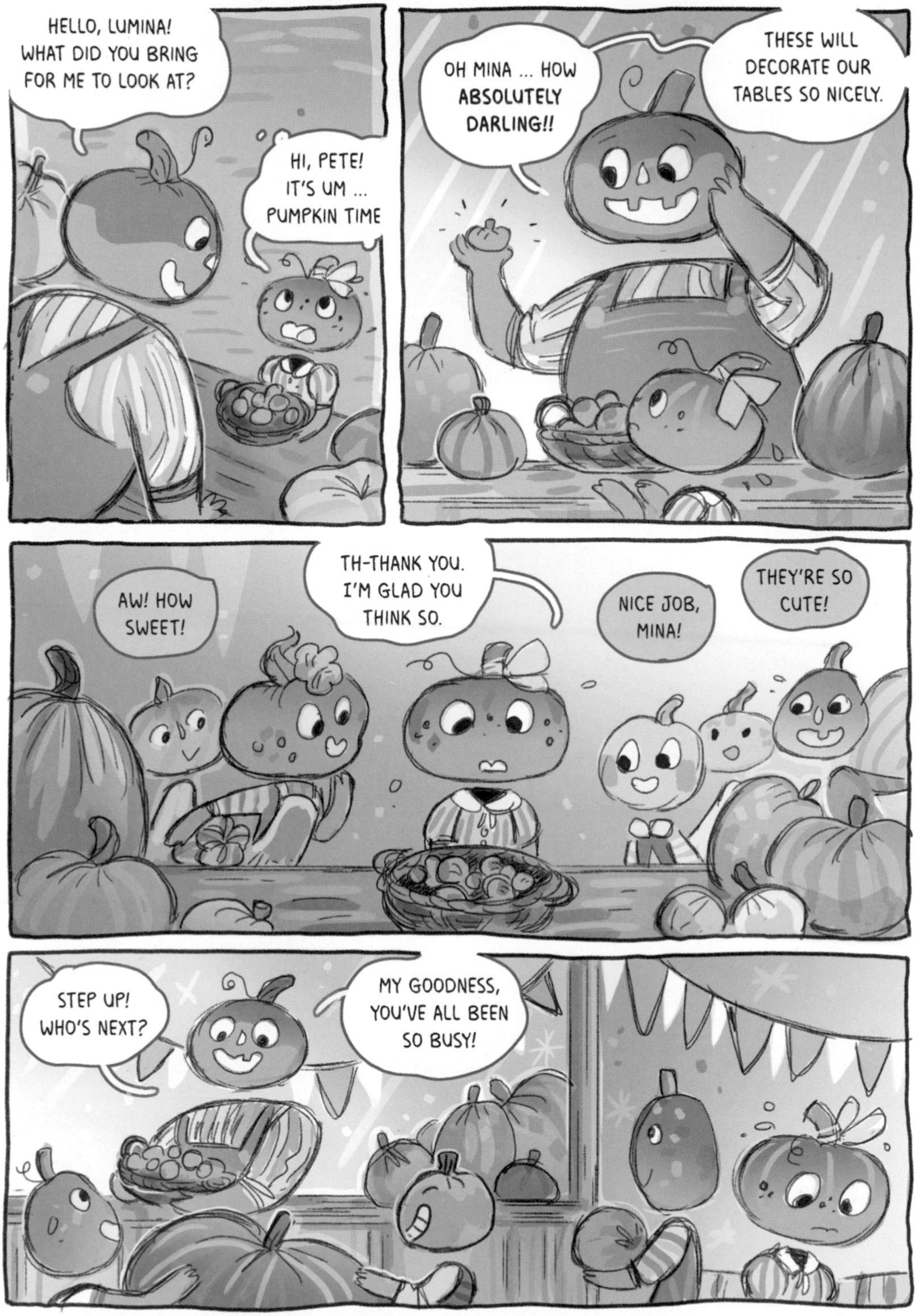
HELLO, LUMINA! WHAT DID YOU BRING FOR ME TO LOOK AT?
HI, PETE! IT'S UM ... PUMPKIN TIME
OH MINA ... HOW **ABSOLUTELY DARLING!!**
THESE WILL DECORATE OUR TABLES SO NICELY.
AW! HOW SWEET!
TH-THANK YOU. I'M GLAD YOU THINK SO.
NICE JOB, MINA!
THEY'RE SO CUTE!
STEP UP! WHO'S NEXT?
MY GOODNESS, YOU'VE ALL BEEN SO BUSY!

KAETI VANDORN IS AN ILLUSTRATOR AND CARTOONIST WHO LOVES DRAWING COLORFUL LANDSCAPES AND ADORABLE MONSTERS. SHE SPENT HER CHILDHOOD CHASING FIREFLIES IN KANSAS, THEN BEING CHASED BY MOSQUITOES IN ALASKA. SHE HAS RECENTLY MOVED TO VERMONT, WHERE SHE LIVES AT THE TOP OF A BIG GRASSY HILL. SHE STAYS INDOORS MOST OF THE TIME TO AVOID THE TERRIFYING INSECTS OUTDOORS. (ALSO, THAT BIG GUY, SASQUATCH.)

SHE HAS A DEGREE IN ILLUSTRATION FROM THE ACADEMY OF ART UNIVERSITY, WHICH SHE ACHIEVED THROUGH ONLINE CORRESPONDENCE. HER CASUAL INTERESTS LAY IN BOTANY AND HERPETOLOGY; IF SHE WASN'T AN ARTIST (AND NOT SO WARY OF BUGS), SHE WOULD PROBABLY BE A NATURALIST, STUDYING THE BIZARRE AND WONDERFUL CREATURES OF THE WORLD.

AS A FREELANCE ILLUSTRATOR, KAETI HAS THE PLEASURE OF WORKING FROM HOME, WITH AN EVER-CHANGING VARIETY OF TASKS AND THEMES . . . SHE LIKES THIS A LOT! HER DRAWINGS HAVE BEEN FEATURED IN ART BOOKS, INDIE ZINES, AND GALLERY SHOWS ACROSS THE UNITED STATES, AS WELL AS DRAWN COVER ART FOR ALBUMS BY THE MUSICAL ARTIST NANOBII.

KAETI BEGAN SELF-PUBLISHING COMICS ONLINE IN 2014. CRABAPPLE TROUBLE WAS ADAPTED FROM THE SHORT STORY "LUMINA," WHICH CENTERED ON A PUMPKIN GIRL STRUGGLING WITH A SIMILAR THEME OF "LOSING HER HEAD" WITH ANXIETY OVER FRIENDS AND EXPECTATIONS.

CRABAPPLE TROUBLE IS HER FIRST PRINTED BOOK, AND SHE HOPES YOU ENJOY IT VERY MUCH.

PROTEIDAES.TUMBLR.COM
🐦 @PROTEIDAES
📷 @PROTEIDAES

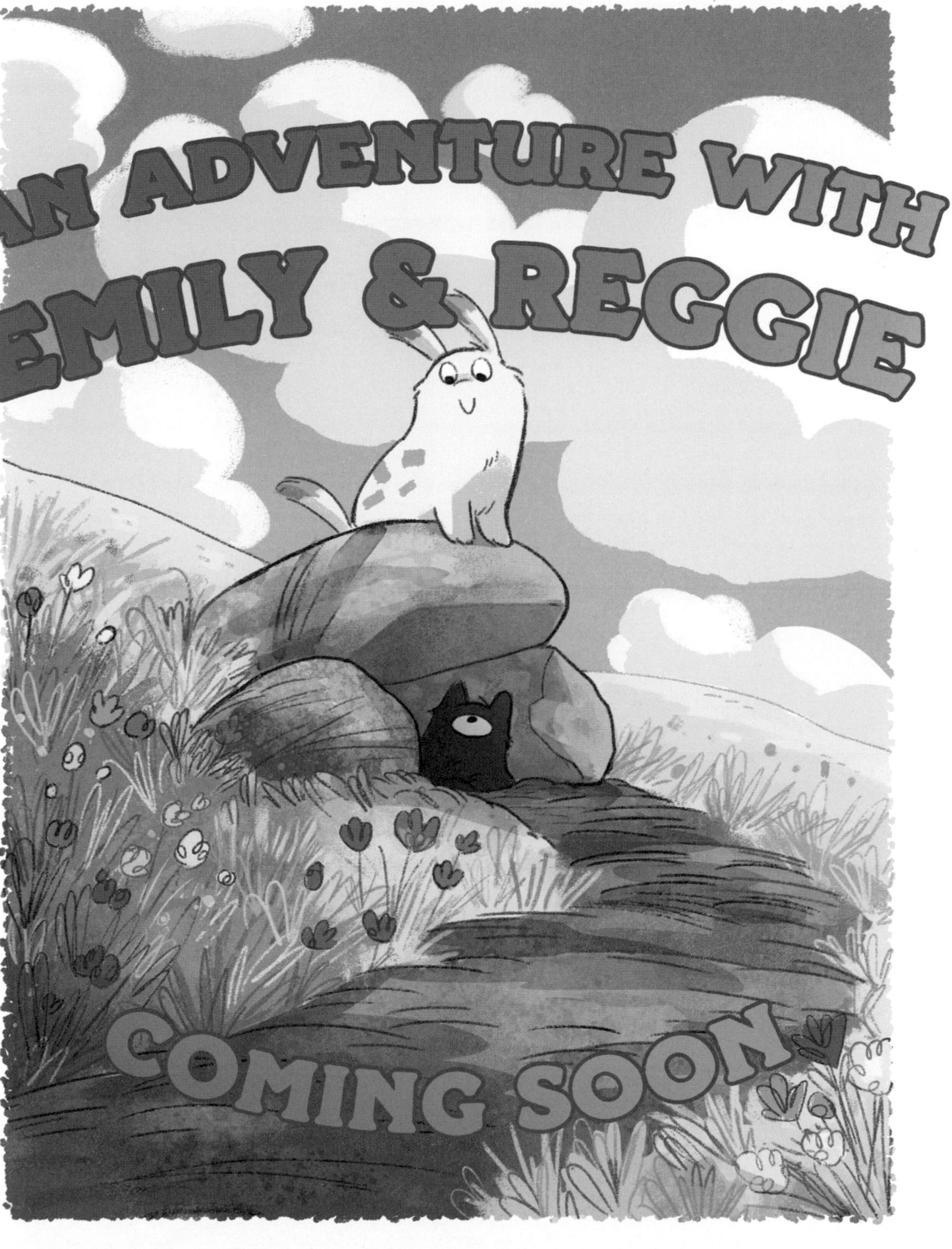
AN ADVENTURE WITH
EMILY & REGGIE
COMING SOON

RH GRAPHIC

THE SUMMER 2020 LIST

CRABAPPLE TROUBLE
Kaeti Vandorn

CRABAPPLE TROUBLE

By Kaeti Vandorn

Life isn't easy when you're an apple.

Callaway and Thistle must figure out how to work together—with delicious and magical results.

Young Chapter Book

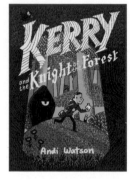

KERRY and the Knight of the Forest
Andi Watson

KERRY AND THE KNIGHT OF THE FOREST

By Andi Watson

Kerry needs to get home!

To get back to hs parents, Kerry gets lost in a shortcut. He will have to make tough choices and figure out who to trust—or remain lost in the forest . . . forever.

Middle-Grade

STEPPING STONES

By Lucy Knisley

Jen did not want to leave the city.

She did not want to move to a farm.

And Jen definitely did not want to get two new "sisters."

Middle-Grade

NEW YORK TIMES BESTSELLING AUTHOR
LUCY KNISLEY
STEPPING STONES
Peapod Farm
Berries
Flowers
Granola

SUNCATCHER

By Jose Pimienta

Beatriz loves music—more than her school, more than her friends—and she won't let anything stop her from achieving her dreams.

Even if it means losing everything else.

Young Adult

Suncatcher
JOSE PIMIENTA

FIND US ONLINE AT @RHKIDSGRAPHIC AND RHKIDSGRAPHIC.COM